Bound...

'You're mine,' said Ross. 'You want to be my slave. My pet. My little alley-cat. So I make the rules. Sign here.'

He placed a document on the table and I twisted in his lap to open it. Inside were two sheets of paper filled with close type. I read them with slowly mounting horror. It was identical to the one in *Venus in Furs*. There was lots of stuff about vengeance and retaliation being forbidden, the need for total submission, the presence of cruelty and occasional mercy. The only let-out was to be a word of surrender, spoken in true desperation, which would end the whole game: Marquise.

'I'm not signing it,' I said, suddenly feeling distinctly stroppy. 'It says here that you're going to change my name: I will not be called Puss!'

'You'll do it because you want to,' said Ross. 'You'll do it because it's the most exciting thing that's ever happened to you. Above all, you will do it because I say you will – Puss.'

By the same author:

STAND AND DELIVER

Bound By Contract

HELENA RAVENSCROFT

BLACK
lace

Black Lace novels contain sexual fantasies.
In real life, make sure you practise safe sex.

First published in 1999 by
Black Lace
Thames Wharf Studios,
Rainville Road, London W6 9HA

Typeset by SetSystems Ltd, Saffron Walden, Essex
Printed and bound by Mackays of Chatham PLC

ISBN 0 352 33447 9

Contents

Part One

Negotiation

Chapter One

'You want to be my slave?'

Ross Peterson, my dangerously handsome cousin, raised one eyebrow and gazed across his desk at me with mild amusement. It was the third time he had asked me the same question – he obviously couldn't quite believe what I was proposing.

I had been toying with the idea for months – ever since picking up a copy of *Venus in Furs* in an old bookshop on the Portobello Road. It was the jacket which had initially attracted me: plain blue with a sepia-tint photograph of an unfashionably curvaceous brunette. Identifying with this odalisque had been the first step on the path to obsession. Even the title of the book seemed an omen: it was the same as a record by the Velvet Underground which I had almost worn out by playing repeatedly – very loudly – in my first student lodgings.

I had bought the book and been instantly captivated, reading half of it on the Underground on the long journey home. The tale of Severin and his desire to be mistreated by the beautiful Wanda Von Dunajew had enthralled me. I dreamed of re-enacting the roles.

And when Ross's interest in me had shown signs of starting to wane, I had decided to put ideas into practice.

I glanced at Ross as he shifted slightly, and watched him lean forward in his chair to rest his elbows on the desk. His half-amused eyes were fixed on mine and I felt a familiar thrill of anticipation bite into me as I met his gaze. Behind him, rain lashed the window panes, smearing the usually pleasant view of the harbour and boats. The Lifeboat Station was on a windy promontory, and the full force of the storm that buffeted the little building was an instant reminder of the danger of Ross's job.

He was everybody's local hero, not just mine. I studied him with interest and noticed, not for the first time, that he looked the part of a true Action Man with his cropped hair and the navy T-shirt that stretched over a muscular chest. Gorgeously handsome, strong and dark with just a hint of the subversive – George Clooney on a good day was not a patch on my cousin Ross.

'Well?' he prompted.

Unable to hold his gaze, I let my eyes drift downward, feeling a tense heat curl around my insides as I watched the way his fingers pressed together to form a steeple that hid his wide mouth. I took a deep, steadying breath, and let my gaze drop to where the edge of the desk hid what I knew to be an impressive package of hard thighs, neat hips and bulging faded denims.

'I think it'll be fun,' I ventured.

'Come off it, Sam.' His grin was broad now, no longer merely half-amused. 'You as a slave? Don't make me laugh.'

'Why not?' I was indignant. 'What are you trying to say?'

'Well, we've got a lot of history, and the one thing I

4

know you *aren't* is a natural submissive. I seem to remember that it was always you who took charge in all the games we used to play in your garden. Remember Action Jim?'

I made a face. Action Jim had been this crazy game we'd played as children. A version of Truth or Dare, except that I'd always made up the dares, and Ross and my brothers had always carried them out. Under duress. Seeing the boys performing dangerous feats of physical strength had given me a strange thigh-clenching thrill that still flavoured my relations with Ross in adult life.

'Forget Action Jim,' I said. 'That was a long time ago. Come on, Ross. The slave game will be fun. And very, very different. You'll love it.'

I leant on the edge of the desk opposite him. Only three feet of polished timber separated us, and I could smell his masculine scent: that evocative mixture of tobacco and spicy aftershave that never failed to arouse me. Ross and I had been playing our own version of Action Jim ever since my eighteenth birthday, except now the dares were solely confined to the bedroom. My dad and stepmother would have had a fit if they'd known, but that was partly what made it so much fun.

'Come on,' I breathed, aware that if I leant over just a fraction more, Ross would have an uninterrupted view of my cleavage and the very top of the gravity-defying bra that contained my breasts. I saw him swallow hard.

'Come here,' he said, his voice made hoarse by desire.

'Oh no.' I braced my arms and dipped my back, arching my body so that my shirt fell open a little more and the honey-brown curves of my breasts were thrust forward. 'Not until you tell me what you're going to say.'

5

'I need to think.' His teeth clamped on to his bottom lip, then he flicked his eyes quickly to my face before settling back on my décolletage. 'I can't tell you now.'

'You can. It's a simple decision. Just say yes, and let the game commence. Just think, Ross, you can make me do whatever you want. Whatever you need. Come on.' I raised my hands and slipped the fastenings from my hair, letting the thick, chestnut-coloured skeins fall around my neck and brush my cheeks. I knew Ross liked my hair. He spent hours twisting his hands in it, smelling it, burying his face in it, winding it around his cock.

The thought of him doing that now, here in his office, with several lifeboat crew only a wall thickness away, made a jolt of arousal hit me like a freight train. Electricity surged up and around my scalp and I felt that familiar slow-burn somewhere in the region of my thighs. Ross, staring at me, seemed to sense it: the amusement was suddenly chased from his face and his body became tense. He reminded me of a wild beast. Poised and ready to pounce.

'Come over here,' he murmured.

I hitched myself up on to the desk, then slid over until I could drape my legs over his, straddling him but with no contact except for the soft inside of my bare thighs resting ever so lightly on the rough fabric of his denims. Skirts were the thing for me – did it every time I saw Ross. Diaphanous fabric, lots of room to lift and cover. And always naked beneath: the sensation of juicy skin sliding and slipping as I walked was pure heaven and I wasn't going to let a little social nicety like underwear interfere.

Ross's hands came up and rested on my knees, his palms dry and warm, his thumbs gently stroking in tiny circles. I leant back on my hands and looked at him with sleepily lowered eyelashes, giving him my special Ross look: a lazy curving of my mouth that's half pout and half smile. He loved it. I could see him hardening under his fly: the buttons shifting as his length manoeuvred of its own accord and strained, rod-like, towards his pocket. I moistened my lips with the tip of my tongue.

'D'you want me?' I breathed. 'D'you want me here?'

'I always want you.' He tried to look away, nervously patting the pocket on the breast of his T-shirt, as if feeling for a packet of cigarettes. I smiled teasingly.

'You gave up, remember? New Year's Eve.'

A guilty pink flushed across his jaw and I wondered whether he'd been cheating already. It also made me wonder how voluntary the smoking ban had been, or whether he'd been coerced into it by the pretty piece of arm candy I'd seen him with at Christmas.

'Have me instead.' I was only half joking.

We'd never done it in his office before. Usually, on my weekend visits to the coast, we went down to the boathouse. It was empty and private, and the smell of briny sea mixed with engine oil always drove me wild. Since Ross had been promoted, I had only visited his office twice. On the previous occasion the little room had been filled with burly men in oilskins and boots.

The presence of the men had turned me on, but Ross was rather busy that time: a merchant vessel was in difficulty out in the channel and his was the nearest station available to the Coastguard. The crew had quickly disappeared down to the slipway to launch the rescue craft, leaving me to twiddle my thumbs and flip the pages of an ancient copy of *GQ* magazine.

But now I was there with the proposition of a lifetime, and it seemed like the perfect opportunity to christen the desk.

'You know I always want you, dirty little alley-cat.' His hand fell to his lap and he cupped his package with the palm of his hand, squeezing and lifting his muscular buttocks fractionally off the seat. I held my breath: what I wouldn't give to fall on him now and tear those buttons open, take his hot cock in my mouth and drown in the gorgeous taste of him.

Steady, Bentley, I thought. You're here to get him to agree and – as Anne Boleyn found out – a man's far more likely to say yes if you don't let him sample the goods too soon.

'Look.' I lifted the edges of my skirt and slipped them up over the satin of my thighs until he could see the very edges of my sex. Newly shaven, plump and perfumed, I knew I looked and smelled like paradise so I widened my thighs to show him. His reaction was quick: the sharply inhaled snatch of breath and the single-handed grasping of his denim-clad cock that followed it made me realise that he and I would have to do it – whether he said yes or not.

But he didn't have to know I was that easy, did he?

'Ross. Look at me,' I said, kicking off my boots and sliding out of the skirt. 'All shaven. Just how you've always wanted me. I'm all yours if you say that little word. Come on.' I was beginning to wheedle, I could hear it. My own desire for him had given me a short fuse, and I was ready to blow. Come on, Ross, say yes! I silently screamed.

'OK. One month, you little bitch.'

He hardly paused, grabbing my hips and jerking me forward on to his face. His tongue was rigid, hot and hard. I gasped, trying to quell the sudden lack of control as he buried himself in my sex. He was good. Much better than good, but I knew that anyway. Ross was no angel: he'd gone through all the girls in my class before he'd finally consented to touch me. Our parents' strict moral codes had been drummed into us since childhood; and while it was not strictly incest, it

8

was still pretty daring to screw your father's sister's son, wasn't it?

'Oh God, Ross. What about the door? It's not locked.'

'Forget the door.' His voice was muffled, dulled by the embrace of my juicy sex as he burrowed into the creases between my lips. His fingers had joined his tongue – I didn't know when – and he was engaged in a firm two-stroke of my hard little clit. I could feel his thumb, easing in between so that it slid suddenly and quickly into me and I cried out.

'Shush!' His hand was over my mouth, sealing it tight. For a moment I struggled, afraid that I wouldn't be able to breathe. I didn't like it. But then my nostrils flared, and the sudden intake of my own sexual scent from his hand made breathing seem a pointless irrelevance.

I relaxed against my out-thrust arms. My bare feet were braced against his shoulders, my knees as wide as they would stretch without hurting, my sex thrust forward and up to his face while his tongue worked its volcanic heat into me. I could feel the waves of a trembling climax shudder somewhere deep inside my body, and I tried to force them away.

Not yet. Not yet, I prayed silently, it's too soon. I pulled away a little, putting some air between me and Ross's mouth. He glanced up, his eyes piercing and alert.

'I said "yes". Didn't you hear me?' He took a deep breath as if to calm himself, and frowned at me in a way that made me melt inside. 'Come on, Sam, you can't back off now.'

'I'm not,' I murmured. 'I just don't want to come yet. I want to make it last, but you turn me on too much.'

He stood up and I entwined my arms around his neck, revelling in the stubbly brush of the short-cut hair that grazed my forearms. He was so sexy, so clean and masculine. If I was going to act as someone's slave, no other man would do.

His mouth sought mine and I crushed his lips with my own, my ardour rising through my body. I wanted him so badly that I didn't care how many lifeboat men there were in earshot. I lowered myself back on to the table and jerked his button fly open with one hand. His cock sprang out, tightly covered by the soft cotton of his Calvins, and I fumbled with the fabric, desperate to find the opening that would reveal him to my hands.

'Let me,' he murmured.

'No! Let me! Put your fingers back on my breast.' Submission has never been my strong point. I could hear him chuckling against my neck and I jabbed his ribs with my free hand. 'Stop it! We haven't signed the contract yet, so I can behave how I like.'

He began to laugh, louder this time, then gasped and became abruptly silent as I caught his bare cock in my fist and slid my fingers up and down its steely length. He was so ready that I felt a warm dab of pre-come spill on my stomach. I squirmed beneath him. It was too bad, no more foreplay, I had to have him inside me now.

I dragged my bag across the desk and rummaged for my little mauve box of condoms. Ross bit back a sound that was half-gasp, half-sob as I slipped one on to his charged and ready cock.

I gripped his hips with both hands and curved my legs up over his hard buttocks. He was so athletic, so fantastically fit from leaping in and out of boats all year round: it was just like GI Joe had met the good fairy and she'd made him come to life. That's why it gave me such great satisfaction to feel him yield to me in every way.

And that's why being bound by a slavery contract

would be so much fun. Role reversal for Ross and me was going to re-ignite the touchpaper, and make him see that it was me he wanted, not that milky-white creature, Louisa, that he'd brought to the family Christmas party.

At the thought of her, the green-eyed monster reared up and I determinedly closed my eyes and pulled Ross on to me. Into me.

His cock entered my creamed and ready sex with all the strength and rigidity of a policeman's baton. I inhaled sharply as he thrust all the way in without a pause. I urged him with my hands on his shoulders and my ankles at his hips until he moved to my rhythm. Quick. Slow. Double time. Gradually easing open the throttle until we pumped against each other, hip to hip, and my body was humming. Faster and faster until I thought that the desk would move across the floor and hit the wall. I gasped.

'Oh God, Ross, you make me feel so –'

I didn't have time to finish my sentence. As if in preparation for the month when he would be master, Ross suddenly pulled out of me, stripped off the condom, and pumped his cock in one hand. His hot come spilt in jerks and thrusts across my bare stomach and thighs, burning and searing into my skin. I cried out, frustrated and unfinished.

'You don't like that, do you?' he said. 'Get used to it. The slave-game starts here.'

With one stride, he had tucked himself in, crossed the room and opened the door. I watched, still horizontal and aghast on the desk, as he spoke to someone outside my field of vision. I let my head drop back on to the wooden surface, feeling the cushion of a sheaf of papers beneath my spilt hair.

When I next looked up, it was to see a man in yellow oilskins, boots and a navy sweater standing just inside the door. He had dark-blond hair, a two-day-old stubble and he didn't look terribly clean. Ross closed the door behind him and smiled slyly at me.

'Go ahead, Mike. You want her, she's yours.'

I struggled to sit up, then crashed down from the desk, grabbing up my skirt and boots as I hit the floor running. Ross reached me in a second. I shoved my boots against his chest to fend him off and tried to wriggle free. I needn't have bothered. It was just as if I wasn't moving: he was like a piece of granite. Immovable.

'Sam.' He held my face between his hands and I was forced to meet his gaze. His eyes were like black fire – boring deep into my soul and momentarily making me stop my struggling. 'Trust me. Have I ever hurt you?'

I shook my head, my eyes fixed on his.

'Do you trust me, Sam?' The serious look on his face and the emphasis he placed on the first word showed me how important this was to him.

I considered it, thinking about how well I knew him. We went back such a long way. The years of shared history and the childhood games, the tenderness and the thrill of the on-off sexual side. It must mean something. It must all add up to what he had just said: trust. I wasn't sure, though, and that little niggle of doubt made it all seem so much more exciting: the spice of potential danger. I pressed myself against him slightly and nodded.

That was enough for Ross. I felt his strong arms immediately pin mine to my sides as he turned me and thrust me forward over the desk. Then his hands pushed my hips and slid my naked bottom sideways so that Mike could see me. I felt very exposed, very bare, and I could feel two sets of eyes burning into my smarting cheeks.

'Go on.' It was Ross again, but his friend needed no further urging. His booted feet were between mine

12

and kicking them apart to spread me even before the sound of Ross's voice had died away. Thick fingers were rough on my back and I could feel his hands reach under to my sex, stretching and probing, thrusting upward with what felt like his whole hand. I yelped and there was a crinkling sound, then a strip of cloth was bound around my mouth. Ross's face was close to mine, his mouth by my ear, and I could see the clean white gleam of his teeth as he spoke.

'Come on, Sam. You know it'll be fun. Enjoy it – slave.'

His fingers slid between my shirt buttons and my skin. He eased my breasts from my bra so that he could pull and tweak them to full, raspberry-red erectness. Behind me, Mike had opened his oilskin trousers and I could feel the wide, hot stump of his cock pressing against my thigh.

I heard a tearing sound, and knew then that the slight movement behind me meant that he was sliding a condom on to himself with the fingers of one hand. I glanced down at the discarded wrapper, on the floor by my foot, and saw that he favoured Mates Superstrong. A careful guy. I smiled and shivered slightly with anticipation. This was going to be fun. Unexpected, but fun.

His hands cupped my buttocks and he lifted me slightly, opening and stretching me before he lowered my body on to him.

'She's so wet,' he muttered. 'Did she do this or did you butter her for me?'

'It's all her,' replied Ross. His hands engulfed my breasts and squeezed. 'Go ahead, Mike. You'll like her, she's so hot. She'd do it with anyone, the dirty little cat.'

I could hardly believe what I heard, and I opened my mouth to protest, then abruptly closed it. His words had given me an inexplicable thrill, and I decided to keep quiet and see what else he had to say.

'Tell me how good she feels on you. Tell me what it feels like to fuck her. If you make it good then I'll join in. Maybe I'll get the lads in to watch.'

An audience? Perhaps that was going too far. Since when had Ross made me the public property of his crew? Since when did he share? He'd never once, not in all our time together, suggested anything more group orientated than a quickie in my room while my brothers were busy with their Airfix kits in the next bedroom. And now here he was planning to gang-bang me with Mike the mechanic from the boathouse and considering an invitation for a crowd of burly men to look on.

I hated it.

No, I lie. I loved it. When Mike forced his thick cock into me from behind I creamed him with all the enthusiasm of a skin-flick star. The sexiness of his sweaty smell and the stickiness of the oilskins that stuck to the back of my thighs made up for any lack of finesse in his technique. He thrust and rutted behind me, gripping my hips until they hurt, and banging me against the side of the desk until I felt bruised. But I didn't care. I was lost in the heady sexual sensations of pleasure.

Ross had my breasts, and then freed my mouth from the cloth. He put his mouth near my ear and I closed my eyes to enjoy the warm feel of his breath on my neck. He whispered little words of endearment that made me feel special; wanted; beautiful. I rested my head on his shoulder and whispered back.

'Please, Ross. No one else. I don't want anyone in to watch.' I opened my eyes and tipped my head back, holding his gaze and staring at him with mute appeal. He remained very still for a few moments, then took a deep breath.

'OK. No audience – this time.' I sighed with relief and caressed the length of his cock lovingly with one hand. 'Now suck me, Sam. Suck me good and hard like only you can do.'

When he knelt up on the timber and thrust his shaft in my face, I fell on it as if I was born to do nothing but suck cock. His balls were so tight up under him that I thought they'd disappear, so I reached forward and wound my fingers around them, gently pulling and easing them until I could get them close to my lips.

My throat felt stretched and tight, the angle he was at making his glans thrust at the back of my palate and on down, but I loved it. The tightness and the near gag-reflex was bliss and I felt a fresh wash of my milky juice slick around Mike's cock just as he became stiff and tense behind me. His thighs were rigid against mine and I felt him lift me off the floor and force me forward on to Ross's crotch as he came: hot, pumping, muscular jerks that sent an echoing thrill and shudder deep through my body. I almost sobbed when he'd finished.

It didn't stop there. He withdrew and spun me round, ignoring Ross's yelp of dissatisfaction as my mouth left his cock, and crushed me to the floor so that he could brace his boot against the small of my back.

'Get down on the floor, darlin'. Kneel for me,' he muttered, the coastal lilt of his voice thick with lust.

My face was pushed into the carpet and the stench of cigarette fumes and years of dirty footwear almost made me retch. My hips were yanked up and my buttocks thrust out, then I felt him broach my bottom with one finger. It was horrible but fantastic.

'You like that, don'tcha? You like my finger in your sweet little arse.' He probed long and hard in my anus, his finger widening and stretching me until he

15

could introduce a second. 'D'you want more? D'you want to feel my cock stretching you?'

Then I heard him urge Ross, who clearly needed no second bidding because he sank to his knees behind me. I felt the tentative fumbling as he took the second condom from the pack on the table and moved nearer to introduce his cock. He hesitated, so that Mike quickly became impatient and grasped his friend's dick, pulling him so that Ross's hips bumped my buttocks and the head of his cock was hot against my tight little flower.

I moaned and widened my mouth around my own forearm. Anal had never been a big thing with me. I'd only done it a few times, just to please Ross who was crazy for it. I got off on knowing how – right now – he was probably ready to blast at the sight of my smooth, round buttocks and his big cock probing between my cheeks. I hardly needed Mike's clenched fist on my back to arch me further and make me thrust my bottom upward.

Ross slid into me slowly, hesitant at first, coaxing me with little whispers and murmurs of how much I'd like it, how I'd come when he was in me. I have to admit that the extra pair of hands and eyes did a lot to arouse me further and I could feel myself lubricating around him, some mysterious deep part of my body lusciously easing his passage.

'That's it,' he murmured. 'Open up for me. Oh, you feel so good. You're so hot and wet.' I felt the warm scrub of his balls against my shaven sex and knew he was all the way in. I felt so full, so stretched. Ross was a big guy and he'd filled me to capacity.

I heard an animal groan, a feral sound that was partly muffled, and I realised that it was me, moaning against my forearm as I gripped my own flesh with my teeth. God, it felt good. I was creamy and swollen and my flesh was pouting around his rigid prick. The thought of both men there, behind me, worshipping at the rounded altar of my behind, made me anticipate my approaching orgasm with relish.

I squeezed my eyes shut, panting hard and feeling the rutting thrusts inside me get faster and faster. I was going to explode. I was going to come. I braced my arms and threw my head back, crying out as I came, feeling my insides shuddering on to Ross. Letting my muscles clench on to Mike's fingers that were suddenly thrust deep into my sex.

Ross waited for me to finish, one warm hand stroking my hair as he leant forward over my body. I could feel his fingers toying with the silky, slightly curling ends and I preened like a cat under his caress. When the last undulations of my climax subsided, he began to move. Slow, slow, drawing out with care then easing gently back in. It was like being massaged with golden syrup, it felt so sweet and good.

I concentrated on the in-stroke. It was fabulous. It made me close my eyes and rest my forehead back down on my arm. The inward strokes are always so much better than the outward, so much more intense. There is such promise of fulfilment and ecstasy. Ross's cock was so hard, so satin-smooth. His movements were so perfectly timed. I felt a repeating echo of my climax tingle through my lower body and I tightened on to him.

I heard my careful breaths coming thick and deep, almost in time with his movement, then I began to drown in pure sensation as Mike's fingers were curved inside of me. He put gentle pressure on my g-spot and slid his hands about in my juiciness. The pressure made me feel like I needed to pee – it was so strong and strange that I shivered and bucked with the combined ecstasy of Ross's cock and Mike's frigging fingers.

'Sam, you're so wet. Does that feel good? Jesus, I

can't hold out much longer.' I could feel Ross swelling inside me, his cock reaching rock-hard proportions as he swivelled his hips and screwed me a little quicker. His balls were pressed tight to my sex with each inward thrust and I could hear the slicking sound of my lips pouting up to meet him around Mike's hand.

'It feels fantastic,' I whispered. 'Do it faster. Let me move for you.' I began to rock with him, careful not to let myself get out of rhythm with Mike's heavenly fingers. I felt Ross's hand grasp a hank of my hair and he pulled it, stretching my head up and back so that my scalp was on fire and my eyes smarted at the corners. He started to move fast, pumping himself in and out until it almost hurt and I cried out, unable to stay silent.

Hands came from nowhere to gag me, covering my mouth with strong male fingers, and I breathed hard through my nose, feeling an echo of my earlier climax shuddering deep within my sex. Ross seemed to sense it, for he gave a last, hard thrust and buried himself deep in me, pulling on my hair and squeezing one side of my buttock hard with his free hand. I felt his cock stiffen and jerk inside me, throbbing and arching with searing heat until he collapsed forward on to my perspiring back.

Mike's hand became still, his thumb jammed up against my rock-hard clit, his dick held tight in his other fist as he pumped himself off over my thighs. His come was hot and sticky and beautifully sweet, like condensed milk that just begged to be lapped up by the dirtiest cat in town – I just wished I could bend round that far.

I contented myself with lifting a trembling hand to his now half-mast cock, which was surrounded by curly blond scrub, and teasing a little drop with my forefinger. It glistened on my oval nail, pearly-white against the pink nail-bed: infinitely precious and special. I lifted it to my lips and tasted him: he was salty and bitter, like the freshest hand-prepared Japanese sushi.

He would do. I silently vowed to have him again, alone, some other time when Ross was not in town.

The contract in Sader-Masoch's *Venus in Furs* was very wordy: Severin had agreed to obey Wanda almost to the death, renouncing his rights unconditionally. I, the physical coward that I am, had decided to tone it down a little. Sex with Ross was worth a lot, but certainly not worth dying for.

I had written and rewritten until I got it just right, and there was a single sheet of paper with my neatest handwriting in carefully parallel lines. I was quite proud of it, and I smiled at Ross as I slid it out of the envelope.

'Sign here.' I twisted the thick, creamy vellum on the polished table-top and watched as Ross shrugged his shoulders, then marked on the dotted line with his familiar sparing hand. I signed below with the usual flourish, then we smiled at each other in the twilight. Co-conspirators in the greatest sexual adventure of our lives. I lifted the paper to my mouth and sealed it with a kiss, then walked slowly around the desk to sit in Ross's lap.

'One month,' I murmured.

'One month,' he said. 'No more, no less. But under my terms.'

He held the creamy paper at the top, inches from my face, and slowly tore it down the middle. I stared, first at the paper, then at him.

'Hang on –' I began.

He silenced me with a shake of his head.

'You're mine. You want to be my slave. My pet. My little alley-cat. So I make the rules. Sign here.'

He placed a document folder on the table and I

twisted in his lap to open it. Inside were two sheets of paper filled with close type and I read them with slowly mounting horror. I could feel Ross's breath on my neck as he read it over my shoulder.

It was identical to the one in *Venus in Furs*. There was lots of stuff about vengeance and retaliation being forbidden, the need for total submission, the presence of cruelty and occasional mercy, and a mention of torture for the sake of whiling away time. The only let-out was to be a word of surrender, spoken in true desperation, which would end the whole game: Marquise.

'I'm not signing it,' I said, suddenly feeling distinctly stroppy. 'And it says here that you're going to change my name: I will not be called Puss.'

'Yes you will. That's to be your name from now on.'

'No it's not.'

'Of course you will. Severin had a name change. Wanda called her slave Gregor.' He stood and unceremoniously brushed me off his lap on to the floor. 'You'll do it because you want to. You'll do it because it's the most exciting thing that's ever happened to you. And above all, you'll do it because I say you will, Puss.'

We left for the country a week later.

Chapter Two

'*H*ow much holiday did you get?' I asked Ross. He had driven up the previous day and spent the night with me in Kingston. We had lazed in bed late, and then hit the South Circular after lunch.

We were travelling together partly for companionship and partly because I had no car: my beloved ten-year-old Golf had finally given up the ghost just after Christmas. I remained carless because the first few months of the year are never a good time for a major purchase. In fact my bank account was still positively reeling from all the last-minute present-buying back in December.

'I've got a whole month off,' Ross said. 'What about you?'

'Same.'

I smiled happily at him, feeling a warm glow inside at the thought of spending four weeks alone with my favourite cousin. I pressed a few buttons on the car stereo and when I found nothing but idle chat, I rooted around in the glove compartment for a tape.

'This is mine,' I said accusingly, pulling out a faded Echo and the Bunnymen cassette.

21

'I know.' Ross grinned. 'I pinched it from you years ago.'

'You sod. I spent ages searching for this. Does it still work?'

'Yeah, I think so. Put it on.'

It worked. I turned up the volume and rested my forearm on the window, letting the long-forgotten album take me back to my sixth-form days in the early eighties. When my favourite song ended, I snuggled down in the passenger seat and watched the muscles in Ross's forearm twist and bulge each time he changed gear.

'Imagine you getting four weeks off,' he said after a while. 'How did you manage it? I though you estate agent types only got the regulation fortnight plus bank holidays.'

'We do.' I couldn't help a smug grin. 'But the market's had a bit of a rush. It must be early spring fever. I finalised three sales in as many days, and Larry was so full of the joys of commission that he was a walkover.'

'You should have asked for longer. You could do with getting out of the city; you look tired.' He reached over and rested his warm palm on my thigh.

'I'm happy with what I've got,' I said, lightly stroking the back of his hand with my forefinger. 'Just think, a whole month to do exactly what we want.'

'Exactly what *I* want,' he corrected. I wrinkled my nose and let him delude himself.

We stopped just outside Swindon for coffee and bacon sandwiches, then Ross let me drive for a while. I loved getting behind the wheel of his car. Although it was old and dented from numerous accidental run-ins with harbour bollards, his BMW had more power and guts than most of the other cars on the road. It got us to Bath in record time, where we swapped seats again before heading on.

Three-quarters of an hour later, Ross pulled into a lay-by screened with trees and asked me to step out of the car. I only did as he said because I had no idea of what was to follow.

I stood on the tarmac by the hedge and watched him as he opened the boot, took out my suitcase and turned to face me.

'Strip,' he said.

'Ross! What the hell are you doing?' I stared in horror as he opened the catches of my case and unceremoniously threw my possessions over the hawthorn hedge into the field full of bemused cows beyond.

'You're a slave now,' he reminded me patiently. 'You don't need any of that.'

The suitcase was one of my favourites. A battered blue leather job that had been with me since college. It followed the clothes over the hedge, and then Ross took a step towards me, his usually genial face a blank mask.

'Strip off. Hurry up. Move.'

Trying to tell myself that it was all part of the game, I drew my sweater over my head and dropped it on the ground. My skirt made a drift of creamy fabric next to it and I stood still, waiting for the next command, a warmth swelling in my belly at the thought that any passing long-distance trucker could pull in and see me half-naked.

Ross stepped forward, slipping warm fingers across the surface of my skin so that he could snap the clasp of my gorgeous new wonderbra. I sighed as it flew over the hedge, and then shrugged. What the hell. My job showing prospective buyers around other people's houses was as good as an aerobics class any day so I had no need of the wonderbra to keep me rounded and pert.

The cool air caressed my nipples and tightened

23

them into appealing little buds. I smiled beguilingly at Ross. He gave my almost-naked body the once-over and I saw a muscle flicker in his jaw as if he were holding on very tight to his self-control, then he slipped his fingers into the side-seam of my knickers and gave them a harsh tug.

There. I was naked. Somewhere on the A303 with the noisy traffic just the other side of the trees. Did I care? Yes. A little. But it was fun and part of the contract we had signed.

He slipped a sleeveless white sheath over me and smoothed it down my thighs, then his hands lingered at my sex briefly, very teasingly. I thrust myself forward on to his fingers and he grinned at the damp patch that darkened the cloth, then stood up and stepped back. He buckled a red velvet collar around my neck. There was a silver disc attached to the buckle.

'What does that say?' I asked, holding it between thumb and forefinger but unable to see it despite angling my chin in every direction.

'Your name,' he said simply. 'Puss.'

I grimaced and then gave in. If it gave him a thrill to put a cat collar on me and dress me in a shroud, then it was fine by me. His hands warmed my shoulders and he smiled at me, then dropped a tender kiss on my forehead.

'There, my little slave-cat,' he murmured. 'You really do look good in that. I like you better already. Let's go.'

And that was that. I was put in the back of the car, with the heater on high, and he didn't deign to speak to me for the rest of the journey.

When we arrived it was nearly dark. A big moon slipped up behind the trees that edged the property, casting a candlewax sheen on the long gravel drive and house. A low building of indeterminate age, it

24

had been rented in Ross's name for the month, and he swung the keys casually from his forefinger as we walked up the path.

'The bags?' he prompted. 'You may have no luggage, but I certainly have. See to it.'

Huffing and puffing, I dragged his bags up to the front porch, wondering whether he had put in a couple of concrete blocks just to punish me. As he put the key to the lock, the dark red door swung eerily open and we both stared – me in amazement and Ross with evident pleasure.

Just inside the door, their pale skin lent a golden glow by the light of hundreds of flaming candles in the hallway beyond, stood two of the weirdest sisters I had ever seen. They were much younger than us, probably about nineteen or twenty. Their faces were identical: perfect ovals relieved only by the merest hint of cheekbone, dark-lashed eyes with a smudge of gothic eyeliner underneath, white-blonde hair parted and plaited into serpentine braids that shone like spun silk. I swallowed hard and let my eyes drift down, aware of a sudden tightening in my fascinated sex.

The sisters were beautiful. Skin like milk and honey with small curving breasts and long legs that gleamed through the diaphanous muslin of their long skirts. They wore nothing above the waist but tiny beaten silver caps which covered each nipple. I found myself suddenly desperate to taste those strawberry-coloured buds. To tongue them and suck the silver from their swollen flesh.

'I'm glad you could make it.' It was Ross speaking. I almost got a crick in my neck as I jerked my head sideways to stare at him in amazement.

'Do you know these people?' I stuttered. He ignored me and spoke directly to the sisters.

'Please excuse Puss. She's had a long day. Perhaps

you would show her where to put the baggage and help her bathe. I'll be up shortly to instruct her.'

He walked past them and strode into the warm depths of the house, out of sight. I stood on the doorstep for a moment longer, then stepped inside to find that the heat hit me like a wall. The humid closeness was very welcome in my undressed state, and I felt an instantaneous prickle of sweat under my arms. The interior of the house seemed aglow, like a great equatorial greenhouse: sultry and humid, and somehow reeking of sexual promise.

One of the sisters stopped me as I entered, her hand gentle and light as it rested on my forearm. I noticed that she wore a single, gleaming silver bangle on her wrist. I waited for her to say something, but when nothing happened and no one spoke, I wondered whether they would show me the way or whether I'd have to prompt them. The one who held my arm stood very close, almost nipple to nipple although she was taller than me by several inches. She placed her fingers on my cheek.

Her hand was warm and soft and seemed to vibrate with some inner energy that transmitted itself to me in an electric shiver. She smelled of citrus scent and fresh clean laundry, and I swayed towards her without meaning to as I felt her forefinger trace over my cheek and up to my eyebrows. She smoothed the flesh of my temple and then ran the light tip of her finger down my straight nose before slipping it between my lips where I instinctively sucked the subtly musk-flavoured nail.

My hands were still welded to the handles of Ross's bags. I could hardly drop them on anyone's toes, so I stood very still and gripped the leather until my knuckles were white, conscious that my mouth was full of the taste of sex and my mind was fixed on roughly the same subject.

Girls aren't actually my thing. Some of my friends had done what they called 'experimenting' at college. I'd never been even remotely interested or tempted to join in. But these pale sisters just screamed sex. It oozed from every pore. I couldn't help but be attracted to them with their decadent looks and their innocent blondeness. Besides, I was a long way from home, and Ross hadn't fed me since the bacon sandwiches in Swindon, so I forgave myself for feeling a little bit unusual.

The other sister walked a complete circle around us, her eyes slipping over my body in such an intimate way that it felt as if she had touched me with her hands. Her eyes were not as kind as her sister's; they were a paler blue that reflected the light of the dozens of candles balanced on the window sills. Eerie. I couldn't even guess at the thoughts that lay behind those eyes.

She was behind me for a long time, not touching, just looking, and I could feel a fierce redness blush all over my body, and a strange crinkling of the hairs at the back of my neck. When she stepped again into my peripheral vision, I saw that she had folded her arms and her breasts were pushed upwards and together, creating an appetising rounded cushion. I quelled my strange, unbidden desire and gazed down at the plush crimson rug beneath my feet. Dazed and confused, as they say.

First they took me to the room that was to be Ross's. Up a flight of stairs that hugged the wall and on to the landing, along a thick warm carpet, past several closed doors to the end. The heat of the house was all-pervading and by the time we reached the landing I had a pearly sheen across my forehead and the muslin dress stuck to my thighs and back.

The first sister – the nicer one – pushed open a pale

door and gestured for me to enter. I walked in and put the bags down on a soft rug just inside the door.

The room was large and had windows on three walls. On the far wall was a cast-iron fireplace with pretty red and salmon tiles and an iron fender, behind which glowing coals made the room hotter than the rest of the house – if that were possible. Behind the door was a bed large enough to accommodate several people with ease. The bedding was soft and white, while over the footboard a generous-sized silk eiderdown had been folded in readiness for the occupant, presumably when the heating failed. I moved the bags nearer to the wardrobe and turned to look at the girls.

'What are your names?' I asked. 'What shall I call you?'

They looked at each other. The nice one lifted her hands as if she would sign something, but the other roughly grasped her wrists and stilled them, shaking her head and frowning.

'Well, I have to call you something.' I felt a stir of annoyance. This was all so mysterious and not at all what I had planned. My mind had constructed an elaborate scenario of Ross and me, alone in the country, eating grapes from each other's mouths and engaging in a little vigorous toe-sucking. Instead he'd disappeared and left me with Weird and Gilly or whatever their names were, and no clothes to change into. To cap it all there were those stiff pieces of A4 with my signature flourished on the dotted line. It wasn't legally binding, was it? He'd hardly take it to a court of law, surely.

But I knew Ross. He would.

Anyway, I didn't want to tear up the contract. Part of me – that perverse dark part that had always got me into trouble over the years – wanted to see exactly how far he'd go with the slave thing. And to pull out would mean that I was a big wimp: I knew from years of experience in our childhood games that wimps were held in the greatest ridicule.

You can choose your friends but you can't choose your family, and Ross fell very definitely into the latter category. I didn't fancy years of painful verbal torture on Christmases and birthdays if I pulled out on day one of our agreement. No way. I was staying put. I'd see out the month, because I wanted to get Ross back: I wanted to supplant the new girlfriend. I wanted things to be like they were before, when I was number one in Ross's life.

'Is this my room too?'

Two pale heads shook and together they backed out of the room and beckoned me with synchronised fingers. I took a deep breath and followed. Did they actually talk or not?

We went in single file along a landing where the walls seemed to exude heat and light, to a door set in the wall that was flanked by two burning wall-sconces. Positively medieval, I thought. Ever the professional, I found myself wondering what their insurance company would have to say about so many fire hazards and how I would compose the house details, then dismissed the thought as we began to climb the tiny staircase beyond; I was at play, not work. And it was obviously all done just for effect.

At the top, the stairs widened out into an over-heated attic room with the regulation sloping ceiling and tiny dormer windows. The blinds were down and securely fastened, the walls were lined with purple silk and the floor warmly spread with a matching wall-to-wall carpet that felt like velvet under my feet. Catlike, I curled my toes into it and experienced the first real stirrings of pleasure that I'd had all day.

At the far end I could see an old Victorian bathtub set in a wood-panelled corner, and a pile of folded towels of the same dark mauve as the carpet lay on a stool by its side. To my left was a black iron bedstead, devoid of mattress or coverings: simply the flat iron-work base. It looked desperately uncomfortable and I silently prayed that someone would see fit to carry a mattress up the tiny stairwell, or else I was going to have a sleepless night. Assuming that this was my room.

It was.

'You'll sleep here during the time that I don't need you.' It was Ross. He had silently mounted the stairs and was standing close behind me, his fingers lightly resting on my shoulders. 'Seph and Sasha will bathe you and ready you,' he said, pointing out which twin was which. 'You will be chained, as a good slave-cat should be, and then you may begin.'

'B-begin what?' Did he think I had some plan as to how the month would progress? Apparently he did.

'Begin your time as my slave. It was your idea, Puss, so I imagine you know exactly what that will entail. If you have any hesitations then I'm sure I shall be able to help you out.'

He moved to where Sasha stood by the nearest dormer window and raised his hand to her breast. I stared with fascination as he moulded his palm to the curving underside and slowly squeezed. Her nipple, complete with its cylindrical silver cap, swelled and rose, and I watched as he dipped his head to fasten his lips on to her warm skin.

A pang of jealousy tempered with adrenalin and excitement shot through my stomach. I was beginning to hate him, this new Ross who held me in such contempt. How dare he? I stalked over and grasped him, pulling at his cropped dark hair and thrusting his head back so that I could stare into his eyes.

'I may be your slave.' I spat the words through my teeth, my tones clipped and precise. 'But I am not your court jester. Get away from that girl before I do something we both regret.'

We both stood very still, eyeball to eyeball. There was a look of surprise deep in Ross's eyes, and I saw him weigh up his options. Then his hand shot out and struck me a hard slap to the face. It didn't hurt but it felled me as if I was a tree that had been struck by lightning.

I was on the floor, staring at the soft mauve pile of the carpet, before I even realised that he had struck me. A righteous fury flared inside me and I wiped my lip with the back of my hand, horrified but aroused to see my own blood streak in a crimson dash across my pale skin.

'You violent bastard,' I cried, staring at his boots. Above me I heard him laugh and, curiously, instead of angering me more, it turned me on in an obscure and scary way. A charge ran through my body and my hair felt as if it was standing on end as I raised myself to my knees and gazed up at him. His dark eyes met mine with an inscrutable look.

'Chain her,' he said. And turned on his heel to leave the room.

Hot fingers fastened on to my skin with predatory firmness and I heard a tiny sigh escape from the pouted lips of one girl. Hands slipped and slid while mouths moved across flesh, leaving warm trails of saliva that dissolved into the soft white foam of the bath-water.

The room was like a sauna – a sweltering dry heat tempered by the steam which rose in thick curls from the bath. Swollen lips fastened on to my nipples and they began to gorge hungrily, drawing and pulling at the tender flesh and making swirls of sexual ecstasy curl around my head and down my back.

I gripped the sides of the bath and let my eyes fall

31

closed, feeling feverish from the heat. They could do whatever they wished with me, I had no objection. They were so beautiful and so skilled, and the room so warm and relaxed, that they could keep me like this all night. I wondered vaguely where Ross was. Wash her and chain her, he had said. If this was washing, then chaining didn't seem like an unappealing prospect.

A firm hand curved under my buttocks and gentle pressure eased me upwards until my hips broke the surface. Almost immediately, fingers and mouths were fastened to my warm wet skin, stroking and probing, and I could hear my own breathing – rapid and shallow – as they smoothed the stubbly regrowth of my pubic hair with their twin tongues.

Sasha moved first, always the leader, and drove her left hand hard between my thighs. My knees hit the sides of the bath and I shrank back a little at the chill of the enamel: it was a shock after the steamy heat of the water. Sasha stared hard into my eyes and I felt myself drowning again in the clear blue irises. She nudged my legs apart once more and slipped the forefinger of her other hand up over my chin and into my mouth.

I sucked on the exquisitely manicured nail, running the tip of my tongue around and under to the tiny ridges that made up her fingerprint. Her hands were soft and smooth, like a soapstone carving, and I sucked as if I wanted to drink her in. Which – by that time – I did, of course.

Her other hand continued to move in ever-decreasing circles, closer and closer to my sex. Her nails made tiny red weals on the tender skin of my inner thighs, and when she finally slipped her middle finger between the groove of my freshly aroused lips, I almost begged her. I needn't have worried: she plunged in, heedless of the thick silver thumb ring that grazed and pressed at my labia. She twisted and frigged with her finger, pressing upward so that I felt that strange urge to pee. I felt as though I was sinking into sweltering pleasure, and entering a tropical territory that I had never walked before. It felt so incredibly good that if I could have died then, it would all have been worthwhile.

One finger became two. The ring that had grazed and hurt a little became the most stimulating clitoral pressure. The onyx stone set in the wide silver band seemed designed to press against my swollen clit, encouraging its reddened length to grow and swell, making my whole being shudder and jump.

To the other side of me Seph smiled and stroked my belly with both of her large, firm hands. Her fingers seemed nimble and clever as she swirled the hot water and encircled my navel. Her tongue followed her fingers and I felt her dive in with her nose pressed to my stomach. Her pale hair began to escape from its confining braids and I watched as it sank slowly into the water to move like tiny eels that curled wetly around my half-abandoned nipples and breasts.

Sasha's fingers twisted inside me, stretching me, and I felt the first waves of unbearable pleasure slip and slide like honey through my limbs. Orgasm was the only goal and I could feel it coming closer, homing in on me, trembling through my nerve-endings and clouding my awareness with a bitter-sweet heat.

I love it. I love that moment just before climax when you can hardly speak, only cry out in that animal way that makes you sound like you're going to die: oh God, this is fabulous –

'I thought I told you to chain her!' Ross's voice sliced through my dreamlike state with razor-sharp precision. I was abruptly dropped back under the steaming water and the two girls sat back on their heels, gazing at him with their limpid eyes while the

33

candles cast strange shadows across their cheeks. 'This slave is no longer a person. Think of her as an animal, just a pet, and treat her as such. If you wish to partake of her, you may – but you must chain her first. Besides –' he leant back against the door frame and gave a slow lazy grin that caught at my heart '– I think she'll learn to like it like that.'

'Never,' I cried, struggling to sit up and look dignified despite my bare breasts and obvious sexual arousal. The sudden lack of orgasm had been crushing, but I felt as if I suddenly held all the cards. Chaining me would make me look particularly attractive to Ross; my arse was shapely and I knew how to stick it out to my advantage. Maybe, just maybe, I could use this submission thing to my own ends.

I stood up and stepped out of the bath, then I grabbed a towel that had been warming on a hot rail nearby and wrapped it firmly around my body. Ross laughed – a low ominous rumble that reverberated around the inside of my head – then strode across the room and unwrapped me again.

'Hey!' I said. 'How come I'm the only one who's naked here?'

There was a moment of silence and I could hear the slow drip drip of the tap on to the soapy bath-water. Then Sasha came and stood very close to me.

'Maybe we should all be naked,' she murmured. 'Then we can see if we like each other.'

In her hands she held a length of narrow golden chain and two leather manacles that had been lined with soft fur. She slipped them around my wrists, her eyes intimate and never leaving mine. I found myself holding my breath and trying not gaze at those beautiful fingers that had given me so much pleasure.

As she clicked the tiny padlocks shut on the manacles, I felt a frisson of excitement that sent ripples over my hot skin and I knew I was covered in goosebumps despite the sultriness of the room.

Sasha stood back and went to Ross's side. She stood still for a moment. Then, at a word from him, she unlaced her filmy skirt and let it drift to the floor. I stifled a gasp. Her body was perfect, like Venus come to walk the earth. Narrow waist, flaring and gently rounded hips, endless legs and a carefully trimmed nest of blonde pubic curls. It made me want to step forward and run my fingers through it, her pelt was so glossy and soft-looking. I wondered briefly whether she bleached it to match her hair, then shook my head to clear it.

'Happier?' Ross's eyes met mine as he spoke, and a smile curved his lips. He looked divine, like a demonic angel, and I felt a tug of pure lust pull at my sex. We stared at each other for a long time. His eyes were full of interest and challenge, and mine – I hoped – met that challenge and raised the stakes even higher.

'Much happier,' I said.

There was a sound to my right and I glanced down to see that Seph, the gentle, lovely Seph, was crouching at my feet and encircling my ankles with matching manacles. The length of chain was slightly heavier, and had a spare length that seemed to trail off to one side for a moment. Then I understood – my ankles were to be attached to my wrists by the means of this long fine chain, restricting my movements. Keeping me bent forward.

Seph raised herself to her knees and fastened the length to the centre of my wrist chain, then stood and placed her hands on my shoulders. Her mouth was so close, her lips so pink and lush, that I couldn't help myself. I leant forward and opened my mouth to hers, taking her petal-soft lips between my own and sucking. She yielded, and I felt her sway even closer to me, her small flat nipples briefly brushing mine with erotic

35

gentleness before she stepped back and went to stand next to her naked sister.

I was consumed with passion, standing there naked in the hot room with swirls of steam curling up from the bath-water behind me. I took a faltering step towards them, then stopped dead. Seph had mimicked her sister and unlaced her skirt, letting it fall around her narrow feet like a drift of warm, pale goosedown.

My eyes travelled the length of her beautifully toned legs, then stopped. I couldn't breathe. My lungs felt taut and tight, my throat constricted to a narrow tube. I clawed the air with one manacled hand and searched Seph's face with mounting incomprehension.

Seph was a boy.

Her legs were muscular and male, her cock as strong and virile as Ross's. He. He. He, I said to myself, silently wondering whether this was one of Ross's tactics to beat me into submission. *His* legs were muscular and male, *his* cock as strong and virile as Ross's. His waist tapered from narrow hips and, now that I looked closely, his breasts were the under-developed bee-stings of an adolescent.

It was only his face that had that oval, girlish beauty; the androgynous smoothness that had made me assume that his gender was the same as his sister's. That, and the silken blond hair that reached almost to his waist.

I looked him fully in the face and he gave me a shy, tentative smile. I kept my lips firmly closed and willed myself not to smile back, but I knew I was fighting a losing battle. Seph's gentle beauty had me hooked and it didn't matter to me whether he was girl, boy, or plain red herring, I still fancied him more than I had a right to. And Ross knew it.

He stepped away from the twins and came to stand in front of me, his body so close that I could see the excited beat of his heart through the sweat-damp fabric of his white T-shirt.

'Hold her still,' he said to them. 'I don't want her to move more than a muscle.'

The twins did as he told them and I felt their hands pressing me until I was bending over the bath with my face dangerously close to the water. The steam and heat caressed my face and shoulders, giving my skin a humid glow.

They strapped a narrow leather belt around my waist and used it to hold me in position. My arse felt high, exposed and vulnerable, and I wiggled it a little when I got bored of waiting. Ross slapped one cheek and it stung like hell. I winced but didn't make a squeak. He'd have to go further than that to make me beg.

But not that much further.

He used a short tawse on me, the leather making gentle 'thwack' noises as it kissed my skin. I wriggled and squirmed, not used to the sensation of stinging pleasure. I could feel my behind beginning to glow with what I was sure was a beacon-like pink. He beat me for a full five minutes, until I twisted and writhed and pulled against my manacles. I couldn't escape. If I was honest, I'd say I didn't want to.

When my skin was blushed and stinging from my shoulders to my thighs, he stopped. I felt him probe between my legs and I thrilled to his touch. The thorough whipping had set my senses on fire and any contact with my sex was bliss. I let him open me with his fingers, then relaxed under his gentle hands as he introduced a smooth dildo. Looking down between my breasts, I caught a glimpse of hard black rubber, about five inches long. It filled me. I gasped slightly when it was all the way in, because it felt so good.

I waited for Ross to move it again, expecting him to screw me with it, but he didn't.

37

'I'm attaching a chain to this,' he said. 'A fine gold chain that fixes to the three tiny rings set into the end of the dildo. One of them comes up between your buttocks and the other two either side of your groin. I'm going to fasten them to the belt and they will keep this in place.'

He did it, then let his hands play over my thighs. I could hear him breathing, even feel the faint warmth of his exhaled breath on my bottom, and it turned me on. As if I needed turning on. I was so hot, so ready for him, that I hardly knew what to do with myself. I eased my legs apart and silently begged him to do more.

'Call me old-fashioned,' he said loudly, for the benefit of the twins as much as for me. 'But I'm going to think of my slave as a non-person. As such, she will have no sexual gratification unless I decree it. This little chastity number should see that she isn't accessible. If anyone wishes to have access to her, they'll need the key.'

I whimpered. Not have sexual gratification unless he decreed it? How could I bear it? I tried to straighten up and found myself pinned down by the twins. Ross stood close behind me and moulded his body to mine.

'Luckily for you,' he murmured, 'I decree it now. You'll come now because I want you to. I want to see you writhe with pleasure. I want to see you shudder and hear you cry out.'

His hand slid to my clit and began a slow circular massage that made my sex swell up to greet his fingers. I was so wet that he had no need to moisten his fingers, but he did anyway, spitting on his hand and smoothing it into my naked folds until I was as slippery as a bowl of warm oil. The dildo moved inside me, the black rubber warming to my body temperature, and I squeezed my insides, gripping it with my sex and thrilling as my flesh folded around it in a tight hug.

'She's such a bad slave,' whispered Ross tenderly. 'She pretends to be submissive but she still gets me to do things the way she wants them, without even speaking.'

His hands were both on my sex now, his thumbs pressing together and pouting my lips so that my clit stuck out like a little tongue. I smiled and circled my hips a little so that my buttocks gave the front of his jeans a little rub. He was rock hard behind the button fly, his erection straining against the faded denim and digging in between my cheeks to press on the fine chain that was fastened between them.

I heard a rustling as the twins moved to him. Seph placed his hands on my bottom and held me wide while Sasha released Ross's cock from his denims and slipped her head between us to take it briefly in her mouth. Having moistened him with her saliva, she let her fingers glide sensuously up and down his granite length as she slid a gossamer-thin condom on to him. Seph squeezed and stretched my buttocks apart, his thumb looped in the chain.

Ross's cock was poker-hot when Sasha held it to me and I could feel the wetness she had spread on the rubber-clad head to ease his passage. As if I needed that. Somewhere deep inside me, in some nameless part of my body, there was a lush soft centre. I lubricated for him like a fresh-cream cake: a delicious éclair that just begged to be split and devoured. I pressed myself out towards him, jutting my hips and tempting him. He took the bait, and my bottom, with enthusiasm and I found myself matching him thrust for thrust.

Seph's hands were warm on my skin, Sasha's hot breath purring in tight little excited exhalations where she was so close. The dildo, deep inside my sex,

39

throbbed and dragged at my flesh. I clung on for dear life until conscious thought eluded me and my thoughts slipped inside one another with confusing speed.

I felt Ross stiffen and jerk inside me. The sensation of his pleasure, pure muscle arcing inside my juicy sex, made me shiver and groan. My vision became raggedly blurred and I could feel all the little nerve-endings inside my head fighting to keep my body upright. I was coming. Coming. Sinking in an ocean of light and heat.

I took a deep, gasping breath, like a drowning man, and let myself come. My orgasm bowled me over, literally, and I found myself face forward in the water, spluttering and half-choking as the sudden lack of breath tipped me into a gasping, shuddering climax that rocked my body and my mind.

One month, we had said. I wished it was one year.

Chapter Three

When I awoke the next morning, I was aware of a burning soreness in my sex and in my bottom. Ross had used me until he was exhausted. Then he had stood by and watched while Sasha took his place and inserted her thumb deep into my ass, pressing hard on the fleshy wall that separated her digit from the dildo. Her actions brought me, almost immediately, to another pelvis-bucking orgasm. I longed to turn and catch her pale pink mouth with my own, to pierce her mouth with my tongue and lick her soft palate all the way back to her throat.

But I was chained so firmly I could hardly breathe, let alone turn around. I could see by dipping my head slightly that Seph had retreated to crouch by the door, just on the edge of my field of vision. His blond hair fell around his shoulders and obstructed my view of his chest and stomach, but behind his knees I could see the slow, long strokes of his hand as he caressed himself. He was gorgeous and I wanted him. I knew that the minute Ross gestured to him, Seph would have me. And I would be weak at the knees with suppressed lust.

Ross didn't make that gesture, and I was not about to beg.

What little sun there was found the high attic windows and inched into the corner of the room, where I had slept. No one had seen fit to bring me a mattress and there was no way that I was going to lie down on the metal springs that stretched like taut barbed wire between the bedposts.

I had dragged a quilt and a handful of soft sheepskin throws over to the warmest corner, the place where the hot-water pipes to the bath ran just beneath the floorboards, and settled down to an exhausted sleep.

I awoke in daylight but had no idea of the time. My mind was soon concentrated on the soreness between my legs, and the knowledge that the rubbery dildo was still firmly chained into my sex.

The dormer window above showed a blue sky streaked with mackerel clouds. The pale blue was blushed with salmon pink as if the season was high summer, despite it being so early in the year. I considered what time of day it might be. Just after dawn? Maybe. But it could equally have been dusk. I wondered what was going on at my office, and felt that unfamiliar, gorgeous satisfaction that came with the knowledge that, whatever was happening, I would have no part in it for a month.

Four whole weeks. A long and very welcome holiday. I let my eyes fall shut and pictured my desk: cheap veneer piled high with house details and photographs, scattered pens and empty coffee mugs, buff envelopes and the odd post-it note. My desk diary would still be open at Friday's entry, but if anyone cared to flick through it – and nosy Kimberly, the receptionist, certainly would – they would see nothing but blank pages for weeks to come. Fabulous.

I hadn't realised how much my dead-end job had

bored me until I had got away. I stretched my arms up above my head and squeezed my sex on to the dildo. It felt good, sensuous and over-full. There were certainly very few opportunities for me to have this kind of experience in the day-to-day tedium of checking house details and soothing irritated clients, I thought, beginning to really enjoy myself.

A bell jangled and made me jump. I glanced towards the source of the sound and saw that an old-fashioned serving-maid call system was still in operation in the house. An iron bell set on a curving leaf of metal was positioned just above the tiny fireplace. I had to assume that I was being summoned.

Grabbing a coarse linen sheet and winding it around my naked body – all my other garments had been removed from the room – I walked carefully towards the door, my normally athletic and purposeful stride reduced to a near-shuffle by the chains that ran between my manacled ankles.

Sighing as I opened the door, I wondered again what I had let myself in for with this slave thing: it was all so much more complicated than I had planned. For some reason I had imagined that I would still be in control of the course of events. Judging by the experience of the previous night, that was some hope.

The heat of the house was still as intense as it had been the previous night, a torrid warmth that seemed to emanate from the very bricks and mortar, drying the air and expanding the silence. I could still hear the frantic jangling of the bell in the room behind me as I shimmied along the polished floorboards of the dark landing.

I found Ross. He stood by the Aga in the kitchen, his brow practically folded in half with a deep frown and his hands thrust on his hips like an angry army sergeant. I knew I was supposed to be scared, but I couldn't suppress a tingling shiver of excitement that raised the hairs on the back of my neck when I saw him.

He had shrugged himself into a long black leather coat which, teamed with a dark pullover and black jeans, made him look like an up-to-date German officer. All he needed were the little steel-rimmed spectacles and he'd be my idea of fun on a Saturday night. With an attitude to match.

'Hello,' I said, more to break the stony silence than anything else.

'At last.' Ross stared across the kitchen at me with cold eyes. 'I rang for you ten minutes ago. Some slave you're turning out to be. And what is that get-up you're wearing? You look like a spare mummy in *Tales from the Crypt*. Take it off.'

'But I haven't got any clothes.'

'I said take it off.' He strode towards me across the flagstones and ripped the sheet away, leaving me with friction burns on the tender skin beneath my arms. I shuddered and stepped back, feeling the edge of a rug beneath my feet and moving carefully to avoid tripping over it. He advanced again until the toe-caps of his boots crushed my fashionably blue-varnished toenails into the thick pile of the rug, and I couldn't move any more.

'That's better,' he murmured, one hand cupping my right breast and squeezing it with firm insistence. 'That's much better. Now show me how servile you can be. On your knees, Puss.'

I wriggled my toes free and sank to my knees. I'd heard Ross talk like this before, and I knew what he wanted. I slipped my fingers over the button fastening of his jeans and felt the hardness of his rigid cock beneath. A tremor of excitement flashed through my gut as I anticipated a nice, leisurely twenty minutes of giving head.

He slapped my hand away.

44

'Follow orders, or I'll have you whipped.'

'What do you want?' I heard the petulance in my voice even before he did. He raised one dark eyebrow and stared down at the top of my head.

'Yours is not to reason why, or to ask. You wait until you're told. And right now I'm ordering you to stay on your knees until I tell you to get up. Put your hands on the floor and show me your backside.'

I did as I was told, wondering whether the contract I had signed would really stand up in a court of law. Indignation and rage seethed inside me, and I could feel my notoriously hot blood boiling away in my veins. God help Ross when I was free, because when I no longer had chains to bind me, I was going to exact a revenge that no normal person would even think of, let alone carry out.

He strode around me, his boots ringing on the quarry tiles, then stepped on to the rug and came to a halt behind me. I felt vulnerable and a little uneasy. The new Ross that had been revealed over the past twenty-four hours was capable of anything, and I wondered what his next devilish trick was going to be.

I didn't have long to wait.

His hands were hot and dry on my thighs, like sun-baked desert rocks, as he prised my legs apart and subjected me to a minute inspection. His thumb grazed and rubbed, and I could feel the tiny butterfly caress of his index finger as he probed and examined my still raw sex and anus. I felt him drizzle half a bottle of warmed, sweet almond oil on to my buttocks and massage it into me.

I held my bottom tight under his fingers, but to no avail. The oil eased the passage of his fingers so much that he slid in without any effort at all. I tightened for all I was worth, but he kept going – and I could feel the touch of his other fingers across the stretched lips of my sex.

'You are so full,' he breathed. His voice was hoarse and I felt a thrill of satisfaction at the knowledge that I could still turn him on so much. 'Jesus, Sam. If you could see yourself now. Your pussy is crammed full of the dildo. A great black thing that stretches and protrudes and makes your lips all shiny and swollen. And your arse, your arse is so tight, but I'm filling it. I can feel you clenching around my fingers. You look so good – so fucking good – so hot. I could eat you up right now.'

His other hand came round and started a slow tease of my nipple, pulling and rolling it between his oiled, scented fingers until I gasped and arched my neck.

'Well, why don't you?' I invited huskily. 'If that's what you want to do, what's stopping you?'

'I want to.'

I felt his warm breath on my back and then the fiery touch of his lips as he kissed my shoulder. His mouth moved along my spine and lit a whole line of crazy tingles that rippled across my skin. It was like being carpet-bombed, with kisses instead of napalm, but the fire that resulted was just the same. The instant his denim-clad cock nudged against my hip, I felt how turned on he was. I was full to the brim and stretched wide with his hands and the black dildo, while the promise of his cock jutted and thrust against my side.

I was in slave heaven.

'I've got to go.' He suddenly withdrew and I heard the slick contraction of my own lubricated bottom. He slapped me once, hard, on the buttock and leant forward so that his mouth was right by my ear.

'Keep it warm for me.' His sharp teeth closed on my ear lobe: hard and painful. Then he was gone. I heard him shout to the twins as he slammed the front door: 'Lock her up.'

I couldn't get up. My knees were like jelly and the chains at wrist and ankle kept me firmly anchored to the rug. The last thing I wanted was for Sasha to find me like that; she was so evil. I prayed that it would be Seph who came first as I heard approaching footsteps in the hall outside.

The kitchen door creaked open.

'Why, look at the little cat.'

It wasn't the voice I had hoped for. Low tones of female malice told me that it was Sasha, and I braced myself as her small, bare feet came into view just inches from my face.

'The master's gone,' she crowed. 'And left the little cat with us.'

She dropped to her knees on the rug in front of me, and suddenly caught my chin in her hand, jerking my face up so that I couldn't avoid her eye. Her translucent blue gaze almost matched the morning – or was it evening? – sky that shone through the window behind her. I still had no idea of the time. It disorientated me.

I saw that Sasha had taken plenty of time to apply her make-up: sooty mascara was thick on her lashes and a sweep of liquid eyeliner enhanced the almond shape of her eyes. She had blushed her cheeks and applied a slick of frosted pink to the lips that were so close to mine. It was a shade that I knew wouldn't suit me – brunettes are so much better with dark shades of mulberry or the brightest ruby – so I tensed when her mouth brushed mine.

It was the lightest kiss: a mere hint of Estée Lauder, nothing more. But the effect it had on me was electrifying. The dislike I felt for her pulled me one way, but desire for her touch jerked me sharply in another. I let my eyelids fall closed to savour the scent of her proximity. Ross's recent ministrations had elevated me back to a state of panting anticipation, and I wondered whether Sasha was now the person to slake my ardour.

I opened my eyes just a fraction, enough for her to see the dark glint of my pupils and the sweep of my thick lashes against my cheeks. I gave her a look that was part mute appeal, part sensual dare. She gazed at me wordlessly for several moments, apparently weighing up which would give her greater pleasure: to treat me badly, or to go for the sensuous touch.

Luckily for me, she chose sensuous. It was as if she had suddenly been transformed from a demon into an angel. Her hands fluttered over my head, touching the skin of my face and tracing the strong line of my nose. Her fingertips were ice-cool – welcome in the lush heat of the kitchen – and lingered on my cheekbones before sliding back to my ears and round into my hair. I let my eyelids flutter closed and basked in the sensuality of her touch.

She stroked my face again, and crooned tiny breathless words. I felt her fingers steal down to my shoulders and then she stroked the length of my arms to the manacles at my wrists.

'Poor little Puss,' she murmured, her pouting lips printing a pale lipsticked kiss on to my forehead. From where I was, on hands and knees, I had an uninterrupted view of the inside of her gaping shirt. The milky curve of her breasts hung unrestricted by underwear, while the flat plane of her stomach stretched away out of sight towards her thighs. 'Do you want me to set you free? Shall I undo you, just for a while?'

I nodded, desperate to reach for her, and she slid one hand into the neckline of her loose muslin shirt. A tiny key was attached to the fine chain around her neck. I could tell at a glance that it was going to fit the locks on my bonds. She swung it in front of my eyes, like a master hypnotist with a very susceptible subject, and smiled with just the merest hint of her previous cruelty.

'What would you do to be free, Puss? What would you do for me? Sssh, don't speak. I don't want to know, I prefer to imagine.' She laid her forefinger across my lips and shook her head, a half-smile curving her lips.

I looked at her mouth and could see that there was a tiny smudge of frosted pink which had smeared when she had kissed me. It made a little crescent-shaped imperfection that drew my attention to the fine blonde down on her upper lip. The attraction I felt for her swelled inside me.

Sasha pushed my shoulders until I was able to sit upright, with my bottom resting on my bare heels. Her eyes followed the contours of my body until she came to my nipples. It felt as though she had reached out with a sharp needle and pricked me there.

My skin was suddenly covered in pert little goose-bumps that tingled and thrilled across my breasts, and my nipples tightened under her intent gaze. I held my breath as she placed the tips of her fingers in the air just centimetres from my tight little buds. Not touching, but holding me rigid just with the anticipation that she was going to.

We stayed like that, both on our knees, for a long time. The clock on the mantel over the Aga ticked loudly in the warm silence that dropped over the room like a thick blanket, then it struck eight times. So it must be morning, not evening as I had wondered.

As if this was a signal of some sort, Sasha opened her arms to me and I fell forward as if I had been struck on the back of the neck. She folded her sweet-scented limbs around my body and her mouth sank to mine in a devouring kiss.

It was so much more passionate than I had supposed, so much more vibrant, this kiss between

49

women. I felt the slicking of excitement and arousal hot between my legs and I lifted my arms to embrace her too. We kissed long and deep, her tongue wet in my mouth and her hands clasping the back of my head. I could feel her fingers tangling in my thick hair. Sasha breathed hard, her breasts rising and falling, rubbing against mine. Delicious. Aching with need, I closed my eyes and submitted.

She was smaller than me, but strong. My ankles were still bound, so I couldn't walk, but she lifted and manoeuvred me until I was up on the kitchen table. The wood was smooth and cool under my buttocks, the ancient surface scrubbed and sanded to a pearly sheen, and I looked down to see my reflected sex – an image of a glistening butterfly. Sasha followed my gaze, then her head dipped quickly down and she pressed her lips to the table and the reflection of my sex.

The lipsticked imprint she left on the polished surface was beautiful: my plump labia, open and juicy, with her pink lipstick pressed over me in a greedy kiss. It looked like a piece of modern art; an acid etching that would probably be found in a Saatchi gallery, called something like *Female Mouths*. I leant back on the table, spreading my knees as far as they would go, and wordlessly invited her in.

This was slave heaven.

'You taste so good, Puss,' she breathed, her mouth like fire on my sex, her tongue snaking around my straining clit. I felt like I had an itch that just had to be scratched, but my bound hands wouldn't let me anywhere near myself. Instead, I breathed gently as Sasha nestled in close and scratched it for me, her fingers smooth but firm on me. The scent of her hair was in my nostrils, and the feel of the polished table-top was like sleek satin under my butt.

Sasha's fingers found the thick root of the black

dildo and she moved it firmly, pumping it into me and then withdrawing it as far as the chastity chains would allow. I groaned and tipped my head back. It felt so good, so sticky, so forbidden: to be there on the kitchen table, taking it while Ross was away.

'The key,' I whispered. 'Unlock me with the key.'

'Oh, I have the key,' she murmured. 'But I won't use it. I'm going to leave you all chained up. It's much more fun that way.' And she thrust the dildo quickly into me, sinking her mouth on to my sex and silencing me.

I squirmed a little, feeling her teeth rub on my protruding clitoris. She moved in closer, relaxing on to my thighs. Her weight pushed my knees that little bit further apart and I felt totally exposed, all cunt and no body, as she warmed to her task and ate me better than any man had ever done. And I felt pretty well qualified to make a judgement on that one.

The torrid heat of the room, the smell of her perfume, and the smooth but solid pump of the dildo had me at boiling point before I knew it. I felt the hairs on the back of my neck lift in anticipation. She seemed to sense it too: that little flutter in my sex, the sudden tension in my thighs, the pulse of my clit under her tongue. She smiled: a feline, secret smile, and I wondered then whether it should be her that was called Puss, rather than me.

Her other hand, smooth and soft, slid along my thigh to my knee and kneaded my flesh. I could feel her breath coming in warm washes over my sex, ruffling the stubby hairs that had grown over my recently shaven vulva. I could hear myself moaning with long exhalations that trembled in time with the rhythmic thump of the dildo. I was going to come. I could feel it building in me. Pulsing energy. Swelling and throbbing. Deep inside. Deep in my body. My breathing became ragged and I gulped air in. My whole world was focused on the thickening sensations of heat in my sex. I was coming. Coming. Eyes shut. Head tipped back. Too much. Help me.

And then I shot over the top. A huge orgasm racked me, beating me into shuddering submission as I cried out and fell back on to my elbows. Sasha sank her mouth on to me and sucked with all her might so that my climax extended into knee-jerking infinity and I felt a gush of hot cream loosen the dildo inside me as my sex gripped hard.

'My, my, Puss-cat. How responsive you are. I can quite see why he chose you.' She licked her lips hungrily, straightened up, and passed the back of her hand over her juice-slicked mouth. I panted hard, recovering, then opened my eyes and stared at her.

'But he didn't choose me,' I protested, breathlessly. 'I chose myself. It was my idea to be here.'

Sasha looked at me pityingly, one fine eyebrow raised in an elegant curve.

'Is that what you think?' she asked. 'Is that what you really believe? Poor little cat, how deluded you are.'

I wanted to scream at her: Ross could never have thought of this, he's a meat-and-two-veg man, I'm the one with the imagination! I'm the one who dreamt this up. And I'm the one in control!

I took a deep breath, but saw the shutters come down over her face.

'I'm bored,' she said. 'Shut up. I don't want to hear your mewing any more. Good cats should be seen and not heard.'

She pulled at the thin blue scarf that fastened her hair and wound it quickly around my mouth so that I couldn't have told her anything more even if I'd wanted to. She held my hand and pulled me from the table-top, smiling at the sound of my sticky buttocks squeaking across the smooth surface. I followed her upstairs, fuming inside.

You'll see, I thought, you'll damn well see who chose who.

I was locked in my attic room for two days.

I shouted. I screamed. I demanded to be let out. On the second day I pulled the door handle so hard that it fell off in my hands. That day the twins brought me no food, probably as a punishment. I was reduced to slaking my thirst by drinking lukewarm water – there was no cold – straight from the bath tap. When it grew dark, I could hear the sombre sounds of Radiohead being played loud with the bass knob of the CD player twisted round to maximum. It depressed the hell out of me.

When I woke up from an exhausted doze, I calculated that it must be Wednesday. Shopping day. Back in the real world, my friend Nicole and I always met after work mid-week. We usually gossiped over tall cups of latte at Starbucks Diner and then did window shopping. This time last week I had probably just tried on those gorgeously flattering, but way-out-of-my-price-range Manolo Blahniks. Spike-heeled and dangerous, scarlet and black, they had been shoes to die for.

What I wouldn't give to wear them now as I kicked Ross's backside and got the hell out of slavery for good.

Ross's backside, however, lived to fight another day.

It was Thursday before he returned. By that time, I hadn't seen a living soul except the twins – who were once again silent and non-tactile – since he had left me that day in the kitchen. I had drunk little and eaten less, and I knew, even without the benefit of a mirror, that the newly jutting bones in my cheeks and hips looked good. I usually look better after shedding a few pounds, but I was too enamoured of comfort food to submit to anything as painful and anti-social as a diet.

The door to the attic swung open and Sasha stepped into the room. She glanced sideways at the broken handle and I stared at her sullenly, willing her to comment so that I could pick a fight. She wasn't playing, though. She simply shrugged and gestured for me to follow her.

At the bottom of the stairs we turned right and I stepped into the sitting room for the first time. Long and low-ceilinged, it was lit with soft lamps and the blaze of an open fire. Ross stood with one foot on the fender, his workmanlike boots glowing in the red of the coals. He had had his hair cut, an even closer crop than usual; a three-millimetre stubble followed the contours of his head, looking barely longer than the five o'clock shadow that darkened his chin.

The haircut suited him, suited his role as master. He looked very hard and lean, as if only the very stupid or very brave would mess with him. I wondered which category I fell into. The brave, I hoped.

He was wearing leather biker jeans and a thick cream-coloured sweater: an Arran that I remembered my stepmother, Moira, knitting for him years before. It made me feel uncomfortable to think about Moira while I was standing naked, laced with chains, with a juice-encrusted dildo still jamming my sex, so I slid my eyes downward to his hands. They nursed a half-full glass of red wine and he waved it towards me.

'Wine, Puss?'

I nodded. The glass was so large that I had to hold it in both hands, but found that the first sip was delicious. What a hit. A regular drinker like me needs a glassful or two of something every day, and I had been going cold turkey for some time now. The alcohol hit my stomach first, then I felt its warmth steal through my veins, all the way to my fingers and toes.

I smiled up at Ross.

'Thanks,' I said. 'Can I have some more. Please?'

His mouth quirked up at one side as if he felt some inner amusement.

'You've changed,' he murmured, narrowing his eyes slightly. 'There's something almost . . . submissive . . . about you. I like that. Yes, you can have some more.'

He topped up my glass, then ran his hand lightly down my side. My skin flickered under his warm touch, like a cat's skin when you stroke it hard, and I felt myself preening. He bent to catch my mouth with his own and the familiar taste of him sent my deprived senses reeling in a maelstrom of bliss and longing. Our tongues touched and the kiss grew deeper until I felt his teeth on my lips. Then Ross drew back. Reluctantly, I think.

'I've brought you a present. Three presents, actually. Two for now and one for later.'

He lifted a small, flat package from the mantelpiece and handed it to me. I struggled with the glass and the parcel for a moment until he gently took the drained wine glass from my trembling fingers. I prised open the brown paper and withdrew a book: a slender volume in dark blue with a sepia-tint photograph on the front. It was my own dog-eared copy of *Venus in Furs*. The one that I had left on my bedside table at home.

I smiled and slid my fingertips over the curvaceous brunette in the photograph.

'Thanks, Ross,' I said, smiling as I wondered how he'd got into my flat. He had never had a key, but I imagined that he had charmed Mrs Favreux from downstairs into letting him in with the spare she kept for me. She must have seen him coming in and out often enough to know that he wasn't a burglar. 'You said there were two presents for now?'

'Yes. I think you'll like the other one even more.'

Pushing himself away from the fireplace with one thrust of his muscular arm, he brushed past my outstretched hands and left me to glance up into the mirror on the chimney breast. I hadn't seen my own face for a couple of days, and the reflection that stared back at me looked like a stranger: newly defined cheekbones from my enforced fast, dark hair that hadn't had any contact with a brush since Saturday, and newly pale lips that still retained their usual swollen-looking pout. Strangely, I looked the picture of health despite my pallor, and I decided that two days' self-denial might be something that was worth enduring once or twice a year.

The mirror was tall and wide, and it reflected most of the room behind me. I gazed past my own reflection at the golden glow from the fire and soft-tone lamps that lit the walls. There were small wood-framed pictures on the walls and the all-pervading, unnatural warmth of the house seemed less suffocating – more cosy – in this part of the house. Huge amber-coloured curtains had been drawn across the wide windows, and this made the room intimate, enclosed. A bowl of incense was set over a small candle on a table at the far end of the room; the perfume that rolled from it in gentle waves seemed soothing and sensuous.

The long, low-ceilinged room looked restful and cosy, and for the first time since my arrival, the house felt like a real home. I felt tiredness and languor creep stealthily through my bones. The thought that Ross had also brought me presents made me feel a swell of something akin to love and I gazed towards the edges of the mirror, searching for his face in the reflection.

He stood with his back to me, bending slightly down towards the sofa. It was a long couch, upholstered in sumptuous Prussian-blue damask, with heaped-up cushions that made you want to just burrow down in them with a good book.

But good books were the the last thing on my mind just then. Because seated there, waif-like and shy, wearing a plain white dress and with her great grey eyes gazing solemnly out from under the sweep of her dark red hair, sat Ross's new girlfriend, Louisa Richmond. She looked like the Lady of Shallot, ghostly and pale, and I knew that she'd come for me.

Furious, scared, starving hungry, and not knowing quite what to do, I sank to the carpet in a dramatic faint worthy of any heroine in a gothic romance.

Chapter Four

'Samantha. Sam!'

I woke up on a soft mattress with a warm eiderdown pulled right up to my chin. For one blissful moment I thought I was at home. Back under my own nice, familiar duvet cover. It was probably a good thirty seconds before the reality came crushing in on me and Ross's face swam before my eyes.

'Hello, sleepyhead. You've been out for a while. It must have been the wine on top of an empty stomach.' His fingers brushed a sweep of hair back from my face. 'You're usually a girl who likes her drink. I'm sorry, it's my fault. I overestimated your ability to take it like a man.'

For some reason, his words needled me. Irritated with him, I jerked my face away from his caressing hand and scowled at him.

'What's *she* doing here?' I hissed, remembering Louisa.

'I invited her,' he said simply.

'Obviously,' I retorted. 'But why her? I thought it was going to be just us. You and me. And then we get here to find you've got two blonds in residence, and now your new bloody girlfriend has arrived. That wasn't in the contract.'

'True. But then exclusivity wasn't in the contract either.' He sat on the edge of the bed and pulled back the covers. With the gentle fingers of one hand, he pushed up the night shirt that someone had dressed me in. His eyes remained fixed on my face while his hand toyed with one of my breasts. 'Remember, I'm the master. I can do what I like. And right now, what I like is to have Louisa around. And you need to re-read your friend Leopold.' He dropped the book on to the bare skin of my stomach 'Just think Alexis the Greek, but feminine.'

I snorted.

'Have you read this?' I asked, tapping the cover of the book with my fingernail.

'Of course.'

'Then you'll know that Alexis was a proud lion of a man. A panther. A master. *Wanda's* master.' I sat up to emphasise my point. 'A cruel and brave leader. Not a mouse like Louisa.' I could feel my lip curling in scorn. Ross shrugged.

'Sometimes,' he said as he stood up and moved towards the door, 'the mouse roars.'

'Yeah, right!' I cried. Finding that my legs were unchained, I threw back the covers and got out of bed. I realised as I stood that the night shirt was a nice flannelette number that certainly warmed me through, but left much to be desired on the attractiveness front. Great, I thought. This really makes me a hundred times more desirable than my rival, I don't think.

I walked over to Ross and glared up at him. 'Listen to me. I want her gone by the time I get dressed, then we can start this thing properly. We've wasted a week. Just take the mouse home, and when you get back I'll have something special waiting for you.'

I let my hand slip over the front of his jumper and

down. My fingers curved over his crotch and I looped my thumb into the space between two fly-buttons, but he wasn't inclined to play ball. His hand was like curved steel as he gripped my wrist and stilled my seductive movements. He pushed me away.

'Get up to speed,' he muttered. 'This thing has already started properly. Nobody is going anywhere.'

Feeling a tantrum coming on, I held my breath. I put on my sternest face and raised myself on tiptoe, imagining that I was wearing those Manolo Blahniks. Ross, knowing me almost better than I knew myself, raised one eyebrow.

'Now then, young lady –'

'Don't say that,' I snapped. 'You make me think of my father.'

'Hmm. That's good. Maybe we can work on that.' He stared at me with a thoughtful expression in his dark eyes. 'Now get dressed and I'll see you downstairs in ten minutes.'

As he left, I picked up a pillow and threw it at the door. It hit a coat-hanger that was hooked on the back of it, which made a harsh clatter against the painted wood. It was then that I saw what I was to wear when I got dressed as Ross instructed, but getting dressed was probably going to take me longer than ten minutes.

The hanger was padded with swathes of creamy tissue and, hanging over the padded arms, was a rubber dress. The smooth latex was a perfect hourglass shape, with narrow shoulder straps and glued side seams. It was in mulberry – my favourite colour – instead of the usual fetish-wear regulation black.

I stroked the rubber with my forefinger and it rippled slightly. The dress was cool to the touch, and slippery with some sort of silicone spray that gave it a fantastic high-gloss finish. I slipped the shoulder straps off from the hanger and held it up against my unattractively flannelette-covered front. It would be a figure-hugging fit, but all the more alluring for that.

Pegged to the hanger were two long rubber stockings. A matt shade of graphite, they too looked my size and I unclipped them with eager fingers. Real clothes. Real clothes for me to wear. Clothes that Ross had bought me. He must have driven all the way back to London and bought these especially for me. This was obviously the third present. The 'one for later'. My heart hammered with excitement and satisfaction as I laid the dress and stockings on the bed. I stripped the flannelette over my head.

I'd never worn rubber before, and it took me at least three of my allotted ten minutes to work out that it was almost impossible to put it on to a warm body. Puncturing the gorgeous dress with my fingernails seemed to be the most likely outcome unless I had some help.

I peered at the inside of the dress and saw that a layer of powder adhered to the inside – that must be part of the answer. A bowl of talc and a huge fluffy powder-puff placed strategically on the bedside cabinet caught my eye and I used it to cover myself with a fine dusting of white, fragrant powder.

Thereafter, it was no trouble. The dress and stockings slid smoothly on to my powdered skin and I gave the ensemble a quick polish with the awful flannelette before easing my feet into a glossy pair of patent-leather spike-heeled shoes that stood on the carpet near the door. I practised walking in them, then swung around to check the effect in the mirror.

I nearly took my own breath away. A stranger looked back at me from the looking-glass, and Alice it wasn't. Five feet seven inches of curvaceous, rubber-moulded goddess stood reflected there.

The dress was very short, hardly covering my bush in front, and I had to stretch it down over my buttocks

61

at the back. The stockings were long, and hugged my legs all the way up to within an inch of the hem of the dress; the shoes were shiny and gorgeous, almost as good as those scarlet Manolos that I'd tried on last Wednesday.

I raised my hands – watching with new fascination the movement of my rubber-encased breasts – and piled my hair high on top of my head, securing it with the narrow ribbon that I had pulled from the neckline of the flannelette. The powder that had clouded all around the room settled on my face and shoulders, giving me a pale, porcelain beauty that was foreign to me. My mouth was stained red with the wine I had drunk, and my eyes were feverishly bright – from a combination of excitement, hunger and fury I imagine. I looked goddam horny, and the slick between my legs told me that I even turned myself on.

I watched myself as my hands moved almost of their own accord to the bottom of the dress. My sex was barely covered, the pout of my lips just visible below the narrow hem, and I could not stop myself.

The pressure of my fingers was light at first, then firmer, as I rubbed over myself and sought the muscular little button of my demanding clit. I was wet, so incredibly wet that my fingers slid with practised ease over my swelling lips and into the sticky warmth beneath.

It was so good. It felt so delicious. Slick flesh and sliding fingers. I moved one leg to give my hand better access and thrust my forefinger deep up inside myself. Just one quick orgasm, I thought. Just one, and I can face anything that Ross and his mouse choose to throw at me. After all, I'm the cat. Cats hunt mice, don't they? I let my head tip back and began to drown in the sweet sensations that made my skin quiver.

A loud gong sounding deep within the house broke into my dreamlike state, and I jumped back from the mirror. My ten minutes were up and I was due downstairs. The gong must be my summons. I raised my fingers to my face and inhaled the metallic scent of myself, then smeared it behind my ears: I knew it was the best perfume. I walked to the door, took a deep breath to calm my fluttering heart, and descended the stairs.

Seph was waiting for me in the hall. It was the first time that I had seen him without his sister and he looked different. He seemed more vulnerable, although that could have been due to the fact that he was naked from the waist up. His bare shoulders and chest – pearled with sweat from the ever-present heat – glowed like the palest ivory and I had to stop myself from reaching out and stroking my forefinger across his tight little nipples.

His shape was almost perfect, tapering and narrow with wiry muscles and long, elegant limbs. I glanced down and saw with interest that he was wearing a richly coloured cotton sarong that skimmed his hips and thighs, the clinging, sweat-damp fabric revealing almost as much of his shape as it covered. His feet were bare and pale against the warm, dark wood of the floor. The single silver bangle he wore glinted on his left wrist.

I paused on the bottom step, smiling as I became aware of the effect that my appearance was apparently having on him. There was a shift under the layers of cotton that swathed his thighs and I saw his fingers curl tautly up towards his palms, as if he wanted to reach out and touch me, but didn't dare.

He swallowed hard, his eyes fixed resolutely on my waist.

'What do you think?' I prompted.

'You – you look beautiful.' His gaze moved slowly over my body and I waited for his blue eyes to meet mine at last. When they did I experienced a strange, almost maternal, sensation of tightness in my chest accompanied by a smothering tenderness that made me want to reach out and take his hand gently in mine. To embrace him. Caress him. Mother him at my breast.

I pushed the thoughts away and concentrated instead on binding him to me. A slave never knows when she may need an ally, and I sure as hell wasn't going to rely on the duplicitous Sasha.

'Do you like the way I look, Seph?'

He licked his lips. I could see that there was a fine beading of sweat gleaming on his stubbled upper lip.

'Yeah . . .' His voice was croaky, like an adolescent struggling with a breaking voice. 'Yes, I like the way you look.'

'Would you like to touch me?' My voice was barely above a whisper. I waited for him to nod, then I reached out and took one of his hands in mine. His fingers trembled a little and a feeling of power surged through my body, exciting me to the point of combustion. I laid his hand on my cheek, then pulled it around so that I could bury a kiss in the palm of his hand. He smelt sexual: musky and young. An animal perfume seemed to cling to the dry, firm skin of his hand and I inhaled it deeply.

'Have you been jerking yourself off, Seph?' I spoke sternly and raised one eyebrow at the crimson stain that quickly spread up over his beautiful face. Oh, damn, slavery was one thing, but I was a natural at dominance.

When I had read *Venus in Furs*, and the idea of a month with Ross had first occurred to me, why had I not had the sense to take on the Wanda role? I would have enjoyed it so much more than meekly bending my shoulders to the yoke of my cousin's desires. The masochistic Severin seemed like a sad loser to me

64

now, and I wondered how on earth I was going to last another three and a half weeks in submissive mode.

Seph, to my delight, fell to his knees and fervently kissed the tips of my patent-clad toes. I put my hands on my hips and stared down my nose at his narrow but muscular back and the ruby-coloured waist-hugging sarong.

I wondered whether to stand him up, thrust my hand beneath the folds of the Indian cotton and finish the job he had so obviously started while waiting for me at the bottom of the stairs. But the gong was sounding again and it seemed more insistent this time, louder and quicker strikes echoing from further along the hall. Seph stood up hurriedly, glancing over one shoulder as if to check that no one had seen him on his knees before me.

'You should come with me.' He took my hands – almost apologetically it seemed – then moved around me and pulled my arms behind. He looped them with a piece of plaited leather to secure them behind my back. Then I was blindfolded and led along the hall-way by gentle touches of his warm hands. The feel of his fingers – first at my waist, then on my arm – as he guided me made me tremble with desire and pent-up lust.

I desperately needed release, and I knew that I was unlikely to get it unless Ross decreed. And would Ross allow a man ten years his junior to satisfy me? Maybe. Maybe not. With the new Ross, there was no telling. I wouldn't have liked to have had to place a bet. I kept my eyes closed beneath the soft blindfold and let Seph lead me to our destination.

The quality of the air seemed to change. There was still the cloying heat but added to that was a sudden pressure in my ears. I realised that we had entered a room and the door had been tightly, but silently, closed behind me. I couldn't tell whether I was still alone with Seph, or whether there were others present, so I didn't speak.

He released my hands briefly, just long enough to bring them in front of my body and stretch them upwards. I was fastened to something above me, probably a metal bar or loop set into the ceiling, and Seph applied his weight to the bonds until I was on tiptoe, stretched and vulnerable with my breasts thrust out and my head tipped back. I could feel that wisps of my hair had escaped from my hastily made top-knot, and the silky tips tickled and aroused me as they brushed my shoulders and back.

Seph came very close to me; I could smell his proximity and feel the warm wash of his breath across my shoulders. I wanted to lean back into him, to curve myself into his slender body, but I was so tightly bound that I could hardly move a muscle.

He dropped a light, almost undetectable kiss on to the pulse in my neck. There was the sound of movement across the room, and it was then that I knew Ross was there, and that Seph had given me the kiss to let me have something secret to hold on to. I shivered and clung to it, that gossamer kiss that seemed to burn through my skin into the hotly beating blood of my jugular.

Warm hands slid down over my hips, then paused at the hem of my dress. The rubber was sticky with my body heat now and I heard it peel away like a snake's skin. He folded it upwards to bare me until there was just the nudity of my bottom and sex. I felt open. Vulnerable. And slightly afraid.

My legs were gently parted and I found my feet placed by other, smaller hands on to platforms about ten inches off the ground and slightly to each side of me. It had the effect of opening me, widening my legs and bending my knees outward. My feet and ankles were then bound as securely as my hands, and I found myself able to relax against the bonds, and hang there.

Being blindfolded was at first an annoyance: I wanted to see these hands that arranged and secured me. I wanted to see the room I was in, to examine the set-up, to inspect the other people who I could sense were present in the room with me.

But then I realised that I could use my other senses much more intensely than usual: I listened for clues that would usually have passed me by, and my skin searched for tactile input that I would normally have relied on my eyes to detect. It was an adventure in sensual detection. I began to enjoy myself, listening, imagining. And above all revelling in the feel of Seph's hands on my legs and feet.

It was a physical shock when narrow, cold, female hands were thrust suddenly between my thighs. My sex was opened and something hard and cool brushed me. At first I thought it was the chastity dildo, being re-inserted for another spell. But no. Too small. And too metallic. I struggled a little but the bonds held me still.

Clips imprisoned my labia and pulled them outward. I was fastened open with what felt like clamps, and a single feminine finger was inserted into me. Sudden and slick, it was withdrawn almost as quickly as it had been thrust in, and I gasped. Someone slapped my bare buttocks and hissed at me to be quiet. Was it Seph or Sasha? I couldn't tell. As if to ensure my silence, a narrow strip of rubberlike cloth was bound around my lower face and I was gagged.

Then the blindfold was removed.

I was in a small hot room, some twelve feet square. The walls were a plain, warm terracotta and the floor thickly carpeted. Directly ahead of me was a low, wide bed, some six feet in width with no discernible head or footboard. A simple creamy silken fabric covered the mattress, unadorned except for a single pale blue box of condoms which had been placed in the centre. There were no windows, and the only light was from a photographer's lamp set up in one corner. It had an orange film fixed across it which cast a fiery glow over the room and its occupants.

Seph was behind me – I could tell that by the feel of his body heat which warmed the length of my back and the vague aroma of the citrus scent he wore. Sasha stood by the photographer's lamp, her arms folded and her feet clad in some amazingly intricate metal-work: silver chains looped and crossed her arches, encircled her toes and slipped around her ankles. She wore matching jewellery on her arms and hands, neck and breasts. I was reminded of chain mail, or Arabian headgear, and the large diadem that sparkled in her belly button completed the look of a harem-dweller.

There was activity in my field of vision to the left, and, trying to see who was there, I turned my head but found my motion restricted. My arms – bound tightly and supporting almost all my weight from above – encased my head at the sides, keeping me still and muffling my ears so that sight and smell seemed the only senses available to me at present. I could just see that the activity was Ross, and his mouse.

Louisa's pale Pre-Raphaelite looks were given a subtle warmth by the orange light, and her hair was set aglow. At the Christmas party, when I had first seen her and dismissed her as merely Ross's arm candy, her tresses had been smooth and straight, as immaculate as Titian silk. But now she was sur-rounded by a flaming halo of curls that rioted around her face and head like fire. I almost expected to hear her crackle as she moved. Her grey eyes were fixed on Ross with something akin to fear, and I wondered how on earth he had persuaded her to be there. Or even why he wanted her there at all.

I looked at him, trying to catch his eye, but he wasn't playing. His attention was riveted on Louisa and I watched with horrified fascination as his hand slid over her hip and up – inexorably up – to her breast. His thumb played over her skin and I saw that, despite her fear, she was aroused, for a tight nipple sprang to prominence beneath the pale fabric, her dark areola visible as she inhaled and strained towards him a little.

I felt sick. How many times had that hand done the same to me? I knew only too well the sensations she felt: the tightening in her belly at his nearness, the breathless expectation as he stroked and teased, the special masculine scent of him that caught in her nostrils as he moved.

Jealousy surged through my limbs, devouring any good will that I felt towards Ross, and making me feel weak and dizzy. A scream welled up and threatened to burst out of me despite the gag. I couldn't bear it. I couldn't stand to see him touch another woman.

I became aware of a sudden light pressure on my waist and I waited, breathing hard through my nose. Gradually, I relaxed against Seph's hand. It's all right, he seemed to be saying. It will be all right. Just watch. And enjoy. This is for pleasure.

'Ross –'

It was Louisa. Her agitation came through in her voice and I could see the glitter of tears at the corners of her wide eyes.

'Sssh.' Ross put his fingers to her lips, then his mouth followed. I watched as he kissed her, my mind an agony of jealousy as I imagined his skilled tongue soothing away her doubts. 'Sssh, Lou. I know. I love you. Trust me.'

He smoothed his hands down over her narrow body, outlining her rounded breasts and her small waist. He followed the flare of her hips and dropped to one knee to caress her ankles and press his lips to her delicately arched feet. As he stood again, he kept hold of the hem of her white dress and raised it until she was forced to put her arms in the air. Then he swept it off over her head and she was naked.

I felt a flash to my stomach despite myself. She was beautiful and the auburn hair that nestled in the V between her thighs caught my eyes at once. It had been trimmed and shaved to resemble a cat's face and I stifled a grin. How very Mary Quant.

'You are lovely,' whispered Ross, and I had to strain my ears to catch his words. 'My Louisa, lovely Louisa.' His hands traced her body and she shivered. 'Are you cold? Shall I warm you?'

He'd never been that caring with me, I thought indignantly. If I was ever cold, then too bad. Big bad Sam could look after herself. A good hard shag would right any wrongs there. I watched, with nausea swelling in my throat, as he led her to the bed and arranged her horizontally on it. He crouched beside her, his hands rubbing her fingers and then chafing her toes like some solicitous Victorian nursemaid.

'Are you warm now?'

She nodded, her eyes still fixed on his. Then suddenly, she seemed to have a change of heart, for she pushed her hand under her head and swept her abundant hair across the cream sheets so that it tumbled over the side almost to the floor. I had an absurd desire to run over and bury my hands and face in the luxuriant red mass.

Louisa was unaware of me or my wishes though. She simply reached out to Ross and pulled him on to her, her pale arms entwining his neck and her hands grasping his close-cropped, dark head to bring his face to hers.

They kissed with gentle passion, and I suddenly saw him as I had never seen him before: Ross the

70

tender lover, rather than Ross the lustful. He was fierce yet gentle, dominant yet caring. His hands were everywhere on her skin, his lips pressed first to her white neck, then to her arms and wrists.

And all the while I seethed and swung like meat in a butcher's shop window. Superfluous and full of sick desire.

He fucked her, of course.

I was condemned to watch as they whispered and murmured together. Her hands bumped his as she pushed his jeans from his hips, then looped his waist-band with her toes and used her feet to push them all the way down his muscular, dark-haired legs. His shirt seemed to come off in one fluid movement, then he was naked and his warmth pressed down on her.

His movements were slow and measured, his hands burying between her thighs and then sweeping up her flanks until they rested, large on her breasts. It was like watching a porn movie on a Saturday night, but so much more intimate. Thrilling. Better.

I kept holding my breath, then reminding myself to exhale, as I watched Ross and Louisa move on the bed. Slowly at first, but with rising speed and rhythm, he brought her trembling to the edge of climax with his fingers and tongue. Her legs were pale against his shoulders, and his face buried deep between her thighs as he licked and sucked her. I could just see the two fingers that he used to gently stretch her, to massage inside her soft flesh.

His hard digits began to glisten with her juices and I heard her sigh. I wanted so much to be her. To be there in her place on that bed with Ross's mouth burning on my clit and his forefinger penetrating my creamy flesh. I tried to look away, conscious of the swelling in my body and the slickness that oiled the emptiness between my outstretched legs. But I couldn't keep my eyes off them.

I watched in feverish arousal as Ross kissed his way up her belly, his eyes meeting and holding hers. I watched as he rose up, supporting himself on his arms, and sank his thick, straining cock deep into her. And as she groaned, she arched herself up so that she was curved under his body, her neck white and exposed, her nipples raspberry red against her milk-pale breasts.

Ross, like a satyr on top of her, was big and strong, his muscular buttocks pumping in time to the sound of her sighs. His thighs were braced and his knees made deep indents into the mattress. Louisa's legs, creamy pale, were hooked over his shoulders and I could see the dark pink streaks on his back where her nails had scored him.

I felt hot and faint as I watched them, the intense humidity of the room almost overwhelming me as I hung from the ceiling, my rubber dress cleaving to my moist skin and my sex creaming thickly as my skin swelled and burnt.

I was in hell. Or it may have been heaven.

My logical, methodical brain told me to yank my arms out of those bonds and get the hell out of there, but my treacherous body refused to move even an inch. I could feel a hot sticky curl of lust sliding around my body, raising the damp hair on the back of my neck and making my heart do an excited little patter that reverberated all the way down to my toes.

Behind me, I could smell Seph. His lemony scent and the soapy aroma of freshly laundered Indian cotton rose to my nostrils and made me as horny as a bitch on heat. I stuck my arse out a little and felt the rigid throb of his cock as it pressed against me through the thin sarong. I was certain Ross would have told him not to respond to me, but there was no harm in trying.

I twisted a little in my bonds until my eyes caught

his and I widened mine with a silent message. He stared at me, his gaze an expressionless blue, then I felt the smooth glide of his palm on my thigh. He worked his way gently under me, his thumb stiff in the crease of my behind and the tip of his finger just looped between the creamy folds of my sex. I moved some more and frigged myself against his hand until I could feel myself burning hot, juicing up against his hand. I was in control again, bound but happy.

Sasha shimmied across and stood in front of me, obscuring my view. I jerked my head to one side, anxious not to lose sight of Ross and Louisa. They were pumping fast, little sighs and groans punctuating their movements. Louisa's pale legs were now wrapped tight around Ross's waist and her fingers dug hard into his back making little white crescents in his flesh. A sheen of sweat glowed across his back.

Louisa's mouth was suddenly widened in a silent scream. I stared at her pearly teeth, vicariously absorbing the beginnings of her orgasm, when Sasha leant past me to kiss her brother full on the lips, her tongue snaking between his teeth and her hands cupping his face.

The shock of what she did caught my attention, as I'm sure she intended. She glanced at me with a look that seemed pretty close to a smirk, then pulled my gag down and pressed her mouth to mine, her little tongue flicking up over my palate and back towards my throat.

'Tastes good, doesn't he?' she said. 'I've seen you look at him. I know you want him. But he's mine, aren't you, Seph? All mine. He'll never want anyone else. It's me he loves, because loving me is like loving himself but more so. He's Narcissus incarnate, aren't you, brother?'

Her hands fell to my nipples, stiffly moulded through the latex, and she slowly circled one with her fingernail. Then she suddenly and viciously thrust her hand between my spread thighs, scratching me slightly as she speared me with her first two fingers. I heard Seph groan behind me, and then his hand joined hers. They filled me and stretched me. Two hands. Four fingers. Thrusting and opening me wide. Sensation flooded through my body and I began to lose myself. I fixed my gaze on Louisa and Ross.

She came then, fluttering against him like a lily in the breeze. Her eyelids flickered and she stretched her head right up so that her throat was long and exposed. Ross held still, his weight supported above her as he watched her come. He looked satisfied yet predatory, his profile making me think of a hawk circling unsuspecting prey.

When she had barely recovered, he abruptly turned her over and I stared, my own sensation almost forgotten, as I watched the seemingly delicate Louisa take it up the arse. Louisa's shoulders were on the bed and her back was arched up, so that her buttocks were level with Ross's hips. Her skin glistened a pearlescent orange in the glow of the photographer's lamp, and I watched them carefully to see how Ross would enter her.

He eased in gently, lubricating her with his saliva and a touch of her own juice. She buried her face in the mattress and groaned a little: a full-throated, animal sound that caught at my guts and made me almost echo it as Seph pressed his thumb to the tight rosebud of my own anus.

Ross's cock was rigid. And way, way too big. His balls were tight up under him and I knew that he was going to blow. Ten seconds, I thought. I'll give you ten seconds to hold it. I knew Ross. He wouldn't be able to stop himself from coming for much longer than that, not with that tight, neat little rosebud clamped around his hard sex.

He went deep into her with a quick screwing motion of his hips, and my eyes flicked to his face to see an expression of pure ecstasy pass over his features. His eyelids were closed, but I could see by the curve at the corners of his mouth that he was in paradise.

She was so tight around him, so small, that it must have been difficult to hold out for any length of time. But he surprised me, for he rode her for longer than I had bet on. She seemed to become wet there, some gorgeous cream lubricating her tight little bottom as he cruised slowly in and out.

Her fingers walked sideways across the bed and grasped handfuls of the cream sheets, bunching them up and pulling them slightly towards her. I heard her groan: the sound was a potent mixture of ecstasy and agony, and it made my chest feel tight and my ears swish with the fast-flowing blood in my veins.

I could feel that Seph's breath was ragged on my ear and I twisted my head. Now that the gag was off, I was able to catch his mouth with mine as he leant into me from behind. Sasha was right: he did taste sweet. Young and clean, minty but milky. I thrust my tongue almost to the back of his throat in my eagerness to possess him.

He responded beautifully, one hand pressed deep between my thighs from behind, the other somewhere in front of me. Belatedly, I realised that it was his sister's breast he massaged, not mine. But that didn't seem to matter. It was wonderful just to be there, hanging helpless but happy between two gorgeous young bodies, with Ross flashing his booty just yards from me.

I could feel the beginnings of a strong climax rising up into the roots of my hair. My scalp prickled and my skin started to goosebump as the orgasm trembled through my body in waves. I gasped and jerked my head away from Seph's mouth, burying my nose in the soft flesh of my extended arms and revelling in the salty scent of my own skin as I came. My body jerked and shook, and I tried to pull my knees inward – heedless of the ankle bonds – to prolong the delicious sensations that shuddered through my sex in muscular waves.

There was a sudden hot dampness in the small of my back and I experienced a moment of sublime satisfaction as I realised that Seph had been unable to control himself. The heat of his spunk spread against the rubber dress, then slid down on to my bare skin to form an oiliness on the curve of my buttock.

I felt echoing waves of another shudder sweep through me and I sagged against the cuffs around my aching wrists. I could feel Seph's hot breath on my shoulder and hear the grunting exhalation he made as he quivered against me. I closed my eyes and tried to seal the scene in my memory. I wanted something to take out and mull over next time I was shut into the attic room.

When I recovered enough to look at Ross, he and Louisa had gone. The bed was as smooth and pristine as if they had never been there, and the twins had slipped downward to do something mysterious and sexual on the floor at my feet. And to think that Ross and I had thought ourselves daringly incestuous with our cousinship. Think again, Bentley, I thought, as I closed my eyes and waited patiently for release from my bonds.

Chapter Five

*T*he morning sun, broken by scudding clouds, pulsed through the window and warmed my back. It was breakfast time. And I, true to my slavery contract, was serving. Only four places had been set at the table and I found it excruciating to hand out warm, fragrant croissants and pour juice into sparkling glasses when I had not yet eaten.

The little radio on the window sill was on. The DJ was doing the usual breakfast show routine to the accompaniment of the new Catatonia single. Humming, I cracked eggs into a frying pan and wiped my slimy fingers down my front. Ross had given me a pair of old grey sweat pants and a white vest to wear, a far cry from the previous evening's beautiful jewel-coloured rubber ensemble.

This morning I felt like Cinderella, right down to the wooden clogs that he had apparently found in some junk shop back home. If I had to wear them all day then I was going to have some nasty blisters . . .

'More orange juice!' He waved his glass at me. I put the pan of eggs back on the stove and obediently poured. He was obviously enjoying himself: a smile played around his lips and a twinkle lurked deep in his eyes. Even at 7 a.m. he looked dead sexy, with last night's stubble still darkening his chin.

There was a knot in my stomach that was a combination of hatred and desire. After all that he had made me do, I still fancied him rotten. Was I mad? I wondered. Probably.

Louisa, meek and mild, drifted through the door like a pale ghost and made for the chair opposite Ross. No clogs for her: she was wearing a soft cotton man's robe in the palest blue and white stripes with obviously very little underneath. Her small breasts pressed lightly against the fabric. In my mind's eye the little circles of her areola pressed and darkened the cotton. The belt was tied tight around her waist, but as she slid elegantly into her chair, I caught a glimpse of milky thighs in the gap at the front, and I tried to quell an unbidden vision of those legs wrapped tightly around Ross's back under the orange glow.

Ross smiled at her, then leant across the table and took her hand, pressing a kiss on to the tips of her fingers. I bit my bottom lip and picked up the egg slice that lay, dripping oil, on the tiled kitchen counter.

'Good morning, darling,' said Ross, emphasising the endearment slightly. I wondered what they would do if I suddenly turned round and started slapping Louisa with the oily egg slice. It might be quite fun. I turned back around and leant my bottom against the edge of the work surface, watching them and swinging the utensil between my forefinger and thumb.

'Morning,' Louisa murmured. Her long hair caught the spring sunlight now flooding in through the kitchen window. It glinted with copper highlights. She had twisted it up on to her head and secured it with a few pins. It looked gorgeous, effortlessly elegant, and I wondered why I couldn't look like that first thing in the morning. She should have been a cover girl, not a

78

doctor. She was wasted being perpetually gowned and masked in a hospital operating theatre.

'Did you sleep well?' Ross asked.

A blush spread across Louisa's smooth features.

'I did,' she smiled. 'You tired me out –'

'Breakfast?' I cut in, keen to interrupt the love-fest before they started reminiscing about their nocturnal activities. Ross suddenly slapped his hand on the table, making me jump.

'Don't interrupt. You will speak to Louisa properly,' he snapped, his eyes a frightening flinty colour and his voice a commanding bark. I baulked at this; then got into character.

'Good morning, Louisa,' I began, with as much false and exaggerated servility as I could muster. 'What would you like for breakfast? I have eggs, bacon, croissants and toast, accompanied by coffee, tea or juice. And strawberries.'

I held out the bowl of succulent fruit for her to see. Goodness knows where Ross had got them. They were out of season and all the more delicious for that.

'Croissant and strawberries,' she said. 'And take that bacon away. I can't bear meat. I don't even want to see it.'

No wonder she was so pale, I thought. She needed rare steak with pepper sauce to put a little colour in her cheeks. Ross was big on meat, so I experienced a twinge of surprise when he nodded curtly to me.

'Get rid of all the meat in the house.'

'But, Ross –'

'Get rid of it. Louisa doesn't like it.'

I glanced at the stove. The bacon was gorgeous, crisp at the edges just like he loved it. No meat? Now, slavery I could stand, although it was already getting irksome, but a month of vegetables and pulses? That was going to be hard. Louisa was almost certainly responsible for Ross's New Year smoking ban, too, I thought.

Taking the hot frying pan, I went outdoors to the bin just outside the kitchen door and flipped off the lid. It was cold outside, a fresh spring breeze cutting round the side of the house and chilling my skin, but I enjoyed it after the febrile heat of the house. I stared down at the rashers of Danish, then glanced behind me to check that they couldn't see me from the kitchen. It was just too good to waste. I couldn't throw it away.

I nearly choked as I swallowed the third piece. Seph came sauntering round the corner of the garden wall, a sack of coal on one shoulder. No sarong today: air force blue combat trousers hugged his lean hips and his pecs were snugly covered by a sweatshirt with a *quiksilver* surf logo on the front. His silver bangle glittered in the early morning sunshine.

Seeing me hovering over the bin with my pan of bacon and a guilty flush on my face made him smile. He drew near and I caught a whiff of his citrus shower gel, and felt a pull at my guts that made me think of sex despite the early hour.

'What are you doing?' he asked.

'Louisa doesn't want meat in the house.'

'Crazy.' He reached out with his coal-dust-stained fingers and scooped up the last slice of bacon. 'Shame to waste it.' His teeth gleamed clean and white as he bit into it.

He popped the last rasher in his mouth, then leant forward to kiss me. He tasted of breakfast and fresh morning dew, and as his tongue passed me the last crispy rasher I felt as if he'd given me something else, something other than a morsel of bacon, some secret sign that he'd see I was all right whatever Ross tried to do. I felt suddenly warm, despite the cold of the

80

morning, but it didn't stop my nipples popping out like fresh-bloomed rosebuds at his proximity.

He saw this and smiled, a slow lazy grin that washed over his face like sunshine. He had tied his hair back and it made him look absurdly young. Neatly trimmed sideburns framed his face and his skin was smooth and newly shaven; either that or he was smooth because he was too young to shave yet. I stared at him.

'How old are you?'

'Nineteen.'

'Nineteen.' I smiled. He was old enough.

Oh, God, what was I thinking? The contract I had signed had turned me into some lust-crazed monster who fancied everyone and anyone who crossed my path.

But he *was* lovely. Adorable in fact. But probably out of bounds. I bit my lip and took a step backwards to put a little distance between us.

'I'd – I'd better get back inside,' I stammered, very aware of his eyes on my face. Seph bent his knees and flipped the lid back on the dustbin for me.

'See you later.' He nodded at me, then walked on past, one shoulder lower than the other with the weight of the coal. I stood gazing at the wiggle of his neat little buttocks until he rounded the corner of the house, then stirred myself. If I dallied outside too long, Ross might come looking. I went inside and shut the door firmly behind me, feeling the hothouse atmosphere close in around me once more.

'You took your time.' Ross tipped his chair back and stared at my chest. 'Cold out there, was it?'

'Freezing.' I smiled merrily at him, ignoring his enquiring look, then dropped the frying pan into the washing-up water with a singing heart. The encounter with Seph had made me mind Louisa's presence a lot less, and I knew that Ross could sense that something had changed. I could feel his eyes burning into my back as I washed the dishes.

Louisa and Ross ate their food and left the table in a mess, obviously on purpose.

'You haven't had breakfast, Puss.' Ross came to stand next to me and cupped my chin with his hand.

'No.' I hoped he wouldn't smell the bacon on my breath.

'Have some, then clear up. There's a job I want you to do. I'll come back in a minute to give you orders.'

Orders. I sighed and frowned at the remains of their food. I was not going to eat their leftovers; being a slave was one thing, but being dehumanised was certainly not in my contract. I opened the fridge door and pulled out the last two croissants that I had hidden in there earlier. I knew Ross so well that I had foreseen his plan to leave me hungry and begging. I slammed the buns into the microwave for twenty seconds and then scoffed them almost without chewing. They were good, but the bacon had been better.

Ross came back after a while to set me the task. He handed me a toothbrush and nodded at the floor.

'The quarry tiles are filthy. Clean them,' he said, his face blank and unsmiling.

'Oh no. No way. I am not cleaning the floor with that.'

'Yes you are.'

'No I am not.'

'Yes.'

'No.'

'You sound like a spoilt kid.'

'So do you.'

I was suddenly reminded of our childhood fights: me with a hideous flicked fringe and Ross in his groovy tartan flares, hands on hips, both mutinously refusing to budge an inch.

Those were the days. A wave of nostalgia washed

over me and Ross, sensing it too, stepped back as if to distance himself.

'You're my slave. You signed up for a month. Are you really saying that you can't hack it for more than a week?' He tutted and shook his head ruefully. 'I guess I shall just have to tear up the contract, then. No more *Venus in Furs*. I'd love to see what the boys'll say when they hear you've got less backbone than we all thought.'

The boys meant my brothers. If he told them I'd even volunteered to be a slave in the first place, then my life would be hell. The butt of all jokes for the foreseeable future. I stared at him. He wouldn't dare.

'You wouldn't dare.'

'Try me.' His face was serious, not even the hint of a smile. He'd dare all right. 'You can go back to normality any time, just surrender. You know the word.' Then he fired his parting shot. 'Seph will miss you.'

He turned on his heel and left. I stuck two fingers up at his departing back, then got on with it. Being a slave had some hideous drawbacks, domestic drudgery being the biggest. But if it meant staying with Ross and having the chance to get cosy with Seph, then, well, I was up for it. Game on.

The radio was still blaring. The sound of the DJ's voice suddenly irritated me and I strode over and snapped it off with venom.

It took me two hours to clean the floor with the toothbrush. I passed the time thinking about Richard Gere doing the same job in *An Officer and a Gentleman*, and it made the task seem more like fun.

When I had finished I was dirty and sweaty and had extremely sore knees and feet. A warm bath was just the thing, and I knew that the solid-fuel kitchen range meant constant hot water, so I headed up to my room for a long, steaming soak. My door was closed and, as I took the stairs two at a time, I saw that a single sheet of white paper had been nailed to the centre panel.

'Crimes and Misdemeanours' ran the heading. Someone had knocked it out on a laser printer and the neatly typed words made a list in bold type:

The slave has been found guilty and is to be punished for the following:
1. for breaking a door handle
2. for persistent rudeness to Louisa
3. for enjoying voyeurism
4. for casting lustful glances at Seph
5. for eating bacon when she thought she was unobserved

I stared at the paper and then tore it from the door. Found guilty? By whom?

Pushing open the door, I saw that a big wooden gym box had been placed in the middle of the floor. It stood at waist height and the top was rounded and padded and covered with old, soft, velvety suede.

It looked exactly like the one in my old school hall that had been dragged out for rainy-day PE, except for one difference: it had some attachments that were definitely not intended for schoolgirls. Wrist and ankle loops were attached to brass rings set into the four corners at floor level.

I felt a flicker of interest despite myself. I slowly closed the door behind me and leant against it.

'Take off your clothes.'

It was Ross.

'Take off your clothes, I said. Hurry up.' He sounded impatient and I whisked the vest over my head. I was braless beneath, and my nipples – taut from excitement – caught his gaze and he stared at them fixedly.

'Drop your trousers.'

I gladly kicked the clogs off and obeyed, getting a thrill out of his commands. He reminded me of a film I'd seen once. Richard Burton and Clint Eastwood had disguised themselves as Nazis with unconvincing sixties haircuts. In a short but memorable scene in a snowbound wood shed, Burton had ordered a bleached blonde girl to strip.

It had excited me then, and it excited me now: the German SS had a great line in mastery with uniforms. I saw that Ross had obligingly put on his long leather coat and I made a mental note to buy him some little steel specs when I was next able to do some shopping.

'Come here.' He grasped my arm and drew me to him so that my naked flesh was almost welded to the front of his coat. It felt warm and soft against my breasts and my body heat soon made it slick with perspiration. I shivered with anticipation as he ran his finger from my forehead all the way down my nose, over my closed lips to my chin.

'I like having you as my slave.' His voice was low, throaty but soft, like warm treacle as you drizzle it over a sticky pudding – my favourite. 'But at the moment, you're a very bad slave, Puss. I shall have to punish you, I'm afraid.'

'Are you afraid?' I asked, unable to resist. I saw a sudden hint of his vulnerability as he met my eyes. It occurred to me then that, although he was doing very well as a master, he wasn't completely sure of his ground. We had always got on so well, mucking around first as children and then as adults, that this serious stuff was probably as weird to him as it was to me.

I slipped my arms up around his neck, enjoying the slight drag of the leather against my breasts, and raised myself on to tiptoes to kiss him. His lips were hesitant at first, soft, gentle, and I got a taste of what Louisa had been enjoying last night.

'We don't have to do this,' he murmured against my mouth, his hands tight on my waist. 'We don't have to do this, Sam.'

I hesitated for a fraction – the man was offering me a respectable way out, after all – then I pressed my nose to his.

'Oh, yes,' I said. 'We do. I want you to. Come on.'

Taking his hand, I led him over to the gym box and made him stand still while I bent over it. It took a little coaxing, but he soon caved in and knelt to fasten my ankles and wrists to the brass rings. I was bent almost double, my hair streaming to the floor and my buttocks thrust high in the air.

'I'm waiting!' I sang. Ross laughed, stroked my bottom with the tips of his fingers, and then reached for the whip that rested against the box.

'OK, Puss. You asked for it.'

The first lash was more of a kiss than a flagellation. The whip landed softly on the bare skin of my buttocks and I felt a sizzling warmth spread under my skin. Mmm, I'm going to enjoy this, I thought, relaxing into it and closing my eyes to wait for the next tap. When it came, it made me jump about three inches in the air. Catching me just in the crease between buttock and thigh, it stung like hell and set up a burning that snaked around my pelvis.

The leather whip was long and thin, a real beast, and from where I was I could see Ross's hand gripping the plaited handle like he'd been born to do it. A gush of wet cream surged through my sex and I felt the next crack of the whip curl under me and touch my protruding labia, making me swell with pain as well as arousal.

'Does that hurt?' he growled. I nodded as best as I could upside down. 'Good. Here's three more just like it. One for breaking the door handle –' it was harder than the others and I winced '– and one for your constant rudeness to Louisa. And this one for enjoying that which was supposed to be a punishment in itself. I saw you when I screwed Louisa under your very nose. You liked it, didn't you? You were so hot I could have fried eggs in your juice.' I held my breath and tried to shrink away from the kiss of the whip.

At intervals, he strode round to the front of the box, pulled me up by the hair and devoured my mouth with his. I kissed him back, sick with desire and longing and pain, my body glistening with perspiration, my tongue thrusting against his and my lips sucking and hungry.

He varied his strokes, so that the whip gave me stinging little kisses all down my spine, then a nasty hard *thwack* across my buttocks. After about ten minutes I began to lose track of how long I'd been there. I could feel a slow, burning sensation that made my bottom hot and my eyelids prickle. It was agony. Torture. And not even sweet torture, at that.

'You're good at taking punishment. In fact, I'd say you were enjoying it,' Ross remarked, gripping me under the chin and pulling my face up to his again. He squatted by me for a few moments, as if drinking in the sight of my flushed face and dishevelled hair. 'Don't forget why you are here.' He strode away, his boots supple and matt black in the dim light. 'Your other crimes, what were they? Ah, yes. Bacon. I expressly forbade meat and yet you ate the bacon this morning.' I could have sworn that laughter bubbled under his voice at that one.

The whip caught me again. Pleasure topped with pain rolled around my body and I gasped. My skin was raw from the unaccustomed beating and I was beginning to feel distinctly unhappy about it. The flagellating thong crackled across my buttocks – he was acquiring some technique now, and it showed.

That's it, I thought. I'm going to scream.

A lash licked right across my back, like a tongue of fire, so that the tip came under and caught the side of my breast. It damn well hurt.

I was going to have to cry out, tell him to stop. I'd had enough. I'd do anything to stop the pain in my screaming nerve-endings.

I opened my mouth and nothing happened. No words, just a gasp and a small, low moan. God, I couldn't say it. I just couldn't. I didn't want him to stop.

'Crime number five,' he said, leaning over my back this time and pressing the unyielding buttons of his leather coat into my tingling, hurting flesh. 'I've seen the way you look at Seph. Don't think I don't know how much you want him. I know exactly how much you need him to bend to your will and prove yourself strong again. I know just how much you'd like him to slide his tongue into your tush and lick you to oblivion.' He took his weight off my back. 'Just think about it, Puss. Think about his hard young cock thrusting into you; his arms holding you while he rides you; his hands on your thighs, spreading them wide; his breath on your neck as you come. You dirty little slut-cat.'

The whip tore under my buttocks this time, winding me and catching me in that vulnerable crease where bottom becomes leg. It was agony but in some obscure way it was ecstasy, too. I knew what my back would look like: streaked with red, pink all over. I knew too what my sex would look like: dark and juicy, swelling between my legs like some tropical, sexual fruit.

The thought of myself, and the response I was having to his words, turned me on so much that I tightened my hips against the smooth suede of the gym box. His hand was suddenly there on my juicy sex, chasing all thoughts of surrender from my mind, and I ground myself hard and then harder still against him until I came in blessed, sweet little waves that left me breathless.

He didn't have to know that part of my mind had converted his physical presence into a hybrid beast – half Ross, half Seph. Their features blurred in my mind's eye until they became one perfect man.

Ross rested his weight on me and dropped a kiss on my raw shoulder. I raised my head to look at him, the hank of dark hair that fell over one eye conveniently obscuring my look of sated gratification.

'You enjoyed that, didn't you, Puss?' he breathed into my ear.

'Did it show?'

'Naughty little alley-cat. I'll have to punish you more often if it makes you this submissive and sweet.' His erection pressed against my buttock and I wriggled against it, loving the feel of his hard cock and the leather that covered it. He roughly pulled the coat open and I heard the button-fly of his 501s pop. The sound nearly made me come again and I waited with bated breath for him to move into me.

His hands trembled slightly, warm and firm on my sex, as he opened me and scooped a fingerful of my juices on to his hand. He raised it to his nose and inhaled.

'You smell so good, Puss. Why do you always smell so fuckable?'

Beats me, I thought. I'm the one who hasn't had a bath today, remember?

He didn't seem to notice this, though, for he bent his head down and put his mouth to me, licking and sucking and covering his nose with my dew. It felt wonderful, like coming home, and I relaxed into it with growing pleasure, pushing thoughts of Seph from my mind and letting Ross take command again.

He stood up behind me and smoothed his hands under me, caressing my sticky creases with dextrous fingers.

'I have to fuck you, Puss.'

Be my guest, I thought. Get right on in there and fuck me till you drop.

He curved into me from behind, nestling his legs against mine and easing himself out of his jeans. I smelt him then. Hot cock: a combination of wet seashell and male musk. He spread one hand wide on my sore, whipped back and I considered asking him to remove it, but feeling his thighs tense behind mine made me forget all sensations but the ones in my sex.

There was an infinitesimal pause as he carefully tore the foil and paper covering from around an Arouser with his teeth, then he entered me slowly, sweet as a nut. His cock was hot. So big and hard, and covered in fabulous latex ribs, that I could feel myself stretching around it as if he were a stranger.

He moved with a sweetly hypnotic rhythm that made me groan with pleasure, and I heard his breath come in short little grunts – barely audible – as his thrusting became faster. I began to move with him, as much as my position and bonds would allow, and we fell into our old pattern with breathtaking ease. It was amazing. Fabulous. And so sexy.

I knew when he was going to climax. I could feel the tension in his body. I knew him so well, our bodies were so in tune. I squeezed him, constricting my muscles with all my might, drinking him in as he thrust and jerked inside me with tight little butts of his hips against my bottom.

He was suddenly still; then I felt him curl into me still more, pressing himself so deep that I thought he would crush me. There was the slick heat of his muscular pumping inside me, and I gripped him even more to keep it in. A sensation of constraint rushed through my body, and then my mind imploded: burning sensations shot along my nerves like a succession of firecrackers as I came on to his still-thick cock in a gasping, shuddering torrent of bliss.

We stayed like that for a while, his face resting on my back and his exhaled breath soothing the weals on my sore skin. Then Ross reluctantly raised himself up and buttoned himself back into his denims. He walked around the box and came to squat down by my face, cupping my chin in his hand.

'We're good together, aren't we?'

I nodded, hardly trusting myself to speak. Then I blew it.

'Of course we are. I don't know why you ever doubted it. You don't need Louisa, you just need me.'

His face closed over and became a blank, expressionless mask. Dropping my chin with such abruptness that I hit the deck and bit my lip, he stalked away and I heard the door slam behind him.

Damn, damn, damn. How stupid. Now I was stuck here, looped hand and foot to the brass rings set in the box and no knowledge of when he'd release me. I cursed myself and my impatience. Five minutes later I cursed him and his intransigence even more as a cooling slick of juice and come slithered down my leg. When was I going to get a bath?

'In here.'

It was Ross's voice. I stiffened as his boots came into view followed by a pair of pale feet clad in buckskin platforms. Now, there are shoes and there are shoes, and these were definitely my kind of shoe. Not quite Manolo Blahniks, but pretty sexy all the same. Black and strappy, with a thick but very high heel and a low platform at the front to give those little feet even more slenderness and vulnerability. I coveted those shoes at once. I also had few doubts about who was wearing them.

Louisa.

'She needs a thorough punishment.' Ross moved behind me and I knew he was flexing the whip. He laid it on my back and I felt a lump rise in my throat.

'No, please. No more.'

He ignored me.

'Hold it like this. Follow the red lines that mark her skin already.'

I tensed and held tightly to the bonds that fastened me to the box. The shoes disappeared from view and Louisa took the whip from him. When she beat me, her lashes were light, tentative, and I relaxed a little.

'Harder,' murmured Ross. I squeezed my eyes shut and silently cursed him. What he said didn't matter, though, because she didn't change what she was doing. Small taps, as light as warm raindrops on my skin. I enjoyed it.

'Come on, Lou. Let me show you.'

'I don't want you to show me. I'm doing it like this. I don't want to hurt her,' replied Louisa.

Good for you, I thought, don't let him tell you what to do. But then she gradually settled into it, striking harder, and my back and buttocks quickly became a quivering mass of pain. A sob rose in my throat and I swallowed hard, hating her but hating myself even more – for in the midst of my pain was a tiny bright jewel of pleasure that glowed and grew with every stroke she administered.

I put up a show of disliking it: pulling against my bonds, writhing on the box and making a few little cries of protest that sounded false even to my ears. She didn't let up, though, and I could hear Ross continue in his encouragement of her at intervals. Louisa may look like a long drink of milk, but she had the strength of ten girls in her right hand that morning.

I can't imagine who started it, but there was a lull and, apparently to fill the gap and pass the time, they kneaded the sore skin of my buttocks. I could feel the different sizes of their hands – one small, soft-skinned, one large, slightly callused – moving over my hips and thighs. Then my sex was pulled wide and something foreign and hard plundered me.

I couldn't see it, and I was in a fever of sickened lust and pain and pleasure, so my mind didn't work as well as it should. It had to be the whip handle. The plaited leather dragged at my soft wetness with grazing brutality. My sex felt full and thick. Ross, or Louisa, thrust it deep into me, then withdrew it almost to the tip before plunging it home again.

It was sensational: harder than a cock and with more ridges. Just right to stimulate even the most hidden parts of a girl's nervous system. I gasped and swallowed, almost choking on my own saliva, as I tried to survive a sudden rush of blood to my head. Being upside down intensified the feelings; I found myself sobbing and begging for mercy. And when I thought I could take no more, they thrust their lubricated fingers in alongside the whip handle and pressed hard on my G-spot.

That was it. I let go and came in a shattering, cunt-grasping, howling stream of juice that flooded my thighs and their hands. It was the best orgasm I had ever had. Mind-blowing. Unique. The pain in my whipped hide gave the climax a bitter-sweet piquancy unmatched by plain sex. I couldn't imagine wanting to try it again in a hurry, but I'd found that whipping and bondage had a lot to recommend them. I closed my eyes and felt the smarting tears that had gathered on my lashes trickle around the bridge of my nose.

I sensed the darkness of unconsciousness trembling

at the edges of my mind and struggled to stay in the same world as my tormentors. Then someone grasped me by the hair and jerked my head up, forcing my lips open and plunging a throbbing, straining cock into my mouth. And behind me Louisa – it had to be her, because it had to be Ross in my mouth – slipped the knobby, juicy end of the whip into my bottom and sent me shuddering into another throbbing, burning climax.

The last thing I felt was the heat of Ross's come as it hit the back of my throat. Salty and searing hot. I swallowed the sudden short jewels instinctively. Oysters had never tasted so good.

After being thoroughly whipped and comprehensively fucked, the long hot bath I had sought so long ago was bliss. Of course, being the slave, I had to run it myself. But Louisa sat on the edge and swirled her hand in the steaming water, watching the turquoise bath crystals dissolve in the warm eddies.

Her face was pale and smooth, no sign of the emotions she must have shown when whipping me. I watched her from the other side of the room, fascinated by the shadow cast by her lowered eyelashes, and by the swollen pout of her lower lip. She didn't move. I realised that she was not ready to leave, although Ross was long gone, so I walked over with as much nonchalance as I could muster, and calmly stepped into the bath.

'Did that hurt?' she asked, her eyes intent on studying the crystals which were becoming smaller and smaller against the white enamel.

I shrugged, anxious not to give her clues about my weak points that she could use against me in the future. When she realised that I was not going to reply, she picked up a bar of soap and rolled it in her left hand. I sat there, my back smarting in the heat of the water, and listened to the mushy, slick sound of the wet lather against her fingers.

'Did you like it?' She gazed at me and must have caught the gleam of something in my eyes which she took as an admission. 'You did, didn't you? Was it that good? Would you do it again?'

I really didn't want to answer that, partly because I didn't want her getting ideas. The meek persona seemed to have been pushed down inside her somewhat, and the woman who had whipped me had been anything but mild. She still looked the same, but there was an inner spark that hadn't been there before – her passive detachment had been replaced by something else.

'Did you do this because of me?' she asked. Her gaze met mine and I was suddenly aware of the central force of her personality, the quiet strength and composure that shone behind the calm grey of her eyes. It made me feel small inside, insignificant and quite afraid. I could see now what Ross saw in her: she was like a soothing balm, a cool, calm oasis. A peaceful haven from the danger of his work and the tempestuous switchback ride of life with me.

Looking at the porcelain smoothness of her flawless skin and the sweep of her auburn hair, I realised that I had lost him before this had even begun. Lost him as surely as if he had gone out in one of his lifeboats and never come back. Lost him to her, this Lady of Shallot.

I had always disliked that poem. When we'd read it in the fifth year at school I had found it ominous and eerie. It had filled me with strange presentiments and a sense of foreboding that seemed to have come back to haunt me. It was as if I had always known that this would happen.

I sighed, and sank down in the bath so that the water came up over my ears. I didn't want to answer

Louisa's question, but I knew she wouldn't leave until I did.

'Did I do this for you?' I hoped I sounded condescending. 'You were the last thing on my mind. I did this for me. Everything I do is for me.'

It was supposed to be a parting shot, but she didn't move.

'Yes.' Her voice was as smooth and fluid as silk. 'So Ross says.'

She smiled and passed me the sticky bar of soap before walking away.

Then I was alone.

Part Two

Exchange

Chapter Six

'*I*s she leaving?' I could hardly keep the satisfaction from my voice as I watched Louisa close the boot of her red convertible.

I had walked up behind Ross, who was standing in the sitting room looking out of the window. A bowl of snowdrops and crocuses glowed white and yellow on the wide sill, giving a promise of spring sunshine and rebirth. That, and the apparent evidence of Louisa deserting us, gave me a bubbling feeling of optimism.

Ross turned to me, both hands thrust deep in his trouser pockets.

'She should be gone by the time you get back.'

'Oh? Where am I going?' My heart sank.

'For a walk.'

He took my shoulders and turned me round, gently pushing me out of the room. I was steered to the garden door at the end of the hall where there were a collection of muddy boots and a rack of coats.

It was so cosy and warm in the house that I didn't really want to go out: it had rained all night and I was only too aware of my pitiful lack of clothing, but Ross obviously wasn't taking no for an answer. I didn't try to fight as he buttoned me into a shirt, jeans and a fleece-lined overcoat three sizes too big and thrust some socks and wellies on to my feet, because there was something vaguely paternal in his gestures. It warmed me through and made me want to say, can I have some pocket money as well, please, Dad?

The freedom I experienced as I reached the end of the path that led from the back of the garden to the open fields was bliss. I took several deep breaths of glorious ozone and could hardly contain the feelings of joy that threatened to burst through my chest in a shout. Grinning like an idiot, I slammed the little gate behind me, making the fence rattle, then set off down the lane.

I could hear Louisa's TR4 roaring into life at the front of the house, and the thought that she would soon be far away made me start singing. I happily thought about Ross and sang all the way up the lane at the back of the house, enjoying the squelch of thick ooze under my boots.

The track was muddy. Inches of brown water filled every rut in the tractor trail that seemed the closest thing to a real path that I could find. After a few hundred yards, I climbed a gate and struck out across the empty fields. I followed the line of a hawthorn hedge for about a mile, conscious that I was heading uphill. I imagined that the view from the little copse at the summit would be breathtaking. The countryside and I don't usually mix – give me the sordid pollution of an inner city every time – but that day I was as happy as a sand-girl, with my chunky socks and wellington boots, tramping along like an apprentice cow-herd.

I found a stick under the hedge and carried it with me as if I did that sort of thing all the time. I used it to turn over interesting stones on the ground, to beat down nettles and poke at things in the hedge. After a while, my fingers were filthy and the legs of my borrowed jeans caked with mud. But I didn't mind one bit. At the top of the hill I squatted down under a tree, with my back braced against the trunk, and gazed around me.

The house we were staying in looked small from where I was; a long, low, rectangular building with a couple of stone out-houses. It was at the very end of the winding lane. At the bottom of the garden a narrow brook curved and meandered, followed the back lane for a few hundred yards, then veered off on a path of its own.

The pot-holed, partly gravel-laid driveway at the front was shadowed by tall trees. It stretched straight and true for a few hundred yards, then curved abruptly before ending in a five-bar gate that I had a vague recollection of pushing open for Ross on our arrival.

That seemed a long time ago, now. I did a bit of mental arithmetic and calculated that today must be Saturday. Well, I'd lasted a week. And had three left to go. Three more weeks of being totally enslaved to Ross. Things hadn't been going quite as I had planned, but now that Louisa was gone everything would be better, I was sure. Ross and I could settle back into being Wanda and Severin, with some extra-hot sex thrown in for good measure. Somehow, I would be able to seize the initiative once more.

A cold east wind cut across the hillside, chilling my cheeks and making my lips feel sore and chafed. I dug in my pocket for the miniature pot of lip-balm that I kept there, then belatedly remembered that this wasn't my coat. I sighed and shrugged the collar up around my face. Having nothing to call my own was very odd. I loved my creature comforts, and having to rely on hand-outs was strange. But on reflection, I suppose that it gave the slave thing a lot more authenticity.

In fact, if I really thought about it, having no possessions was probably pretty liberating for a perpetual hoarder like me. The lack of responsibility and property meant that I had nothing at all to worry about.

All of my things were still back at the flat. I felt safe in the knowledge that the borrowed jeans and boots were only temporary. And three more weeks without worrying about work, or commuting, or my social life, or making normal adult decisions was undoubtedly a good thing. A total de-stress.

My friend Nicole had once paid hundreds of pounds to get the same effect at some health farm in Surrey. And I knew there had been no sex there. In comparison, I'd got a pretty good deal. Especially now that Miss Mouse had left.

With Louisa gone, I could relax and enjoy myself a little more. Sasha had not been much in evidence in the past twenty-four hours, either. So much the better: the idea of being alone in the house with just Ross and young Seph was pretty thrilling. To be the filling in a sandwich where those two made the bread had distinct appeal. I could feel an electric tingle in my sex just at the thought.

I pondered on the fact that I felt so much more at ease with the men. Sitting there under the tree, watching the clouds part themselves for a watery sun, I thought about my circle of friends. The truth was, I didn't seem to mix with other women very much. I had one close friend, Nicole, whom I had known since nursery school, plus a few female acquaintances from work that I went drinking with on a Friday night. Otherwise the people I chose to spend my time with were all men. What did that say about me as a person? I wondered.

I leant my head against the bark of the tree and stared at the streaked metallic sky. It probably meant nothing at all. Perhaps having my dad and the boys to myself until I was eight, and then having to bear the arrival of an incoming wicked-stepmother type, made me resistant to all forms of apparently friendly female overture.

My brothers had welcomed the arrival of someone to pick up their boots and wash their football kit, but I hadn't trusted such a pushy newcomer. Moira and I had spent ten years on opposite sides of firmly drawn battle lines. Our constant rows had coloured my view of other women: I just didn't trust them. Not then. Not now. I didn't trust Louisa Richmond. She was the same type. Coming in and elbowing me aside, taking what was mine.

I wriggled my hands in the pockets of the coat and listened to the metallic jingle in the depths. I sighed and wiped my nose on the cuff, pushing comparisons of my stepmother and Louisa out of my head. Too much time on my own was making me introspective and heavy. It had to stop. I needed company again.

Standing up, I brushed bits of wet grass from the seat of the coat and began to walk down the hill again. Away to the west a small village nestled in the loop made by a river, of which our garden brook was a tributary of sorts. I decided to wander into town and see what I could make of the local inhabitants. Every hamlet had a pub, and I had a sneaking suspicion that the jangling in my coat pocket was being made by somebody's long-forgotten loose change. I palmed it and took a look: a two-pound coin and some tens. I could afford a drink. Brilliant.

The village public house was a tiny thatched building with one room and a crackling log fire. Two elderly locals were hunched at the bar and when I walked in they stopped talking and turned to stare at me over the rims of their personalised tankards. I felt horribly out of place and the leary looks they gave me suggested they knew I was a townie.

I glanced superstitiously back over one shoulder. I had two choices: turn and beat a hasty retreat, or brave it out and get a liquid lunch. I took a deep breath and chose the latter.

'Half of cider, please.' I wasn't going to show the barman my urban pedigree by asking for a vodka Red Bull.

The cider was murky and I examined it carefully for living things, but it tasted all right so I took it over to a high-backed settle near the warm fire. The locals slowly swivelled on their stools to watch, then equally slowly turned back to their brew and ignored me. I flopped off the big green wellies and propped my sock-clad feet on the fender. It would be nice to doze here for an hour, I thought, closing my eyes.

The pub door opened and closed, letting in a draught that made the fire flare and crackle for a second. A few minutes later, a slender hand set a dark pint down on a nearby table and sank into the seat beside me.

'Hey.'

It was Seph. He looked very pleased to see me, his eyes wide and fringed with pale brown lashes, his generous mouth curved in a smile. He was wearing the same clothes as he had on his coal-scuttle trip the day before – I couldn't forget the tight fit of his combat trousers and the way they cupped his package.

I dropped my gaze to his lap and smiled inwardly. Everything looked very neat there. All hot and bulging. And just waiting for me. It made me go warm inside and the crotch seam of Ross's jeans got a sticky addition as I felt a thrill run right through my stomach and down to my sex.

'Hey,' I said in reply.

'What are you doing here?'

'I might ask you the same thing.' I snuggled down

a little and let myself move closer to him on the wooden seat. He eased himself slightly away.

'Just came in for a drink. It's my local.'

'Mmm. Maybe I'll make it mine while I'm here.' I met his gaze and felt my pulse skip a few beats. He looked young and unsure, undecided about whether to touch me. He was the picture of an innocent boy who had an angel on one shoulder and a devil on the other.

I reached up and laid my forefinger on his lips. He unexpectedly shot out his tongue, looped my finger into his mouth and bit down hard.

'Ouch!' I jerked my hand away and he laughed.

'Ssh. Be quiet or they'll ban you,' he whispered.

'Who cares?' I whispered back, my eyes fixed on his and my heart giving a skipping little leap.

'I do, for a start. I live here, remember? I'll have to keep coming in here long after you've gone home.'

'Well, I'm not going home for a while yet. So let's be as quiet as mice and maybe they won't ban us.' I slid my bottom further along the wooden seat which had been polished smooth by generations of village bottoms. Seph tried to ease away again, but there was nowhere for him to go; he was wedged into the corner of the seat with the carved timber sides keeping him prisoner, my prisoner. I leant against him a little and saw his excitement and nervousness in the visible beating of a pulse under the warm skin of his neck.

'Seph, do you like me?' I asked, spreading my fingers on his thigh. He dropped his hand to mine and gripped my fingers, crushing them against his leg in a futile attempt to stop my stroking movements. But I wasn't stopping. Because I had plans for this boy.

'Do you like me?' I repeated, curving into him and pressing my chest against his. He swallowed, then licked his lips nervously and glanced over the high back of the seat. The two men at the bar were nose-deep in their pint mugs and oblivious of us.

'Of course I like you. You know I like you,' he whispered.

'Will you do something for me?' I asked.

'That depends.'

'No it doesn't. Will you do something for me?'

'I don't know what it is. How can I say?' He frowned a little, an adorable little crease appearing between his two straight brows. I slid my hand further up his thigh, ignoring the pressure of his hand which tried to tell me to stay put.

'You can't say,' I replied. 'You just have to agree to do it. You'll have to trust me when I say that I wouldn't make you do anything you didn't want to.'

'How can I trust someone I hardly know?' His eyes were full of amusement tempered with anxiety. One part of him was desperate to do whatever it was I wanted, another part of him was very keen not to encourage any trouble. I took my hand off his thigh and slid myself back along the seat, purposely pouting my bottom lip and staring sulkily into the fire. I took a slug of my cider, feeling it burn my throat and then warm the inside of my chest. I waited to see what Seph would do, wondering just how far he'd let me manoeuvre him before he gave in.

I could see him out of the corner of my eye, gazing at me with big eyes, his long fingers plucking at the button that fastened the leg pocket on his combats. He was torn, I could tell. But he'd obviously need a final push before he jumped.

I sighed and glanced at the big clock on the wall.

'I'd really better get back to the house,' I said, slowly raising my arms and stretching so that my breasts pushed out against the man's shirt I wore. I piled my hair up on top of my head as if I were hot and held it there, letting him take a good long look at my slender neck. Hopefully he would also see my nipples, hard and pointed, pressing against the fabric of the shirt. He looked, all right. He looked for a long while, swallowed hard, and then made up his mind.

'OK.' He shuffled towards me. 'OK, I'll do it. But first tell me what it is. Will it get me into trouble with Ross?'

Curiouser and curiouser, I thought. Ross has obviously been taking the role of master very seriously, even when I wasn't around. I studied Seph with renewed interest. Exactly what was my cousin's relationship with the twins? That was something which deserved further investigation.

'Maybe it will. Maybe it won't,' I said, dropping my arms and turning sideways to smile at him. 'It depends on whether you tell him about it. Come here.' He slid along the seat until we were thigh to thigh, hip to hip. His shoulders bumped up against mine and he was so close that I could see the paler flecks in the dark blue of his eyes. I laid my fingers across his lips. 'Sssh. It'll be our little secret. Just you and me.'

I kissed his mouth lightly, my eyes fixed on his, then lifted my coat from the seat on my other side and laid it over my lap. I took his hand and slid it under the coat, pressing his fingers between my legs.

'Like this,' I murmured. 'Do it just like this, Seph.'

He gazed at my mouth, as if seeking inspiration of some sort. I guided his hand, pressing him and directing him until he took the initiative and began to move of his own accord. His hand slipped from under mine and his fingers eased open the fly of Ross's denims.

I held his gaze for a few moments longer, then that was it, I was gone. My eyelids fell closed, my head dropped back against the carved wood of the seat back, and I relaxed as he slid his fingers through the short tight curls of my pubic hair and into the lush heat of my sex. He seemed to grow in confidence at the signs of my pleasure. The devil on his shoulder had definitely won.

'What are you drinking?' he asked. I kept my eyes shut as I answered him.

'Cider.'

'Nice. It's made you very relaxed. You feel so sweet and creamy when you're relaxed. The other night, when you were hanging from the ceiling, I could hardly stop myself from –' he paused, then lowered his voice almost to a whisper '– from opening you wide and plunging my face into your sweet little cunt.'

I feigned shock, then smiled and slid my bottom forward a little on the seat to give his hand a better angle. I liked the way the once-reviled c-word sounded on his lips. It was a word that my friends and I had screeched and squirmed about in college, hating its derogatory-sounding hardness.

But during the past week I had heard it – and thought it – more times than in the whole of my life previously, and I liked that. If a word could have a natural habitat, then it was here, in this situation. It was like reclaiming it, making it nice again. A nice dirty word that dripped off the tongue. Like 'cream', 'cossack' and 'cuckold'. Cunt, cunt, cunt, I said to myself, and almost laughed out loud with the thrill of naughtiness that the word made me feel.

Seph's hand was deep in my jeans, his silver bangle crushing back the button fly. The smooth part of his knuckles was jammed against the pleated seam in the crotch and the juice that slicked the fabric there was making his skin sticky and sweet. I let my knees fall open under the rustling jacket and felt his forefinger slip wetly through my arousal. I was honey-sweet and as sticky as a cream éclair under the pressure of his fingertip. The slow rub and circle of his callused pad was sending streaks of blue electricity through my hips and belly, tightening me inside and making my breath become slightly ragged around the edges.

'You are so sweet, so lovely,' he crooned, his lips almost touching my ear and his breath warm on my neck and face. He was getting bold now, and I liked it. 'So sweet and wet. You were made for this, weren't you? Made for opening your legs to anyone. Anyone who'll put their fingers in you and bring you off. You don't care who it is, as long as they frig you good and hard.'

'Oh, yes I do.' I opened my eyes and stared at him, seeing my own wide-eyed reflection in the dilated black of his pupils. 'I care. They have to look just like you. Talk just like you. Now, push harder.'

He did as he was told, and I sighed in an ecstasy of heat and light as my body melted and opened up to him. He whispered in my ear: barely audible mutterings of how sexy I was, how beautiful, how wet and juicy.

I could smell old beer and the wood-smoke from the log fire. I could feel the hard wooden seat under my buttocks. I could sense the excitement that emanated from Seph in waves. And I knew that the two men at the bar could walk over and see us any time they chose to. My arousal was swelling like good music in my head, while a deep shuddering vibrato pulsed inside my body.

The world seemed warm and safe and comfortable, and Seph's hand movements wonderfully predictable as he pushed me ever closer to the ultimate goal. My breath came more quickly, my heartbeat thudding in my head as I started to slip and slide into the trembling heat of climax. He was so careful. His hand was warm and soft, yet hard when it counted, and I could feel myself collapsing on to him, my creamy slickness easing the passage of his fingers.

The sudden thought that this was forbidden, that

Ross would be so angry if he found out, urged me into a deeper state of arousal. I imagined his face if I were to tell him: his angry frown, the way his mouth would get those two little white creases either side that ran from nostril to lip, the way he would stand with his strong legs planted wide and his fists on his hips.

Oh, yes, that was good. Ross was fabulous when he was angry. Like a tightly coiled spring just waiting to erupt like hellfire and hurt someone. And that someone would be me. Oh, yes, I thought, feeling the tension tighten inside my body, I like it when he hurts me. It's like a kiss, a very special kiss.

Seph was leaning against me now, his weight crushing me into the corner and his breath warm on my throat. I felt a sweeping tide rise up inside me. It was so strong that it threatened to engulf me and sweep me away. He seemed to sense the sudden tautness of my body, for he thrust two fingers deep into me. Pushing and parting me. Stretching me wide.

I gasped and bit my bottom lip as I came hard on to his hand, my own reaching down to grip his wrist and pull him deeper into my grasping, tightening sex to make it last. To make it last as long as possible because it felt so fabulous. I was becoming an orgasm junkie. The hit needed to be long and deep. And this one was good. In fact it was better than good, it was one of the best.

Seph dropped a clumsy kiss on my nose, then sought my lips. I opened my mouth to him and took his tongue deep into my throat, sucking and gorging myself on him, my lips moving with the promise of what I would do to his cock when I had a chance. He tasted delicious: young and fresh, smooth clean teeth and a hint of the dark, creamy Guinness he'd been drinking. I could have eaten him up there and then and still been hungry for more.

His fingers remained inside me and the weight of his thumb was pressing on my clit. Little electric tremors of post-orgasm tingled there, like lightning in a summer storm, and I softly bucked my hips up to catch the sensation. I slid my hands around to the back of Seph's head and pulled him closer so that our kiss was long and deep.

When we broke off for air, he nuzzled my neck and gave me tiny little nips under the chin. I snuggled into the curve of his neck, breathing the scent of his long hair and stroking my fingertips across the lean breadth of his shoulders.

'I want you, Seph. I want to fuck you so badly,' I whispered, my words slightly muffled by his hair. It spilt over his shoulders like golden silk, and smelt of fresh air and shampoo. I could have spent all day just burying my nose in it, but I pulled away from him and buttoned up my jeans. 'Come on, let's go.'

I stepped into my boots, shrugged on my coat and hitched up my jeans almost in one movement. I grabbed Seph's hand, downed the last of my cider, and dragged him from the bar without so much as a sideways glance to the locals. He grinned and pulled me back, sank the other half of his pint, then pushed me through the door with an enthusiasm that almost matched mine.

'Where to?' he asked, squinting against the watery sunlight that seemed so bright after the dimly lit pub.

'I don't know, you're the local boy.'

We stood at the side of the road for a moment, on what the villagers probably called a pavement but what was actually just a muddy track at the edge of the tarmac.

'Back to the house,' he said. 'There was no one there when I left. Come on.'

We went back the road way, striding fast along narrow lanes decoratively strewn with mud and cowpats. The weak sun had given up trying to press through the clouds, and the sky was low and full of malevolence. There was probably a storm coming, but I didn't care. I had so much excitement and anticipation flooding through my veins that I could have gone through a tornado and come out the other side with a big smile intact on my face. The feel of Seph's warm young fingers clasped in mine and the powerful looks we kept exchanging made up for any country-side whims like storms, or mud, or cold wind. Still, I was glad when we turned into the gravel drive that led up to the house.

'Wait,' I said, pulling at Seph's sleeve. 'Kiss me. Kiss me here.'

I wound my arms around his neck and pulled him to me so that our bodies were almost fused together. His narrow, girlish hips pressed hard on to mine and I felt the long slenderness of his cock pressing into my jeans' fly. The feel of his body against mine was very arousing and I could feel a rush of heat and energy sweep my lower body in anticipation of the time when there was no denim or combat trousers between us. Just skin on skin. Hard to soft. Wet, open sex to thrusting rock-hard prick.

My thoughts made me shudder with pleasurable anticipation and I slipped a hand between our strain-ing bodies and cupped him. He may look girlish from some angles, I thought, but what I have in my hand is all male – and then some. I squeezed slightly and he groaned, his lips pressed hard to mine and his hand tangling in my hair. I could feel the prickle and thrust of my hard nipples against the front of his sweatshirt, and longed for the feel of his bare chest on mine.

He read my thoughts pretty well for a novice, because his hand slid up between us, taking my shirt with it until the cotton was scrunched under my chin, then he fixed my nipples between his thumb and forefinger with a pincer-like grip. It hurt, but I had recently discovered the pleasure of a little pain and I exhaled hard, pressing myself into his hand. He grasped the shirt in one hand and stood back, letting the cold air play across my hot skin for a moment, then bent his head and took me in his mouth.

The sensation was like fire and ice mixed up in a devil's brew. His mouth was hot and wet against my dry skin, his lips soft but his teeth hard as he teased my swollen nipple to dark pink erectness. His hand slipped to my other bare breast as if he didn't want it to feel left out, and I strained towards him, my ribs thrust out to give him maximum access. He was a wizard with his teeth, a veritable magician, and I could feel my hungry body crying out to him. I wondered whether we could do it there, in the drive-way, against one of the trees that were dotted so conveniently along the hedgerow. There was no one about, no sound except the rustling of the wind through the bare branches of the trees. I decided to chance it.

'Oh, God. Come on, Seph. Let's do it here. Over here,' I said, pulling away a little so that his teeth grazed my nipple and pulled it out to cork-like ripeness. 'Seph, let's hurry.'

'Not here. Up at the house,' he murmured, his mouth clumsily seeking mine for an instant, then diving back to my breasts. His tongue felt like the lash of Louisa's whip as he snaked it around my nipple and downward, into the curve of the underside of my breast. I could feel my knees starting to go weak with the strength of my desire, but we weren't moving anywhere. I had to get to the house, or I couldn't be held responsible for wrenching his trousers down and making him fuck me right there.

I grasped the waistband of his combats and hauled him closer. Nose to nose.

'What?' he said.

'Up to the house, soldier. Now.'

We practically ran, the creamy crotch of my jeans slipping against my lubricated sex. As the house came in sight, I felt a burst of pleasure, a thrill of anticipation flooding through my body. I grabbed his hand and pulled him to me for a lingering kiss. The delay was minimal, but it seemed to add to the unbearable pleasure a hundredfold. I was drowning, slipping and spiralling into a pool of lustful intentions and I didn't ever want to come up for air. Nothing was going to stop me from screwing him senseless.

But a car horn sounded behind us. An all too familiar convertible careered around the curve in the drive. Head-lamps glowing and roof down. Red and predatory, it slowed alongside us, the tyres slewing in the wet gravel.

'Out of the way!' yelled Louisa, her pale face blushed with the cold wind and her red hair whipping up and behind her. 'Get up to the house, slave. I've come back and I shall need you.'

She was like Cruella de Vil on a bad-hair day: all temper and definitely none of her previous shyness. I frowned at the smoky pump of the exhaust pipes of the car as it sped on up the drive.

'What is she doing back?' I muttered. 'I thought she'd gone.'

Seph shrugged, then stroked my face. He bent his head and pressed his lips to mine for a tender, resigned kiss.

'Better go on up,' he said, softly. 'You don't want to be punished for not doing as you're told.'

That was debatable. All punishments so far had fallen into the category of pleasurable experience. But I did what he said, albeit with some reluctance, ignoring my swollen and disappointed body as I trudged up the drive.

114

The gravel sounded damp and crunchy under my boots, and I realised that it was only my footsteps I heard because Seph had stayed where he was, letting me go on alone. I willed myself not to turn round and look at him. I started to walk faster, and as I went round the bend of the driveway, I broke into a run.

When I got to the house, I was windswept and breathless. The front door was wide open and I kicked off my boots and followed the scent of Louisa's perfume along the hallway to the overheated sitting room. She was alone, standing behind the sofa wearing a long cream fur coat – unbuttoned – and a dangerous smile.

'What are you doing back?' I asked, my annoyance showing in my tone.

'Tut, tut,' she said, one of her pale hands propped on her hip. 'You obviously haven't learnt your lesson. You're not supposed to be rude to me, remember?'

I stared at her with one eyebrow raised. She suddenly seemed to have a lot of guts and I was surprised at the change in her. I jammed my hands into my pockets and waited to see what she would do.

She did nothing. Just eyed me from the other side of the sofa, her expression unreadable and decidedly unmeek. There was a long silence, then she thrust a hand into her coat pocket and pulled out a soft-pack of cigarettes.

'Smoke?' she asked. I was tempted to tell her that she sounded as if she were in a fifties *film noir* – and a bad one at that – but I couldn't be bothered. I shook my head.

'Light me,' she said, propping a Camel Light between her beautifully painted lips. I watched her but didn't move. 'Come on. You are the slave, after all. Light me.'

I reluctantly leant forward and rested one knee on the sofa, took the old-fashioned Zippo lighter from her fingers and snapped it open. There was a powerful petrol smell, then a lovely flare as it caught. She dipped her head and I watched her nose narrow to a point as she drew on her cigarette.

She straightened up and exhaled, not bothering to direct the smoke away from my face. It stung my eyes but I stared straight back at her, willing myself not to cough or wave it away. The smell reminded me powerfully of Friday nights in West End bars. Nostalgia and homesickness hit me like a fist blow to the belly and I wished I had a bottle of something strong and blunting to hand to drown my sorrows. That measly half of cider now seemed a long way off.

'Thank you,' I said pointedly, hoping to remind her of her manners. She tipped her head back and flicked her abundant hair over one shoulder, then took the cigarette from her mouth. Another lazy stream of smoke trickled from her nostrils.

'I don't have to thank you. You're the slave,' she said sweetly. 'Take off your coat.'

'Why?'

'Don't fuck around, Puss. Just take it off. The heating's on in here.' She gave me a piercing look. 'It seemed to me as if you were about to take off more than your coat back along the driveway, so why don't you oblige me? Take it off now.'

I tossed the old Barbour on the sofa and then stood very still, waiting for her to say something else. I could sense she was playing with me, but I didn't know what her game was. She held all the cards. I hadn't a clue why she had come back.

All I knew was that she seemed a different person to the meek and mild Louisa that I had thought was my rival for Ross's affections. The woman standing on the other side of the sofa was strong and in control. I wasn't sure whether I admired her or hated her in her

116

new persona. Her next words went some way towards making up my mind.

'I've decided to stay here,' she said. 'I like you. And Ross likes you. It's a good game and I think I'd like to see what happens.'

I didn't like the proprietary way she spoke Ross's name. And I didn't like the way she thought she could control what happened. In my game, too. It was my game. She'd probably never even read *Venus in Furs*.

'The game has changed, however,' she said, resting one hand on the sofa back. 'The roles have changed. Oh, don't worry, you are still Severin, you poor fool. But Ross is no longer Wanda Von Dunajew.' I was a beat ahead of her and it made my hair curl. 'I am.'

'No. No way. That's not how it goes.' I stepped away and found my back up against something very hard and unyielding. Twisting, I saw Ross, his face inscrutable and his hands reaching for my arms.

'No. NO!' I struggled and tried to sidestep him, but he was way too strong for me. He caught me easily and jerked me back round so that I could do nothing but stare at Louisa. She took a deep drag on her cigarette, ground it out in a glass ashtray on the table beside her, then flicked the collar of her coat up. She looked magnificent: the flame of her hair flared against the waxen blond fur of the coat and her great grey eyes fixed me under her thick black lashes. She walked slowly out from behind the sofa and my eyes dropped involuntarily to her feet.

Shoes. It was always shoes. I don't know how she had done it, how she had known, but the shoes that she wore were the same Manolo Blahniks that Nicole and I had drooled over. Red and black and spike-heeled, with a great vamp to the way they made her walk. I stiffened against Ross and tried to breathe deeply, a red mist of fury clouding my mind.

Those are mine, I wanted to shout. My shoes. They

practically had my name on them. Take them off. My toes curled inside the thick woollen socks that enveloped my feet, almost as if they were embarrassed.

'Gorgeous, aren't they?' she said, following my gaze. 'Sex on heels. Ross bought them for me.' There was a definite gloat in her voice and I hated her as I had never hated anyone before. I wasn't going to be her slave. I wasn't going to be her slave for anyone. Not even for Ross. No way. Never.

'You're mad,' I murmured. 'I'll never be your slave. Never in a million years.'

'Never say never, Puss. You know you don't mean it,' Ross said. I could hear the smile in his voice and it made me hate him almost as much as I hated her. Even when he bent his head to kiss me.

Chapter Seven

*R*oss's tender lips on my neck made me waver a little in my determination to hate them both, and I jerked my head away. I didn't want to be seduced by his sweet kisses. The terms of the contract had changed. This wasn't what I had signed up to, and I protested again.

'You can't change things. You've no right.'

'Actually, I think you are the one with no rights.' Louisa slipped a hand into her pocket and drew out a long, folded piece of paper. 'Let me just refresh your memory. Here we are – just like in the book. Do you remember the bit about unconditionally complying with every one of Ross's wishes? You are – just like Severin – bound by your honour. And I haven't heard anyone utter the safety word yet, have you?'

'You don't really want this to happen, do you?' I twisted to try and catch a glimpse of Ross's face but he held me fast. I could feel the curve of his thighs warm against mine through my jeans and it made me feel weak and helpless. 'Please, Ross, tell her. This is our game. The contract is between you and me. The safety word is ours.'

'Yes.' I could feel his breath on my ear as he bent his head to speak to me. 'You're right – the contract is between you and me. But you *are* bound by that contract, and it does say that you will comply with my wishes. My wishes, not yours. And what I wish at the moment is for Louisa to be happy. If you want to say the safety word, you go ahead and say it. If you really want to end this.'

I twisted my head so that I could see him properly. I felt like saying it just to defy him. Just to see the look of shock on his face when I said the word. But I knew that I wouldn't, just yet. He looked so proud, so arrogant and yet so vulnerable with his chocolate-brown eyes melting my insides and his curving, lop-sided, oh-so-kissable mouth.

He leant forward and fastened his lips to the side of my neck, and I knew my resolve to fight him every inch of the way would falter if he carried on like that. His proximity, the warmth of his strong body, and the tenderness of his mouth against my skin were too much for me to bear. I shook my head and struggled in a vain attempt to loosen his hold on me, my fingers turning white as they gripped on to his wrists.

'She's very unruly, Ross,' remarked Louisa. 'I think she needs to be reminded who is master and who is slave.' She moved a little closer to me and I could smell her perfume: a subtle mixture of scent, body lotion and clean hair that mingled with the cigarette smoke to make me feel light-headed and wanton.

I mentally pulled myself together and tried again to shrug Ross's hands from my arms. He was gripping me so tight that it almost hurt, and I could feel his tension in the rigid steel of his thigh muscles as they tightened against the backs of my legs. His breath was burning hot on my neck, and the racing of his heart was palpable against the cotton-clad skin of my back. We were pressed so close together that there was no air between us, and the intense heat that our bodies generated added to the sultriness of the room until I thought I would pass out.

Louisa stood very close in front, the fur from her floor-length coat brushing the backs of my fingers with a sensuous touch. I dropped my hands away from Ross's wrists and stuffed them back into my pockets. I stared at her, trying to look fearless but knowing that my weak soul would shine out through my eyes and give the game away. Then she would know that I was filled with fear, and loathing, and desire.

'You are a useless slave,' she hissed. 'Very bad.'

Her hand, the nails glistening with silver gloss, reached up and rested on the neckline of my shirt. I watched as her thumb toyed with the top button, and felt an echo of the arousal I had felt earlier with Seph. A sensuous heat curved up and trembled through my senses. Her fingers were almost perfect: slender and pale with beautifully manicured cuticles and short, oval nails.

'Do you know,' she said conversationally, her forefinger sliding down the front of the shirt between my breasts, 'in ancient times slaves were branded to show who they belonged to. Have you been branded?'

I shook my head, my eyes fixed on hers. What horrible thing was she dreaming up? It didn't bear thinking about. The nearest I'd come to branding was going to a tattoo parlour in Muswell Hill with Nicole, to give her moral support. But when he'd started, I'd suddenly found the buzzing of the tool and the hot smell of Nicole's flesh far too scary, and had beaten a very hasty retreat to the local pub.

Nicole had come out later showing off a delicate alchemist's symbol etched in dark blue-grey on her shoulder-blade, swearing that it hadn't hurt. I didn't believe her then, nor when the scabs of her skin started falling off a few days later. She had loved it though, deeming it worth the pain, and wearing cut-away vests and spaghetti-strapped dresses to eye-catching effect all through that summer.

That had been twelve years ago, when she had been a wilful rebel before rebellion was fashionable, before every other twenty-something sported a tattoo and a nose-stud. I had never been quite as outrageous as Nicole, preferring to bask in the shadow of her reflected glory and watch her bloom under the scandalised glances of her elderly relatives.

'It seems the little slave-cat has been struck dumb,' Louisa murmured, cupping my chin with her free hand. 'How odd. I thought she had plenty to say when I was here earlier. What do you think, Ross? Do you think that her silence means that she likes the idea of branding? Hold her still and let's see.'

Ross stiffened behind me, his hips thrusting into my buttocks and his curled fingers like granite around my upper arms. I made a token struggle as Louisa tightened her fingers and gripped the fastening of my shirt. She gave it a vicious tug, ripping it suddenly from breastbone to hem. I gasped and flinched at the sudden warm feel of her breath on my chest.

'Delicious,' she whispered. Then bent her head to lick one of my nipples. I was rigid with horror and shock, my back arched against Ross's unyielding washboard stomach. My nipples had tightened with involuntary arousal at her touch, and I held my breath, praying that she wouldn't notice.

Her tongue felt strange, different from Seph's recent male caresses. Smooth and narrow, and very pink, it stiffened and rubbed quickly against my areola, then trailed a path of flickering fire across my sternum to the other breast.

'Stop it,' I hissed, my teeth gritted. 'Stop it. You

have no power over me, I'm not your slave, I'm Ross's.'

'How sweet.' She straightened up and her grey eyes seemed to bore into mine with some sort of challenge. 'How very touching. But you're wrong. You see, Ross is going to lend you to me for a while, aren't you, Ross?' His stubbly cheek was pressed to mine and I felt him nod. 'So, for the time being, you're my slave. I can do what I want with you, provided I hand you back undamaged.'

Her words made an unwelcome thrill fizz along my veins and I shook my head.

'No. The contract is no longer valid,' I said forcefully.

'Such spirit,' she said, smiling into my eyes. 'What a little wild-cat you are. You really are an inspiration. I'll have to ensure I'm the sort of mistress you so obviously need.'

She reached for the waist of my jeans and jerked my hips forward. I tightened and jerked them back. She laughed, and pulled me very firmly towards her again.

'Don't fight me,' she said. 'You'll enjoy it more than you think you will, if you just let go of your little middle-class schoolgirl inhibitions. Now, I want something to show that you are mine. Branding? Hmm, maybe a little too permanent.' She pressed one finger to her lips. 'I wonder. I know. Ross, bind her, please.'

I fought him as best I could but he had the strength of two men at the best of times, and the heat inside the house had sapped my strength. I was quickly bound with a combination of leather belts and short soft cords from the curtains, and then strapped to an upright wooden chair with my knees forced wide apart.

The jeans had been stripped from me, so I had only the torn pieces of shirt to cover my modesty – what was left of it – and I felt horribly exposed. Very vulnerable and small. But the warmth of the room seemed to kiss my bare skin, making it flushed and glowing, and I knew that the goosebumps that puckered my skin were not due to cold but to a strange excitement that I couldn't control.

'Sasha, bring my bag, will you?' Louisa strode across the room and held the door ajar. There was the sound of scurrying footsteps and Louisa waited impatiently, the toes of her gorgeous red shoes tap-tapping on the floor. Sasha came briefly into view but did not enter the room. She merely handed a modern, black, very shiny doctor's bag to Louisa and turned away. Louisa closed the door with the toe of her high-heeled shoe.

'I don't want you to be afraid of this,' she said, opening the bag on the table next to me and laying a selection of small sealed packets out in the turned-back lid. 'Everything is perfectly sterile. Strictly single use. And perfectly legitimate. I have carte blanche with wide-bore needles in my job.'

She snapped on a pair of latex surgical gloves and advanced towards me, then dropped to her knees and inspected me closely. I could feel my naked sex blossoming under her gaze and I tried to close my legs but the bonds that held my knees to the chair legs wouldn't budge.

'Hold her, Ross.'

'Help me, Ross,' I echoed, twisting in the chair and looking up at him beseechingly. 'Stop her, she doesn't know what the hell she's doing.'

'Actually, she does,' said Ross in a conversational tone. 'She's a surgeon, so she's more than qualified to put a neat little piece of gold through your labia.'

'Pierce my labia? You're crazy!' I struggled in earnest now, fear flooding my veins and making my limbs weak and useless. 'Ross. Stop her. Stop this. Stop it now, this wasn't in the contract. I don't want anything that hurts. Ross!' My voice rose to a squeal as she moved to brush my skin with a wet piece of gauze.

'Say the word, then.' He seemed almost to be goading me, daring me to give in. 'Say it, Puss, and it won't happen. She'll stop as soon as you say it.'

His pupils were wide and black, bottomless pools that made me feel like I was drowning into his eyes. I stared back at him, my mind spinning while words of venom crowded unspoken on my tongue. I felt like spitting at him, or leaning forward and biting him. He was so close that I could almost have done it, but Louisa was closer still and her proximity made me hesitate. I felt her fingers part me and apply the swab.

There was a roaring in my ears as my heart-rate powered up to about one hundred and twenty as she touched me. The smell of the alcohol that soaked Louisa's gauze swab was medicinal. It reminded me of hospital corridors and squeaky-soled shoes.

I sat still and rigid, feeling the tingle in my sex that told me that her rubber-clad touch was turning me on despite myself. The bonds that secured me to the chair took away every ounce of control that I felt I had. I was powerless, and the sensation of powerlessness was a strange aphrodisiac, piquant and compelling. I could feel pulsing fear buzzing through my veins, and sweat was making my armpits prickle, but I found that I didn't want to say the safety word. Not yet.

I closed my eyes and breathed hard through my nostrils. I felt faint, but tinglingly aware of everything around me. All my senses were on full alert, everything charged up, sensations ablaze. The feel of Louisa's alcohol swab was cool on my skin, a refreshing cleanser that dried almost immediately on contact, but left my sex in a cold menthol buzz.

When I was cleansed to her satisfaction, she held up something that glittered in the light. It was a tiny gold ring with a five-millimetre gap where a golden sphere would be placed to close the circle. It was fascinating but frightening and I stared at it, unable to speak.

'What do you think, slave-cat? Do you think that this will show that you're mine? Just imagine how pleasant this will feel, rubbing in the sticky cotton gusset of your knickers.' Her voice dropped to a hoarse whisper. 'It could make a girl come just from walking if it's positioned correctly.' She sat back on the high heels of her scarlet shoes – no, damn it, they were mine – and raised one eyebrow enquiringly. 'What do you say? Shall I do it? Do you trust me?'

Did I trust her? Hell, no. I didn't know the woman, and had certainly never seen the qualifications that made her a doctor. But something in her eyes – her self-confidence, perhaps – inspired me and I glanced back down at the little gold ring. It lay in the palm of her hand and caught the weak wintry sunlight from the window. The daylight cast a tiny golden halo on to the pale skin of her hand, like buttercups do when held under the chin. Glowing, warm and attractive.

I was tempted. But my fear of pain held me back. I stayed silent.

'North American Indians use piercing,' Louisa said, gently, her eyes meeting mine and probing my thoughts. I found it impossible not to listen to her voice; it was low and hypnotic, warm and full of something that pulled me in and wrapped me up in safety. I felt odd, as if I were someone else, someone not actually inside the body that she intended to penetrate with her needles. 'They use it as part of tribal ritual to increase enlightenment, or seek visions. Piercing the body can release bad spirits and encourage the entry of good ones. Maybe a bad spirit needs to leave your body so that you can realise the pleasure of the game you've started. You certainly don't seem to be enjoying it much at the moment – so perhaps you have nothing to lose by trying this. It might get rid of some of your resentment and let you have fun with us.'

'It'll hurt me.' My voice snagged on the second word. I'm such a physical coward, I hadn't even dared have my ears pierced when all my contemporaries were sporting sleepers at age ten. My feelings of pleasure when Ross had whipped me so soundly had surprised me, but that didn't mean I was going to submit to body piercing. No way.

'Pain is such a subjective thing,' said Louisa. She rested one hand on my knee and stared into my eyes. 'If you are really afraid of pain, then I can give you some local anaesthetic. But you should know that the body has its own pain reliever: endorphins. Just like opiates, they make you euphoric, but with no chemicals. Have you ever done a really hard aerobic work-out and had that natural high afterwards?' Aerobic work-out? Me? I almost laughed out loud then, but restricted myself to nodding. 'Well, that's the body's natural chemical reaction to physical stimulation. You'll feel a rush, a natural high. You should try it.'

I wasn't totally convinced by her words. Chemical highs I'd tried in my twenties, in college; and while they were great when you were out partying with a crowd till 4 a.m., the come-down the next morning was not something I wanted to repeat in my thirties. I shook my head. I'd stick to my orgasm fixes, thank you very much.

But I couldn't help glancing down at the little gold ring which still glowed on Louisa's palm. It looked very attractive, gently glowing against her pale skin. Maybe the local anaesthetic would help.

'No.' I kept my voice firm.

'It would look so good on you, Puss.' It was Ross. He bent down behind me, his hands on my shoulders, his mouth near my ear. His lips nibbled my tender skin, then his tongue looped around my ear lobe and drew it in for a tentative, spine-tingling five seconds. He didn't know it, but I was more than half-way to being convinced. I took a deep breath and stalled, hoping that he'd try other ways to persuade me.

His hand slipped from my shoulder to my neck, then down to my breast. He cupped it in his hand, testing its rounded weight before tweaking my nipples between thumb and forefinger. Then he leant further over me and slid his palms firmly down over my stomach to my sex.

His fingers gripped my labia and pulled them, then settled on the right lip, rolling it and teasing it outward until it was stretched so wide I could see it without inclining my head. It looked cute, all pink and shiny, peeking out from under the short re-growth of glossy pubic hair.

'See it, Puss?' he murmured. 'See how pretty it is? Louisa – and I – wish only to embellish it. Imagine it flanked by the gold ring, with the ball rubbing you for constant stimulation. Mmm, gorgeous. Something to lick and suck when I next go down on you. Something to rub when you ride on top of me. A little gold collar for a little gold cat.'

He nuzzled my neck and inhaled deeply, as if savouring my body scent, then opened his lips against me and sank his teeth into the sensitive muscle that ran from my shoulder to the base of my neck. Now, there is a sweet spot. I sighed and dropped my head to one side, offering my neck as a sacrifice. His teeth raked my skin, delicious and enticing.

So, I was putty in his hands. I hardly heard myself murmur 'yes', but it didn't matter because the pleasure his mouth was giving me, coupled with the sticky heat that came from his fingers as he pressed on my clit, was so good that in my head I was singing 'yes, yes, yes', at the top of my voice.

I didn't feel a thing after she sprayed me expertly with the local anaesthetic. Just some pushing and pressure. Then a little pop. Within two minutes I was probably the only girl in a fifty-mile radius with a gold hoop through one of her sex lips. What a claim to fame.

The endorphins suddenly seemed to flood through my body. A natural high, Louisa had said, and she was right. I was up. I was buzzing, my heart-rate racing and my mind flying high above my body. I felt like Samson before he had the haircut: super-strong and ready for anything.

Louisa remained on her knees before me. She had stripped off her surgeon's gloves and they lay discarded on the floor beside her as she crouched and frowned at her handiwork, examining me for side-effects or unexpected swelling. There was neither. She gave a secret, satisfied smile and raised her gaze to meet mine.

Her irises gleamed a curious deep grey in her pale face and I could see that her pupils were dilated, her lashes wide and her eyes shining. There was a visible pulse shifting under the ivory skin of her neck and I could tell, without even counting, that her heart-rate was almost identical to mine. Adrenalin. Endorphins. Who needs chemicals? I thought, as I watched Ross bend forward to kiss her.

Louisa led me upstairs for a bath afterwards. She filled the tub with steaming water and poured in half a tub of kitchen salt, which she said had absolutely no basis in research, but seemed to make her patients feel happier about their wounds. I wallowed in the balmy saline for half an hour or so, while Louisa and Ross talked in low voices at the far end of my little attic room.

My whole body felt very weird, and when I slid my hand down between my thighs I found that the swollen skin of my labia had puffed up around the gold hoop like an armful of silken pillows. It began to hurt quite a lot as the local anaesthetic wore off, but I could tell that it was going to feel nice later. Very nice.

Knowing that I had been pierced gave me a real ego boost. I could hardly believe that I had put myself in Louisa's skilled and gentle hands, and that she had penetrated the most intimate part of my body. Amazingly, I hadn't cried, or screamed, or made a fool of myself. Partly that was due to her: she had been good. Very good. Maybe she'd do my ears some day. I suddenly felt brave enough for anything, provided it was Dr Richmond who was doing it to me.

'Hey, cut it out you two,' I called, feeling good-natured but a tiny bit cross as I saw that, across the room, Louisa had entwined herself around Ross like a serpent. Her pale fingers gripped the black fabric of his jeans and her flame-red hair cloaked over her shoulders. They ignored me, but I watched them with hungry fascination.

Louisa seemed to be putting on a show for my benefit. She ran her narrow fingers over Ross's chest, down his tapering waist to the crotch of his jeans, then cupped the outline of his cock with her hand.

She sank to her knees and tugged at the buttons of his fly, released him from the prison of his trousers and shorts, and began to caress him lightly with her fingertips and tongue. I watched, unable to move but with a worm of jealousy oozing through my belly. He was hardening, growing, under her sure touch.

She slipped back his crinkled skin and revealed the shining head of his cock. Her tongue flicked over him, lightly, adeptly, then she closed her lips and opened her mouth over him. I watched her subtle movements as she drank him in, and then proceeded to draw him slowly to full erectness.

I saw Ross's chest rise and fall as he sighed and

relaxed, his dark eyes falling closed and his head tilting slightly back. As I watched Louisa give head, my heart swelled almost to bursting and I could feel the thud of my pulse slow to a steady fifty.

It was one of the most gloriously erotic things I had ever seen. Ross laid his hands on her neck at first, then widened his fingers up to cup her head protectively. His thumbs were strong and large, guiding her movements, easing her gently forward and then away. I could just see the jut of her chin and the line of her jaw from where I was, and I watched the swelling pout of her lips as she sank on to him: sucking, drawing him deeply into her throat.

I felt turned on, and divinely jealous. Aroused, but angry. He was mine. Ross was mine. And yet everything that had happened over the past week had taken him further and further away from me.

Louisa was still wearing the long fur coat, despite the tropical heat. She'd obviously done her homework, read the book, and was intending to live as Wanda for as long as it amused her. The pale fur seemed to flow around her shoulders and neck, the cuffs falling back along her arms to reveal her narrow wrists and forearms as she slid her hands up over Ross's hips. She hitched her thumbs into his pockets and hung there, her head thrown back and her wide mouth full of muscular cock. Stretched. Crammed. God, I could almost taste it.

The steamy room was almost silent. The only sound I could hear was my own slow pulse and the slick-slick of her lips on his sex. I closed my eyes briefly, but opened them when I found that I couldn't bear not being able to see what they were doing.

Ross was standing straight, taut, his eyes closed and his face creased into a grimace of pleasure. His hands were bunched into the silk of Louisa's hair, twisting it into his fists as if the long sheaves were the reins of a horse that he was riding. His jeans were shucked down to just above his knees and I could see the powerful curve of his thigh muscles, with their shadowing of dark hair, and the lean sweep of his naked hips.

He was such a man, such a delicious piece of male meat, that I almost stood up in the bath, carried upward by my emotions. I wanted to stalk over there, slap away my rival and sink to my knees. I longed to take that gorgeous, thick cock in my mouth and suck it so hard that he exploded. To gorge on him until I felt the hot salt of his orgasm surge across my palate and down my gulping throat.

But unfortunately my week as a slave had chiselled away some of my bravado, and I lay there in the rapidly cooling salt water, one thumb on my sore labia, the other rammed in my mouth as I played it out in my head instead.

I became Louisa: I thought myself into her so that I could almost feel the waves of Titian hair brushing my shoulders. Ross's cock was hard and it strained against the flat of my tongue, his glans was shiny and primed as he held it back. He was going to come, I could feel it. Just one more hard suck and a little finger-play and he'd blow. His balls were tight up under him now, kissed up to the base of his cock and taut with readiness.

I imagined it all, but I could see that they were going to beat me to the climax. I watched, the thumb pressure moving to my clit and becoming painfully insistent, as Louisa curved her neck and took him all the way in so that her nose was buried in the coarse dark hair of his groin. Her hands swept up and under his balls and she cupped them, milking him. I could see the suction as her cheeks curved inward and I knew by Ross's sudden gasp and moan that he was about to come.

His hips did a neat little double-time thrust and his

buttocks tensed as he pressed himself forward into her face. Her neck was a pale sweep of precious ivory that gulped and swallowed, her Adam's apple bobbing under the sudden rush of hot come. I held my breath. I could feel frustrated, jealous tears pricking my eyelids as I saw the look he gave her from under sleepy eyelids.

But then he raised his eyes – full of tender concern – to me, and it seemed that he pulled me in, locking me into his erotic triangle: Ross, Louisa and me.

I saw then that I hadn't lost Ross at all. Instead, I'd gained Louisa. And I realised that there was no end in sight.

That night I had to serve Ross and Louisa at dinner, dressed only in the mulberry rubber dress, stockings and high heels, with the obligatory cat collar around my neck. I fetched and carried and poured wine, and I seemed to be doing quite well, because I caught Louisa giving me several approving glances. I became even more careful and solicitous after that, because it suddenly seemed very important that I please her, that I do everything to her satisfaction.

Each time I removed the empty plates, Louisa would smile and nudge the toe of her pointed shoe against my leg. It felt good, and somehow secret from Ross who leant back in his chair and watched me with an amused smile on his wide mouth, unaware of her little caresses. I took his plate and wiggled out of the room to fetch the next course and a fresh bottle of wine. They had been drinking steadily throughout the evening and I was hoping that they might not notice if I stole some for myself from the next bottle.

Having taken a few gorgeously illicit mouthfuls of fruity claret, I carried the two dishes of dark chocolate mousse and presented them to Ross. He ignored me. I laid Louisa's plate in front of her but she ignored me, too. They seemed to have eyes only for each other and I was beginning to feel left out. Wondering how I could get back into the triangle, I glanced from one to the other, then remembered Severin spilling wine across Wanda's table. He was punished for it, but he got her attention all right.

I waited until they had lifted their spoons, then I picked up the decanter and poured a little less carefully than usual. A dark, crimson pool washed across the pristine blond wood of the table and I waited for them to notice it – and me. There was a silence which lasted several heartbeats, then Ross dropped his cutlery and stood up abruptly as the wine trickled over the table towards him. His chair crashed over behind him.

'You clumsy little cat,' he muttered, his voice hard and tightly controlled. 'Clean that up. Right now.'

'I am so sorry, master,' I said, thoroughly enjoying myself. 'I'll get a cloth.'

'Do that.' He stalked away from the table and stood by the fireplace, one elbow resting on the high mantel. Louisa, however, didn't move. She sat very still in her chair, her eyes fixed on me, with a quiet smile curving her lips. Her silver spoon glittered in her left hand.

'No, wait,' she said. 'She doesn't need a cloth. I think she should be made to lick it up.'

How did she do it? She was growing into her role of mistress with a sureness that was breathtaking. It was amazing to think that she had been hiding her dominant light under a patina of submissiveness for so long. Had Ross been fooled, or had he known her for what she really was? I glanced across at him and saw him regarding her with a look that glowed with admiration and approval.

Perhaps he hadn't known before, but he was discovering it now, and he seemed to like what he found. Having his two women exhibiting such extremes of human nature purely for his benefit must be particularly thrilling. I wondered whether there was space in the emerging dynamics of the triangle for Louisa and I to take the control away from him. Girl power had distinct possibilities, and the thought of turning it round and making Ross our slave made my breath catch in my throat with excitement.

But right now that would have to wait. I was still the slave, and I was getting my instructions.

'Get up on the table, Puss,' said Louisa. 'Go on. Lick it up, you know you want to. I've seen the covetous glances you've been giving the glasses of wine. You must be so thirsty after all your hard work.' She stood up and prowled around the table to stand next to me. Her cool hand was pressed against the small of my back and I could feel that the metal of the spoon she still held was sticking to the hot rubber of my dress. 'Up. Up now. Tell her, Ross.'

But I didn't need to hear it from him as well, and he knew it. He remained silent, gazing at us from near the smouldering fireplace, his eyes dark and watchful. I drew the nearest chair away from the table's edge and stepped carefully up on to it, pausing for a moment to pull down the hem of my dress.

'Leave it.' Louisa swept my hand away, her fingers brushing lightly across the exposed area of skin between the dress and my stocking tops. I took a deep breath and tried to ignore the throb that set up in my sex as I knelt on the table and bent my head forward.

I knew that if she cared to look, Louisa would see my juicy quim peeping lusciously between my thighs as I bent over. It made me hot to imagine what she could see, and when Ross pushed himself away from the mantelpiece and strolled lazily around behind me, I shivered beneath the promise of their combined gaze.

'That's it, Puss. Bend right over,' whispered Louisa. 'Lick it all up like a good cat.'

I did as she said, my lips slipping across the smooth surface of the table as I applied my tongue to the pool of wine. It tasted delicious, even better than the stolen mouthfuls in the kitchen, and I lapped it up until the surface of the table gleamed. Ross took the decanter, swirled it in one hand and then tipped it so that a further rivulet of staining red trickled across the table towards me.

'Drink,' he said. 'Drink it all up, Puss. Go on.'

I hesitated, unsure of myself for a moment. Were they trying to get me so drunk that I'd do my usual trick of falling asleep when I had imbibed too much, and then they would be free to play alone? Or were they trying to get me just drunk enough, so that my resistance was lowered and they could have their wicked way with me?

I met Ross's dark eyes with mine and tried to read what lay behind them. I couldn't tell. Either I had lost the knack of predicting his every move, or he had changed so much that I no longer knew him.

'Do as he says.' A stinging slap from the silver spoon smarted across my buttocks and I jumped away from Louisa's hand.

I glared at her, then remembered that I was supposed to be the meek and submissive one. I drooped my eyelids and watched the wine spread across the table until it reached my fingertips. I had to trust them. They were all I had now. There was no one else. No white knight to come and rescue me, unless you counted Seph. And he seemed rather too slender to ever successfully do battle with my muscular cousin.

There really was no one else. There was just me, and Ross, and Louisa. I looked up into Ross's inscrutable gaze, then lowered my face to the table and prepared to drink.

Chapter Eight

As I dipped my head to the table, I was aware of the blistering heat in my sex and the low thud of my heartbeat. I waited for them to come closer. The dark, rich wine seduced my tongue and I drank it all up without caring whether it got me drunk or not.

Ross moved to me first, his hand slipping over my shoulder and up my neck to cup my face. He bent his head to catch my lips and devour my mouth before I'd even swallowed the last mouthful of wine, and I could feel the overflow trickle from the corner of my lips as his tongue entered my mouth.

He sucked thirstily, drinking the wine from my mouth and licking it off my tongue until I felt weak and helpless, my lips inflamed under his, and my hands trembling against the wooden surface of the table.

The kiss lasted for a long time. Deep and very penetrative, it was as if Ross was fucking my face with his tongue. Behind me, I could hear Louisa breathing deeply as she watched, then there was the smooth stroking of her fingers at the hem of my dress. I knew that she had bent to kiss me when I sensed the soft caress of a loose tendril of her hair stroke across the back of my thigh, then I felt the humid warmth of her breath against my skin.

I tensed, but made myself relax. The wine had warmed my bones and made me light-headed and open to suggestion, so I let her kiss along the rubber at the bottom of the dress while I drowned in the sensuous movements of Ross's mouth on mine.

I opened my eyes as I felt Ross move away slightly, and saw that he had scooped a handful of the chocolate mousse from his glass dish and smeared it across the table where the wine had been spilled.

'More cleaning, Puss,' he said, one eyebrow raised as if he were challenging me.

'Oh, dear,' I murmured. 'Then I'd better clean it up – master.'

I placed my hands either side of the sweet mess and dipped my head, aware that as my shoulders went down, my bottom went up. I arched my back a little – all my inhibitions soaked in alcohol – and felt my skin goosebump with pleasure as Louisa's lips moved involuntarily from the rubber fabric of my dress to the skin just below the hem. She pulled away, obviously confused for a moment, and I heard Ross encourage her in a low tone.

Her lips fastened back on my buttocks, just above the little crease at the top of my thigh. I felt the flicker of her tongue against me. Then I sensed a coolness, metallic and strange, as she pressed the head of the spoon just next to her mouth. I wanted to move away. But I made myself maintain my position, licking up the delicious dark chocolate mousse, as she slipped the spoon round so that it cupped my sex.

I could just imagine what it looked like: some sort of space-age cap, silver and shiny in the curve between my thighs, just covering the entrance to my sex. It was cold in comparison to my hot flesh, which was swollen and pouting against the silver, but it felt good and I transferred my eager tongue from the table-top to Ross's fingers which were spread just inches from my face.

'Lick it up,' he said, obviously approving of my initiative. 'Lick it all up. I love the feel of your tongue, Puss. It's just like a real cat's tongue. Little and narrow. You've always been capable of great things with your tongue.'

His words seemed to give him an idea, because his other hand went to the fastening of his black trousers. I gripped his wrists, stilling his movement, and my eyes met his for a moment. I wanted to do it. I wanted to unzip him and cradle his hot, hard flesh in my fingers. As he stared at me his pupils dilated slightly, then constricted, and his hands fell to his sides. He let me undo him and cup his semi-rigid cock in my hand.

He was hot and sticky, his skin slipping under my fingertips as I eased him out of his fly. I reached for the bowl of chocolate and dug my fingers in, scooping it up and carrying it to my tongue for a moment to steal a quick mouthful, then encircling his sex with my chocolate-covered hand. I slowly pulled him to erectness, watching him grow and widen until his bevel-headed glans bloomed out from under his pale foreskin, all eager and ready to play. I resisted the temptation to lean down and let my tongue rim the salt-tasting slit. Instead I let my thumb glide over it and allowed myself a secret smile as he gave a sensitive little buck of his hips.

The chocolate mousse was deliciously smooth and smelled gorgeous. It mingled with Ross's cock scent to make a tangy, peppery, chocolate fragrance that would make girls cry with desire and sexual greed if chocolate makers packed their foil-wrapped bars with it. It was all I could do to stop myself from falling forward and gorging myself on him – but I wanted him to wait a bit. And besides, Louisa had turned the spoon over and was using it to stroke across my pouting, juicy lips, stimulating me so much that I could hardly concentrate on the job in hand.

'Suck me,' whispered Ross, unable to wait. I ignored him and closed my eyes to savour the firm pressure and tiny stroking motion of the curved spoon across my sex.

'Suck me,' he repeated, impatience and need trembling in his voice. I opened my eyes just a little and watched the various emotions play across his face: desire, desperation, wanting, irritation, and finally a humbleness that took me by surprise. I think if he'd said it again, I would have capitulated instantly. There's nothing more irresistible than a gorgeous man who asks you nicely to suck his cock. Unless it's a man who begs you to.

And actually Ross looked like he wanted to beg. The sight of his favourite cousin getting her butt kissed and her sex spooned by his favourite girlfriend had put all thoughts of masterful behaviour out of his head. He just wanted a good old-fashioned blow-job. I waited a little longer. He was silent, his eyes fixed on mine. Then he parted his lips and I saw his tongue rim the dry edges of his mouth.

'Please.'

Luckily for him, chocolate-flavoured dick accompanied by the p-word is pretty near to perfection, so I opened my mouth to him with genuine greed.

He tasted so good. Ross always tastes fabulous anyway, even when he hasn't had a shower all day and his bag is all sweaty and hot. But spread a little Bournville around and you have the perfect pudding. Or hors d'oeuvre. Or even main course, whichever way you want to structure your meal.

I cupped the head in my mouth, letting it just past my lips so that I could rub the eye with the tip of my tongue, then I sucked my way off and went underneath, nosing my way down to where his dark hair curled protectively around his root. I took a good long lick from balls to tip, then slipped down again and repeated it until I could hear his sharp intake of breath.

Carefully, I eased up from the table and slipped my hands into the waistband of his trousers. I shucked them down a little, just so that I could feel the curve of his buttocks with my palms, then I let my mouth engulf him.

Behind me, I knew that Louisa was turned on by what I was doing; the movements with the spoon had stopped and I could feel the weight of her hand on my back. She was paying no attention to my needs at all, she was just mesmerised by the way my lips slid up and down the muscular length of Ross's cock, and by the vulnerable and oh-so-sexy look on his face as he let his eyelids flutter shut.

I sucked him until he was clean of chocolate, enjoying the sweetly sticky glide of the mousse against the back of my throat. He was breathing pretty hard by the time his cock was pink again. I could feel his helmet swell and bloom against the back of my throat with each downward stroke.

It turned me on so much that I wished Louisa would start up the thing with the spoon again. She wasn't very good at mind-reading though, because I had to push myself back against her several times before she got the hint and stroked the spoon under me.

She seemed to hesitate, fighting shy of actually doing anything with it, so I reached around behind me with one hand and gripped her wrist. She stiffened, unsure of my intentions, then let me guide her hand closer to my sex. The spoon was solid silver and beautifully rounded. It felt lovely as it slid easily into my juicy sex, completely swallowed until I felt the pressure of the rounded back of it bump against my G-spot.

Louisa held it still, then I began to move her hand for her with slow, leisurely strokes. When I could feel her getting into it, I released her hand, letting her take control, and she carried on smoothly slipping it up and down inside me. What she was doing to me was blissful, exquisite. I had to concentrate really hard to get myself back into cock-sucking mode.

Ross looked as if he could barely hold on: his balls were tight up under him, his face was flushed and I could feel the heat of his body emanating outward to warm my cheeks. His half-closed eyes were fixed on the arching, rubber-clad skin of my back. I tried to catch his gaze, to connect with him, but he was lost in his own little world of sin and dependency, his eyelids slightly puffy and sleepily lowered so that I could see only the dark glitter of his irises.

The table under my knees felt smooth and hard, comfortable at the present, but maybe not for long. But I knew I would stay there as long as it took. I wasn't planning to move out of this little circle of sensation, not if my knees depended on it. I listened to the sounds of the room: a piece of burning wood shifting in the fire-grate, the slow, efficient ticking of the old-fashioned German clock on the mantelpiece, and the juicy slickness of lips sliding across hard flesh. Tiny breathy sighs. The sound of sex.

Ross watched Louisa, and the rhythmic movement of my hips. I could tell that he was nearly ready to come because he mirrored my movements with little tense thrusts of his pelvis. I swallowed around him and got him in a really good deep-throat position, then I curled my fingers around his balls and gently massaged them, sucking hard as if he was the biggest lollipop I'd ever had.

He came then, thick lye pumped into the back of

my throat, and I nearly cried at the sound he made. It was a low, sexy grunt, almost like he was in pain, and when I glanced up I saw that his eyes had fallen closed. His hands clasped my hair and held my face tight around him, his fingers tenderly pressing under my chin as he moved his hips in a fucking, grinding motion. His face was pale, but flushed at the edges as he thrust himself forward in my mouth and spasmed into my throat. I swallowed and swallowed; he tasted divine.

I had almost forgotten his flavour – it had been quite a while since I'd had him in my mouth, almost a week in fact, but the memories came flooding back with the salt of his hot, creamy come and I closed my eyes and inhaled through my nose, adding his smell to the sensations that filled my brain. My fingers left his balls and slid round to curl into the undercurve of his buttocks, softly stroking the coarse little hairs there and holding him so that he could not escape from my mouth.

I knew how sensitive the head of his cock would be when he'd finished – how red-raw and agonising it had been for him once, a long time ago, when he'd come across my belly. I had been so hot for him, so desperate and unsatisfied, that I'd made him go back in and fuck me again straight away. He had shouted and roared with a pain that was close to ecstasy but he hadn't been able to come again so quickly. This time I intended to suck his over-sensitive glans and see whether he could get beyond the pain and climax again.

I held his buttocks tight and slipped my wet lips to the end of his dick. He jerked under my mouth, his hips seeking an escape route, but I held him fast.

'Oh God, no. Sam, no,' he groaned, his hands cupping my head again and trying to move me back. I ignored his plea and sucked on, milking him with a rolling movement of my tongue on the underside of his cock while my top lip went up and over his glans repeatedly. The little slit was open, like it was begging for more, and I looped my tongue up and made the tip hard as I frigged it in and out, as if I could fuck him with my tongue. He gasped, cried my name and tried to pull out, but I could feel the long muscle in his cock swelling slightly under my fingers as if he was getting primed again, so I didn't stop.

Louisa was watching. She seemed to realise what I was doing and instantly improved on it. I felt her take the spoon out of me and turn it around, dipping the thin, dainty handle into my juices to catch as much lubricant as she could. Then she silently pointed to Ross, who had his eyes closed, otherwise I'm sure he would have stopped me. At that moment I had the urge to slide my middle finger deep into his arse. This took him by surprise but had the desired effect.

It was amazing. He cried out and grasped a handful of my hair in one of his powerful hands. I ducked down and encased his balls with my lips, sucking hard. He groaned once, bucked his hips and then exploded against me, his come shooting in ragged ejaculations across my shoulder and arm. I felt a tight constraint in my chest – joy and arousal, I think – as he climaxed, and I stayed very still as Louisa moved to his side and covered his mouth with her own. She kissed him long, deeply, her lips crushing against his in a bruising, devouring embrace.

Eventually they came up for air.

'Where did you learn to do that?' Ross looked from me to Louisa and back again. She shrugged so I copied her and occupied myself with wiping his thick white come off my arm with my forefinger. It was strange, more watery than before, and I tasted it experimentally.

Before I had made up my mind whether or not I

liked the taste, Louisa bent her head to my hand and closed her lips over my finger. The sight of her sucking Ross's spunk from my hand was incredibly erotic. Intensely stimulating. I felt such a dragging heaviness in my sex, such a desperate longing for release, that I reached for Ross and pulled his face down to mine.

'Make me come,' I whispered, covering his cheeks and jaw with tiny butterfly kisses. 'Make me come, please.'

'Naughty little slave,' he murmured against my hair, his voice thick with tenderness. 'Slaves can't ask. Slaves beg.'

'No,' I whimpered, curling my legs under me and rising up so that my body pressed against his and my breasts flattened against the front of his shirt. 'Don't make me beg – make me come.'

Ross leant back away from me, his warm hands cupping my face and his eyes searching my face. I thought for a moment that he was going to refuse, and my heart twisted inside my chest. I felt needy and vulnerable, as if I was lost out in the wilderness somewhere and would never find my way back to comfort and security. Then he relented and the corners of his eyes crinkled upward in a smile.

'Darling Puss,' he said. 'Come here.'

'You're developing into a very good slave,' Louisa whispered in my ear.

She rested her arms lightly on my shoulders and the silk of her Chinese dress slipped like wet fabric across the rubber-moulded swell of my breasts. We had been dancing for a while. Ross, sated from his unexpected twofold orgasm, had put the new Blur CD on and stretched out on the couch to watch us. We had, he said, fulfilled his every fantasy.

'A very good slave indeed,' continued Louisa.

'Perhaps a little too good. You might want to try a little disobedience again. It was fun, punishing you.'

'Fun for you,' I murmured, conscious of the jut of her hips as they bumped lightly against mine. We had moved close to each other, cheek to cheek, and it felt almost too close for comfort: it made me nervous. The fact that she had held my most intimate organ between her fingers earlier in the day kept surfacing in my mind, and the memory made my face burn.

The little gold ring was painfully in evidence, although the swelling was slightly better since the salty bath. My sexual arousal during the Ross-sucking episode had helped ease it a little, and the orgasm that he had brought me to afterwards with his fingers and tongue had made me feel so high as to make me ignore the sensations of pain – those magical endorphins again, no doubt.

'And fun for you, too. Don't deny it.' Her cheek brushed mine. 'Have you noticed that we are almost exactly the same height?'

'Strange, I always think of you as smaller.'

'Oh, come on.' Louisa sighed impatiently. 'I thought all that one-upmanship was behind us. We're both five foot six, give or take a few millimetres on a kitten-heeled shoe or two.'

'What one-upmanship?' I drew away from her so that I could see her reaction. 'I've never needed that sort of thing – it must be in your head.'

'It's not in my head. You make me feel as if we're always fighting over something.'

'Something? Perhaps it's some*one*,' I said pointedly, glancing over at my handsome cousin who was draped across the sofa, almost asleep.

'Why do you dislike me?' she asked, trying to catch my eye. I avoided her gaze and tried to look bored.

'I don't dislike you,' I sighed.

'You seem to. Maybe that's your funny way of showing friendship.'

'Maybe it is.' I gazed across the room at the fireplace and then slanted my eyes sideways at her. She was staring into the middle distance behind me, her grey eyes thoughtful and solemn. I felt a twist of regret inside for being mean to her, because I could feel myself growing to like her. Sometimes.

'It's just that Ross complicates things.' I sighed.

'He doesn't have to. It could be so simple, just the three of us here for a month doing what we like. Experimenting with sex. Drinking lots of wine. Smoking some hash – doing all the things that responsible people are supposed to forget about once they hit thirty.'

'Speak for yourself.'

'I am,' she said, a wry curve to the corner of her lips. 'I've had to forget all those things. Being a woman in such a hierarchical profession as mine makes you give up quite a lot of your real self just to survive – and I want to do more than survive. I want to smash through that glass ceiling and have a real career – get a consultancy before I'm forty-five. And to do that I'm having to smother the real me. But here, with you and Ross, I can relax. I can be myself, be young. Doing what we're doing now would cause most of my colleagues to have coronaries.'

She slid in a little closer to me and I let her embrace me, enjoying the smooth glide of her slender arms on my bare shoulders. Her body was willowy and lean, but soft in all the right places. She was the same height as me, as she had observed, and it made things quite cosy. Standing nipple to nipple in a hot room with another girl is a sensation that I won't forget in a hurry.

'Have you ever tried girl-on-girl sex?' Louisa asked.

I didn't answer.

147

She frowned, meeting my eye. 'Well, have you?'

'Have I what?'

'Tried it?'

'No.'

'Never?'

'No way. I'm straight.' I felt indignant that she might even think otherwise.

'So am I.' She turned her head so that her nose brushed mine and I thought for one moment that she was going to kiss me. I don't know whether the goosebumps on my arm when she didn't signalled relief or disappointment. 'But that doesn't mean a thing. The majority of women have at least considered it. A lot have tried it, and some have never turned back to men. Have you never even thought about it? Even once? Doing it with a girl, I mean.'

I remembered Sasha bringing me to orgasm on the kitchen table, her tongue and fingers firm against my sex, and blushed a fierce hot red. 'No,' I said. 'No, I haven't.'

Luckily, she took the blushing as a sign of embarrassment rather than guilt.

'Really? Well, think about it. Go on. Think about it now.'

'I don't want to.'

'Yes, you do. You liked it when I touched you earlier. I know you did. I felt your body get red-hot under my fingers when I was piercing you.' Her breath was warm on my cheek, making my blush even deeper, and I involuntarily drew her closer, telling myself that it was to stop her seeing my fiery skin. 'And when I put that spoon in your sticky little hole I bet you would have liked it to be my fingers. Or my tongue. Wouldn't you?'

'No.'

'You would.' Her mouth was almost touching my ear, her breath warm and fragrant on the side of my cheek. I could feel her nipples hardening against mine and it made my sex give a tight little squeeze. 'You'd love to feel the heat of my lips clasped on to your juicy little flower. Feel the lick of my tongue going up and down the hot slit between your legs.'

I couldn't speak so I just shook my head, wondering how this was going to end. I could see Ross lounging on the sofa a few feet away. He was frowning and pretending to look at the pictures on the sleeve notes from his CD, but I could tell by the bulge behind his fly that he was listening to every word we said.

'Are you sure?' Louisa whispered, her tongue flicking out and touching my ear lobe. I closed my eyes and didn't move. I just stood there, trying not to enjoy the feel of her breasts against mine and the bullet-hard points of her nipples pressing through the latex of my dress.

'I'm sure,' I said, but even to my ears my voice sounded pretty far from sure.

'Well, maybe you'd like to do that to me instead.'

My eyes flashed open and I stared at her. She was so close that I could see every one of her dark eyelashes and the satin smoothness of the skin around her nose. I shook my head, fixing my gaze somewhere around the curve of her left nostril. I could see that she was smiling, then she spoke in a very slow, sweetly innocent voice.

'Oh, I think you do. In fact I know that you're going to, whether you want to or not. You're the slave, remember? And if you don't do as I tell you, then I'll have to smack you.'

She turned and walked away from me. I watched as she blew out all the candles in the room except one, so that there was just the glow from the fire on one side of us and the single flame in the centre of the table on the other. Then she pulled a chair from by the wall and placed it in the centre of the room.

I thought she was going to make me sit on it, and position me as she had done for my piercing, but instead she perched herself on the very edge of the seat. She didn't look at me, or Ross. She just undid the tiny silk-covered buttons of her narrow dress and eased it up over her head.

Underneath she wore some lingerie that I would have coveted had I not been so engrossed in watching her undress. Her small breasts were encased in a lovely emerald-green half-cup bra. Tracing the line of her milky thighs were matching suspenders, with long lace-top stockings and those fabulous black strappy shoes that she had worn to whip me in before.

I stared at her, holding my breath. She looked so beautiful and so desirable. I didn't know how Ross could just sit there and not leap on her. But he obviously knew that if he left us to it there would be a better reward.

'Come here, Puss.' She said it softly. Asking, not ordering.

I shook my head and she cocked an eyebrow at me.

'Do you want me to smack you?' she asked. Actually I did, but I didn't want to give her the satisfaction of reading me so well. I walked over, my head meekly bowed, and stood in front of her.

'Kneel.'

I glanced at Ross. He was no longer feigning disinterest: the CD cover lay tossed on the carpet, and the hand that had held it before was idly positioned on his thigh, near the bulge of his zipper. His long thumb with its lovely, pale, square-cut nail was slowly sliding up and down on the black fabric. He wasn't caressing himself exactly, just doing a slow tease in the general proximity: he knew that he could get hands-on later if the scene demanded it.

Louisa parted her knees and lay back in the chair a little. Her long white limbs gleamed in the low light afrom the single candle, and I could see the dark whorls of her auburn pubic hair – a shade darker than her head – covering a narrow triangle at the join of her thighs. She looked exotic and dangerous, almost predatory, and I felt a frisson of fear. I was getting into something I had never bargained for here. This was way over my head.

But I trusted Ross. And, weirdly, I was beginning to trust Louisa too. She looked so much like the descriptions of Wanda Von Dunajew in the book that I was beginning to feel that she *was* Wanda. And that I was Severin. And that this was all right and proper. It wasn't at all what I had intended, when I had first dreamt up the idea of a contract, but it was exciting and stimulating. And it felt adventurous.

I sighed, feeling an absurd mixture of emotions: confusion, arousal, frustration, impatience.

'Poor Puss. What's the matter?' Louisa leant forward and gently stroked my cheek with the palm of her hand. 'Come on,' she murmured, half-laughing. 'It's only sex. You might like it, if you try it.'

'That's what I'm afraid of.'

Whoops. Did I say that? Well, it was out there now. I *had* said it. I had admitted that I was afraid that I might like having sex with a girl. It was true, but having voiced my fears, I found that I really didn't want to think about them any more. So I clasped her hand with mine to stop her stroking me, and lowered her palm back to the arm of the chair. Then I bent to kiss her stomach.

She smelt different. Unusual. Like me, but not like me. Her warm sex gave off a heavy, salty, metallic smell. She was exotic and almost floral, and I found that, as I kissed my way down the fresh skin of her lower stomach towards the line of her soft bush, I was remembering the tropical heaviness of an orchid house that I had once visited.

Humid and lush, the orchid house had been full of intense fragrances that lingered in the nose for so long that you could almost taste them. The air inside the small building had oozed moisture: the warm, steamy, almost face-hugging air had drifted in swathes, circulated by the lazy motion of a fan set into the ceiling, and the dark, wet leaves had given the atmosphere the cloying sweetness of a virgin jungle.

It had been a cold winter's day outside, and the baking heat indoors had initially made me reluctant to leave. But once I got back outside, I realised that wild horses wouldn't get me back in there: the blooms had been overpowering and strangely sensual, with the seductiveness of the recently dead. I had shuddered and made a grimace at my companion, and then we'd headed for the licensed bar with a feeling of relief.

But this orchid house was different. Louisa's sexual perfume, mingled with the scent of Dove Soap and freshly laundered stockings, made everything seem less claustrophobic than the real thing somehow, and when I reached the dry, soft springy hairs that cupped her mons, I knew that I was going to like this experiment. It was going to be very strange being on the giving end of cunnilingus – but what the hell.

'Go ahead,' murmured Louisa, tilting her hips so that her sex was opened up towards me. Her fresh perfume reached my nostrils in a lingering wave, and I inhaled slightly, then bent my head to press my closed lips against her sex. I could feel a tightening between my own thighs, a strange clench that seemed to oscillate up from my labia all the way to my womb. I sat back on my heels and stroked my fingers from Louisa's knees all the way up her silky skin to the creases at either side of her pubic hair.

'What do you want me to do?' I breathed.

'Lick me, of course.' Her voice was so soft, so hushed, that I could only just hear her.

'But how?'

'Any way you like. Any way you want. Right now all you'd have to do would be to touch me with the tip of your tongue and I'd probably come all over your face.'

What she said was patently true: as I glanced down at the mysterious tangle of her hair and the shiny skin of her sex, I could see her visibly swelling. Everything looked heavy and pouting, and I could make out a tiny pooling of mouth-watering dew in the scooping pink skin at the base. I wondered where to start, but her body told me almost straight away: her clit strained out, shiny and cockle-shell smooth and just begging for some attention.

I dipped my chin down and gave the little pearl an experimental lick. It popped forward and swelled against my tongue, so I slid my fingers up and behind it almost without thinking. The hood was tight and I made it tighter, clasping it around the base of her clit like a tiny, tight collar, constraining and binding it so that it protruded against my mouth and I could suck it as if it was a tiny, sweet, barley-sugar chip.

Above me, Louisa groaned and I glanced up, along the smoothness of her belly and between the gentle curves of her breasts, to see her eyelids flutter shut and her head tip back against the head-rest of the chair. Her breath came in short little sighs, and I could see the rise and fall of her erect nipples as she made a little panting noise.

Pleased by her positive reaction, I increased the pressure around her clit before bending my mouth to her again. She was cool on my tongue, like fresh, raw cucumber. Clean and cool and crisp, her taste felt as if it was cleansing my mouth, a soothing sorbet after rich food. As I went deeper with my mouth, covering her clit first, then her lips and finally her whole sex, I felt as if I would never be able to stop until I had

153

devoured her. She tasted so good, so delicious, so female.

I drew my head away at the sudden harsh little sob that she made, but her hand was suddenly at the back of my neck, urging me forward and on to her again. I slid my fingers under her left thigh and lifted it, spreading her wide and resting her knee over the arm of the chair. She was open and stretched, her flesh glowing a paler pink inside, but the colour deepening as she became more aroused. She was so wet that I could see the sheen on her creases, and I smoothed my forefinger along her thigh and slipped it into her.

'Oh, yes. Fuck me like that. Finger me until I come.'

As I eased my finger in, I tried to memorise what it felt like, because it wasn't very likely that there would be many opportunities to do this with a girl. And I might not necessarily want there to be. I closed my eyes for a moment, feeling the uniform tightness of her sex, the muscular smoothness and the juicy warmth.

She lifted her other leg and I opened my eyes to watch her as she slid her fingers around her knees to pull herself open wider. Her face was flushed and her hair had started to escape in tiny wisps that clung to her cheeks and neck.

'Do you like it like this?' I slid in another finger and scissored them sideways to open her up more. She groaned and nodded, her knuckles whitening as she gripped her knees.

'Yes. Move them, move your fingers. Fuck me with them.'

I did as she said and listened to the little noises she made, the tiny sighs and little catches at the back of her throat. She looked gorgeous: abandoned and sluttish with her legs stretched wide and my hand moving slowly but firmly between her thighs.

I could just see the glint of her grey eyes beneath her lowered lashes. I knew that she probably couldn't see me, because she was in that other realm where sensation is everything and the real world doesn't exist. The only thing that exists is the climax, and the only thing you can do is to chase it until you are there – right up there – on the top of the cliff about to dive.

I could feel my own arousal hot between my legs and I squeezed my sex tight, enjoying a tingling throb that echoed up through my body and made me shiver. My face was warm and I could feel the tiny prickles of perspiration around my temples. I used my free hand to push away a floating skein of my own hair, then dropped my mouth to her again.

I took her clit between my lips and sucked. The creamy, thick juice that wet my mouth and fingers and the rich smell of her sex made me realise why men sometimes jokingly called it clam-diving. The frills and folds of her ripe and pouting lips really did look like a clam, and she tasted like the most exotic and delicious shellfish that I had ever slurped off a half-shell. Fresh saline and sushi, a bitter, bright taste that filled my mouth and made my tongue tingle. I pressed my face into her and drank deeply.

When I felt hard male hands on my hips it was a shock, but I kept myself steady and pressed back against Ross. He stroked his fingers down the length of my spine, then eased up the hem of my short rubber dress.

I carried on licking and sucking at Louisa, listening to her little gasping, intense, half-suppressed sounds of pleasure, while he parted me and pressed his hand between my thighs. His thumb grazed me and I bucked against him, then waited for the heat and strength of his hard shaft.

It wasn't long in coming, pressing between my legs like a red-hot poker, but six times as wide and clad in the reassuring coolness of a condom. He held my hips to steady me as he eased in, and I felt my juicy sex widen and flare over him as he slipped his cock into me. Just a little way. Then a pause. Then in a little more. Then a pause again.

Then slickly all the way in so that I gasped and stopped what I was doing. Louisa's hand was instantly at the back of my head, pulling me back in so that I could do nothing but suck her, and frig her with my straight-held fingers, while Ross thrust hard into me from behind.

'You feel so good. You're such a hot little shag,' he muttered. I loved hearing him talk to me like that. I arched my back and pushed myself back to him, matching his plunging rhythm with my hips and my fingers. Louisa liked it too, because she fluttered her eyes open, looked at us both fucking between her legs, then cried out as she came. She tasted gorgeous, flooding my fingers with extra-hot cream and clenching her muscular little sex on to my hands.

Behind me, Ross was primed. Having watched us getting down and dirty, he was nearly at flash-point, and I knew I had less than a minute to get myself to the same stage as him. I reached up and grasped one of Louisa's little breasts, squeezing it with just enough roughness to hurt her, and pressed my fingers deep into her, revelling in the feeling of wet heat that engulfed my hand.

When my fingers were sweet and juicy with her cream, I pulled out and slipped my juicy hand over my own clit, sliding and rubbing at the little hard muscle, using her fresh, musky scent as a lubricant until I felt the familiar tension in my legs and belly that made me shut my eyes and surrender.

I almost sobbed as I came. My head dropped and I could hardly stay upright. My body was convulsed with a shuddering, trembling, breath-wrenching orgasm that seemed to last for minutes. I felt Ross ram home inside me, his pelvis butting up to my bottom with a final slam as he squeezed my hip bones so hard that it felt like he was trying to crush them.

The jerk and swell of his cock inside me was bliss, and I tightened on to him, Thai-style, to make it as good for him as it was for me. I heard him groan and felt the dampness of his palm against my skin as he trembled against me.

'Oh, you two,' whispered Louisa. 'What have you done to me? I used to be such a good girl.'

I reached up, cupped her chin and pulled her face down to mine for a lingering kiss.

'There's good, and there's good,' murmured Ross, curving his body to mine and sealing our joined mouths with his. 'But this is better than good. This beats good hands-down.'

He scooped me into his arms and then pulled Louisa down into his lap, so that we were an interlaced, intimate tangle of arms and legs, breasts and mouths, biceps and tongues. I stopped thinking about which lips I was kissing and whose fingers were stroking my skin, as all three of us relaxed on to the softly carpeted floor and sought greater pleasure, together.

Chapter Nine

They had been gone for two hours and I had made hardly any progress with the chains that had been locked around my wrists and ankles. I was trying to escape from my bondage, and not getting very far. But I wasn't about to admit defeat.

I wriggled into a slightly more comfortable position and tried again with the hair-grip. The padlocks that fastened my leather manacles were tiny and intricate, and not easy for a novice to pick. The tips of my fingers were getting sore and my temper felt slightly frayed around the edges.

Leaning back against the wall for a moment, I reviewed the day so far: Ross and Louisa had decided to go away for the weekend. Where, I wasn't sure, although I'd heard her say something about an on-call rota: presumably she was going to the hospital.

After the great sex in the sitting room, there had been nearly a week of bliss when we had hardly shifted from the big warm bed in Ross's room. I had been relieved of my slavery duties, and Ross had even forgotten himself enough to call me 'Sam' at more than one point.

We had ignored all the usual social norms like regular meals and bedtimes, preferring instead to sleep when our bodies tired of each others' fingers and lips, and eat when our hunger demanded. No proper food: just chocolate and Bourbon, with a few pieces of fruit thrown in for good measure; it's amazing what you can do with a ripe plum and a bunch of juicy grapes when there are two other delicious bodies besides your own.

I had never had such a relaxing time. Louisa was an expert at massage and Ross had developed a penchant for sucking each of my fingers and toes for hours on end. It was a tender, sensuous and erotic triangle that surpassed anything I may have considered in my wildest dreams. And the fact that it had suddenly been withdrawn without warning or explanation was almost more than I could bear. I had thought about their departure almost every minute since they had gone and concluded that it was another ploy to confuse me and beat me into submission.

'Be good,' Louisa had said, dropping a kiss on my breast as she snapped the little padlock shut on my manacles. 'We'll be back before you know it.'

Ross squatted on his heels in front of me, his hands firm on my thighs.

'Open up,' he had said. 'I'm slipping this back inside. Can't have you seducing anyone else while we're gone.' He slipped the bulging dildo deep into me, making me gasp with the sudden fullness. 'Anyway, I know you liked this last time.'

He bent down and gave my aching sex a long lick, his tongue bumping over the protruding end of the plug-like dildo. I shuddered under his caress, my juices flowing despite the suspicion that he would do nothing further to satisfy me. Instead, I had to watch as Louisa leant across my knees and trapped his head between her hands. She pressed her mouth to his, then licked all traces of me from his full lips. I thought she was amazing. Now that she had been awakened to the possibilities of dominant sex she was insatiable and incredibly imaginative. If I had been a man I would have been totally in love with her.

'Come on,' she murmured. 'Let's go. I have to be there by seven, or there will be hell to pay.' She turned to me and laid a finger along my cheek. 'We'll be back. Forty-eight hours, that's all. Don't fret.'

I know they locked the door behind them because I heard the key click, so I didn't bother to wriggle over and try to open it. I wondered whether they had left instructions for Sasha and Seph to come and give me food and drink. I hadn't seen either of the twins since Louisa had disturbed Seph and me in the driveway. They obviously didn't live in the house, so I had to just hope that Ross had told them that I was still up in the attic bedroom, otherwise I was going to be very hungry when they came back on Monday morning.

I rested my head against the wall and gazed up at the cloudy sky through the dormer window above me. Being locked in an attic reminded me of reading *Jane Eyre* as a child. I had always been fascinated by the madwoman, Rochester's wife. I was beginning to feel a little bit like her. If we were cast in their roles then I would be Bertha Mason up in the attic – all tempestuous nature and wild hair; Ross would be Rochester, not realising the unpredictability of the woman he'd locked away; and Louisa would be Jane, his new muse, although she was hardly the plain Jane of the novel's title.

I pondered on the way things might turn out between the three of us, and hoped that there would be no flames or leaping from burning roofs. I leant back against the wall and turned my face upwards to gaze at the dormer window. Rain clouds had gathered ominously and the sky seemed low over the house.

It soon started to rain. The cold sleet hit against the glass like shattering needle points. Slowly at first. One. Two. Three, three thousand. Dash, dash, dash, pooling on to the little ledge outside and on to the gravel far below. The casement was slightly open, letting in an icy draught and, after a time, a trickle of water. I could imagine the raindrops darkening the stones of the house and flattening the clusters of snowdrops that I had seen on my walk.

I sighed and pulled a chenille rug around me for extra warmth. Slaves are not well-dressed at the best of times, and my little silken slip and hip chains were no protection against the winter chill that had seeped into the house. I felt hopeless and despondent, crushed beneath the unpredictable heel of my cousin's mastery.

Everything had been going so unexpectedly well between the three of us that I was confused and saddened to find myself alone once more. It made me feel sorry for the fictional Bertha Mason; she must have watched Jane Eyre and Mr Rochester from her window and felt utter rage. No wonder she had set fire to the place, although I knew that I wasn't about to follow her lead. I lay down instead, wrapped in the soft, warm chenille, and fell asleep.

Sleeping revived my spirits. When I woke up I decided that Ross wouldn't win, no matter how intricate the game had become. I don't know whether it was my renewed determination, or the rest that I had had, but the locks beneath my fingers were suddenly very amenable to being picked with the old kirby grip I had found under the bed.

I was free within minutes, all chains dropped to the floor – I left the dildo in, though, it felt too nice to be discarded, just yet. It sat deep in my sex, just held there by muscular control and nothing else. I smiled to myself as I thought how Severin had missed out by

161

not being a girl. No dildoes for him, unless I'd missed something on rereading *Venus in Furs*.

I tried the door but it was securely locked and I knew that no amount of manual dexterity with the hairpin was going to shift that one. I went to the window and rested my palms on the narrow ledge. If I went up on tiptoe and angled my neck then I could just make out the world below.

The clouds made the sky almost dark, but the rain had stopped and I could see a solitary figure standing in the corner of the garden near the apple tree. The person was too far away to identify, but the long blond hair trailing down a narrow back spelt out either Sasha or Seph. I just didn't know which one.

I squatted on the floor and thought for a bit. What did I really want? What did I want to do while Ross and Louisa were away? Did I want to stay, or did I want to hitch a lift into town and get the next train home? The latter thought was growing more tempting: I quite fancied seeing the inside of my little flat again, sleeping in my own bed and sitting on my own toilet. Yes, I would borrow some clothes and go home.

But the memory of the pleasure of the past few days kept flickering around the outer reaches of my brain and quelling my desire to leave. Besides, the month wasn't up yet and I wasn't going to let Ross win on that one, either.

No, maybe I'd stay put. And see what they had planned for me when they came back. But in the meantime, I was free. Free to do what I wanted. Free to finish what I had started with Seph. Perhaps Ross would never know, and I didn't owe him fidelity of any kind.

My heart skipped a beat as I remembered Seph's passion when he'd kissed me in the lane, before Louisa had spoilt it all by coming back. Although spoilt wasn't quite the right word; she'd given me plenty of pleasure to make up for it. And now I was going to have Seph anyway, I hoped.

I stood up again and peered out through the smeared window-pane. The blond figure had its back to me now and was leaning forward. I watched for a while, then realised that whoever it was had a garden fork and was digging the vegetable patch. I was impressed. My knowledge of fresh produce was strictly limited to the veg section of my local supermarket. I hadn't realised that people still grew their own.

I watched for a while, growing more and more convinced that it was Seph. Digging was hard work, especially in the drizzling rain, and whoever it was made good progress along a row of humped earth.

After a while, he stood straight, one hand in the small of his back. Then the bulky jumper was stripped off over the head, and I saw by the wiry musculature and neat hips that it *was* Seph. Definitely.

My heart skipped a beat again, then hammered wildly with excitement. He looked so good, so fit and outdoorsy in the damp late afternoon air, his shoulders pumped and muscular from digging, and his T-shirt darkened with sweat around the arms and down the middle of the back.

I imagined running my tongue up the curve of his spine and tasting the saltiness of his fresh young sweat. The thought was delicious, and so heady that I had to squeeze my eyes shut and steady myself against the wall.

I thought long and hard about what I was going to do. Then I went to the door and dropped to my knees. The keyhole was dark: that meant the key was still in the other side.

Maybe they had left it like that on purpose, I thought. Ross and I had played an exciting adventure game once, a long time ago. My brothers had locked us into a shed, knowing that I would scream when I saw the size of the spiders up in the corners. Ross, ever the strapping hero even at eleven years old, had managed to free us by doing a great trick with a piece of newspaper and a stick. He said he'd read it in a John Buchan story: Richard Hannay had slid the newspaper under the door, jiggled the key with the stick, and then drawn the paper – and the key – back towards him under the door. Hey presto! Freedom.

But here there was no newspaper, and no stick. And luckily no spiders.

I did a bit of lateral thinking, and then stripped the silky slip from my already cold body and slid it carefully under the door. I knelt by the bed and freed one of the springs. It took a while to get it straight enough to go through the keyhole, but finally I did, and within seconds the key was mine. It was so easy.

I giggled aloud because I was so pleased with myself, then swallowed hard, glad that no one was around to hear me – I had been spending too much time alone. I had to remedy that with a bit of normal interaction with Seph, or I'd really turn into Bertha Mason, complete with wild hair and a penchant for arson.

I went quietly through the house checking for evidence of Sasha, but there was none. In Ross's room, I powdered the inside of the rubber dress, and my body, before easing into the mulberry latex and the dark stockings. The outfit looked superb, and I found a can of silicone spray in one of the drawers to polish it up. When I had finished, I looked as though I had just been slicked over with dark red gloss paint. Seph wasn't going to be able to resist.

As I pinned up my hair, I thought about Louisa's glittering scarlet shoes and a small smile curved my lips. Those shoes were meant to be mine. I was going to wear them, make no mistake. I found them in the bottom of the wardrobe and wondered why Louisa hadn't taken them with her. Maybe she was temporarily going back to mousedom while she was at the hospital. Fine. That suited me, because while the mouse was away, the cat was going play, and in her shoes I definitely gained claws. Claws; four inches in height; and a spicy dash of sex appeal.

The shoes were fabulous, although a little tight. Tall and spiky with the highest heels and the pointiest toes. I could see the snug space between the jewel-encrusted sides and my arched instep, and thought how good it would feel to have Seph slide his tongue in there. To feel him cradle my foot in his work-dirty hands and slip his lips across my skin. I glanced in the mirror: the look in my eyes was so gloatingly wicked that it made me shiver.

I waited by the back door until I heard the metallic ring of a spade being propped against the wall outside, then I let the door swing open. I watched him pull at the laces of his Timberlands and kick them off. How sweet: one of his thick socks had a hole right over his big toe. It made my insides contract with tender love, and I wondered whether to offer to darn them, even though I had never even seen a darning needle in my life.

As if sensing that he was not alone, Seph slowly glanced up, raised his eyebrows, then gave me his lazy, lopsided grin. My legs turned to quivering jelly.

'Seph. Hi. Is Sasha about?' I enquired, keeping my voice seductively deep and low.

His eyes were like pools of cerulean heaven and the look of innocent lechery that lurked beneath his sooty lashes was carefully hidden, but still excitingly in evidence. He carefully placed his boots by the mat, then straightened up to stand tall and proud in front of me.

'No, she's gone.' He rested his hands on his hips

and let his eyes travel down the length of my rubber-clad body. I could see a shift in the crotch folds of his loose brown cargo pants, and it made me feel hot and cold at the same time.

My gaze travelled over the cotton T-shirt that skimmed the contours of his chest, and lingered at the fatigued leather belt that wrapped itself so neatly around his tapered waist. The manly bulge below was growing in evidence and the steely length of his thighs was enough to cause palpitations in my already racing heart. If this slavery thing lasted longer than a month, I was going to have to consult a cardiologist about my ever-shifting pulse rate.

I moistened my lips and curved them in what I knew was an invitation.

'Would you like to come and have a drink? You must be thirsty after all that hard labour.'

His hesitation was infinitesimal and purely for show.

'Thanks, I will.'

We started in the kitchen, where I poured him a beer and myself a straight Jack Daniel's. We didn't waste any time with the niceties of conversation, just went straight for the physical. It was as though we had not had the seven-day gap since our walk up the drive.

His kiss was fragrant with such a combination of sweat and beer. He tasted so good that at first I thought I might swoon and miss the action. Spreading my fingers wide on his T-shirt, I clung to him and opened my lips to his gently probing tongue. The flash of pleasure which shot through my belly was almost pure ecstasy, and I gasped against his hard mouth as he became braver, curving his hand under the fullness of my breast, caressing my hardening nipple with his thumb.

Suddenly desperate for his work-roughened hands

on my bare skin, I tugged at the narrow shoulder straps of the dress until the fabric slithered down to fall around my waist. Seph's face assumed the hardness of a statue as he stared at my curves, and his eyes travelled an invisible line that started between my breasts and snaked down to the indent of my belly button. I could feel my skin puckering into goosebumps under his gaze and I could hardly control myself.

Hungrily, I gripped his chin with my hand and jerked his face up so that he had to meet my eyes.

'What about it, Seph?' I said. 'Unfinished business. Let's finish it.'

I held his uncertain stare for a full ten seconds, then took his silence for a 'yes' before grasping his belt buckle and tearing it wide. His trousers were loose and folded back easily to reveal the proud lack of jockeys. There, brushing the backs of my thrusting hands, was the rearing evidence of his desire for me. He had a rigid curve, swaying slightly left of true, a cock that was perfectly shaped with a smooth pink head that gleamed and practically begged for my touch.

I pushed the fabric downward and grasped him in my fist. He jerked and strained towards me, and I could sense the heat and feral muskiness of him as I slid my fingers back and forth along his slender length. I didn't know whether to fall forward and take him in my mouth, or pull up my dress, jerk out the dildo and have him ram straight into my wet and eager sex.

Seph took the initiative, sighing deeply, pulling me to him and kissing me urgently. His hands cupped my face and neck, trapping my hair so that he could use it as a rope to pull my head back and press his burning lips to my throat. I closed my eyes and surrendered to his touch, my senses drowning and a bitter-sweet breathlessness spreading outwards through my body.

There was a sudden pause in the sensations, a moment of stillness, and I opened my eyes. Seph had dropped to his knees in front of me. I could feel the arid heat of his breath upon the rubber which covered my secret creases, which contrasted with the cool touch of his silver bangle on the warm skin of my inner thigh.

A small movement of my foot on the polished floor granted him access with his forefinger, and the glide of his callused digit over the sensitivity of my suddenly exposed sex sent a thrill of anticipation through me. He flicked his tongue, long and subtle, over me and I felt my hips buck involuntarily as my silken insides contracted against the hard black rubber of the dildo.

His mouth enveloped me, sucking and giving tiny light bites to my swollen flesh before pressing firmly. Then the flat of his tongue crushed on to my newly healed labia piercing, and I realised that there was a danger I might come right there and then.

I gripped his hair in my fist and jerked his head back.

'Easy, boy,' I whispered. 'Better make it last. I'd like to anticipate things just a little longer.'

I held his head firm with my fist while running the forefinger of my other hand from his hairline, down over his nose to his mouth. I dipped my finger in and smiled as he sucked hard on it. He made me feel weak inside. I slid my thumb under the curve of his chin, feeling soft blond stubble brush against my palm. I cupped his face in my hand and bent to kiss him. He tasted of hard manual labour and my juices.

'Get up,' I said. 'Stand up straight. I want to see you tall and straight, soldier.'

He did as I said, and I let my eyes roam over his

wiry body. He really was a prime specimen: so neat and compact, but with bulges in all the right places. I put my hand under his T-shirt and pushed it up until I could see the pale brown discs of his nipples. They looked like little chips of demerara sugar, just begging to be flipped on to my tongue and sucked until they dissolved. I bent my head and tasted them.

He was so fresh and sweet, but I could smell the tang of the sweat he had worked up while digging, and a vague hint of freshly turned earth. It was curious, but the smell of the land made me feel even hornier than ever. City-bred girls like me don't get out in the fields much, and when we get a whiff of a man who does, it really gets the juices flowing. That's probably why I liked Ross so much, and why the suit-wearers that I usually dated often left me cold. Real men versus artificially gym-pumped town-boys. Is there any competition?

The real man in front of me squirmed and breathed heavily. I could feel his cock nudging against my thigh, the eager head smearing a little tear of moisture against the hem of my rubber dress.

'Please, I –. Do you –? Can you –?' He seemed unable to finish any of his sentences so, feeling slightly sorry for him as well as immensely superior, I pressed the flat of my hand against his chest and pushed him back until his thighs hit the kitchen table. Seven feet long and half as wide, it could have been built to take the weight of a horse, and it hardly groaned as it took the weight of a slender youth and an eager girl. I dragged Seph's trousers off and knelt between his legs.

Lubricating my forefinger with my tongue, I smoothly worked a slender finger into the tight little pucker of his anus. His face contracted with shock at the intimacy of my action, but I didn't care. After two weeks of slavery, I was determined to live this

169

moment of dominance to the full, and I suspected that he was not the type to try and stop me. A guy who habitually lets his sister seduce him is not going to have scruples about screwing his employer's cousin now, is he?

My finger stretched him and sought the hard evidence of the rounded gland that I knew would give him so much pleasure, while my other hand softly stroked and kneaded his tight little balls. His eyes fluttered closed and I heard him sigh. I reached between my legs and slowly withdrew the juicy dildo, enjoying the slow pull and drag at my lips that it gave as it came out. It was wet and slick. Just right for what I planned.

I turned it round on its chains and looked down: it was just as though it was mine. My penis. I was fascinated: the dildo was so tightly strapped to me by the chains that it really looked like part of my body. The thought gave me a rush of adrenalin mixed with power and arousal, and just for a second I thought I could imagine what it was like to be the male of the species.

I withdrew my finger from his bottom and placed the head of the dildo there. He stiffened, his body suddenly tense and taut.

'It's OK,' I murmured. 'It's fine. Let me do it to you. You'll like it, Seph. Just relax.'

He murmured, then caught my free hand and pulled it up to his mouth. He planted a long kiss on to the palm of my hand, his lips dry and warm against my skin. I felt so in control, so dominant, that it gave me a fresh surge of pleasure and power as I eased the dildo into his tight little arse. He protested at first, his muscles taut and his hands gripping my wrists in a vain attempt to stop me. I bent forward and gave the head of his cock a small, tight-lipped suck and felt him relax. After that he was putty in my hands.

He looked so sweet and handsome, laid out there on the table with me between his blond-haired thighs and his loose ponytail tumbling across his shoulder: just like a painting of a Christ-figure, only without the self-denial.

The thought of religion usually bores me rigid, but at that moment it gave me a heat and energy that swept me forward on to his prostrate body. I leant against his belly, my hands slipping over the hair that snaked from his navel to his groin, my mouth seeking the tiny beads of his erect nipples.

As I fastened my mouth on to his skin, I realised by the little thrilling jumps he gave that he was so turned on that his whole body had become an erogenous zone: even his armpits and the little tufts of white-blond hair that grew there seemed alive to my touch. I moved my lips across his skin, licking and nipping and listening to the little sighs and moans he gave.

I wanted him really badly. Badly enough to break bail.

I reached down and snapped the chains that attached me to the dildo, leaving it behind. Then I was free. Free to move and straddle and get up on top of Seph. Free to fuck him like a girl, instead of a hybrid female with a strap-on cock. I was ready to do it, at last.

But there was one thing missing. I hesitated, and he opened his eyes a fraction.

'Wait here just one sec,' I said. I strode across the room to where Ross had left a jacket draped over the back of a chair. Please, I prayed silently, please let there be one in the pocket.

There was. Actually there were two. A couple of glinting gold coins with flip lids that disguised the neatly rolled and ready condom inside. I smiled and slipped one into the cleavage of my dress, then palmed the other and strode back to where Seph lay spread like a butterfly on the table.

I placed one gold coin in the centre of his chest and smiled down at him.

'Enough for two,' I said. 'But we'll have to get fresh supplies for later.'

Then I climbed back up on the table and curved my thighs over his lean body.

I couldn't get enough of him. He tasted so good and smelled so divine that I felt as if I hadn't eaten for a week – that I'd just have to gobble him whole. My mouth moved urgently against his skin, my hands hard against his cock and balls as I leant over him, poised and ready to devour him with my sex.

'You do it,' I said. 'Come on, you do it. Hold me, lower me on to you. Do it your way.'

He smiled, an angelic lighting up of his face that made my stomach do a back-flip and my thighs tremble. His hands felt soft on my legs, gentle and tentative, as if he was unsure of quite how to do it. I twisted my hand into his long ponytail and pulled his shoulders slightly off the table to kiss him. His teeth were hard under mine, little pieces of ivory that tasted delicious against my searching tongue.

'Come on,' I whispered. 'Don't keep me waiting, soldier-boy.'

'I can't –' He broke off and stared into my eyes.

'You can't what?' I trailed my tongue down over his chin and around to his ear. 'There's no such word as can't.'

'Is there such a word as virgin?' he breathed.

I thought I had misheard him at first, but one quick look at his flushed face told me that I hadn't: embarrassment and apprehension lurked in the depths of his blue eyes. There was a white tinge to his jaw that told me he was clenching his teeth very tightly.

'Come on,' I said, my voice catching on a nervous laugh. 'Are you kidding?'

'No.' He shook his head and dropped his gaze. 'No, I'm not. Do you still want to go on? I mean, I'll understand if you don't –'

'Shut up,' I interrupted. 'Shut up right this minute. You are every woman's wet dream and you know it. How the hell you've managed to keep yourself to yourself this long is beyond me.' I looked at him for a long moment, aware of the throbbing of my blood and the heat of his cock against my inner thigh, then I frowned.

'What about your sister?' I asked. 'I thought you and she did this sort of thing?'

'We've never gone that far. I love my sister, but I draw the line and so does she.'

Satisfied, but somehow vaguely disappointed to find that the twins had morals – of sorts – I took his hands in mine and placed them tight to my sex.

'Come on,' I whispered. 'Let's do it.'

His tentative thumbs held me tenderly apart and his eyes fixed mine with a penetrating intensity. He slid into me, paused, then pushed deep. He suddenly looked so young that I wanted to cry.

He moved hesitantly at first, his eyes wide and blue, and so earnest that it made my heart swell. Then he seemed to gain stature and confidence with the feel of my throbbing muscles clenching around the head of his rigid cock. He thrust and swelled inside me, his stiffness lighting a fire which crackled along the inside of my belly and shot upwards to make my chest constrict. I moved against him, searching for his tentative rhythm until I felt the sweetest waves tingle at the edges of my mind. Eventually he relaxed, trusting me utterly as I took over and rode him towards dark oblivion.

Strong, earth-stained hands slid from my inner

thigh, up over the gentle sweep of my stomach to my breasts and cupped the rounded weight in warm palms before he sat forward, bending upwards to suckle my nipples into his mouth. Their long, tubular erectness was made rock-hard by the grazing of his teeth over the puckered flesh and I heard myself call out, crying his name as he swept his arm around my waist and gathered me tightly to him, pumping his loins into mine.

His eyes were fixed on mine. His hands tight on my waist. I could see tiny beads of perspiration flecking the skin under his stubbled top lip, and hear the little grunts he made as he thrust hard. We were so wet together, so juicy and slippery. The slicking sound of my sex on his cock made me close my eyes to concentrate. I tipped my head right back until the stroke of my own hair across the upper curve of my buttocks gave me a narcissistic thrill.

I started to come. I tightened on to him with all the strength in my sex, pulsing hard and drawing him deeper into me. He was so deep that it almost hurt, but that gave my orgasm a piquant edge that tipped me over into ecstasy. I could feel the ripples flooding through my body, pulling at my skin and pulsating the satin sheath of my sex on to his hard cock.

His hands instantly grasped me tighter, squeezing the breath from my body as he lifted me and then jammed me back down hard with a guttural cry. I felt the scorching, thrusting jerk of his cock as he came and I wrapped my arms around his neck and crushed his mouth beneath mine as we came together, thighs tense and chests tight, sex to sex.

We stayed very still for a long time, each in silent contemplation. I was smiling into his shoulder, enthralled at the prospect of two whole days of lechery which now lay open to me in Ross's absence. I planned to do things to Seph that not even his sister, in her wildest dreams, would ever think of.

I decided that we would christen every room in the house.

In the dining room we swept away the lace table-cloth and a vase of flowers, and I lay back on the bare, polished surface. I spent an hour giving Seph guidance on how to go down on me, how to give expert head.

He learnt to hold the little gold ring in my labia between finger and thumb while his tongue slipped over and around it. When I was just about ready to collapse, I told him to thrust his long middle finger deep into me and feel the muscular oscillations of my orgasm.

In the big first-floor bathroom I filled the room with bubbles and steam, while Seph ransacked the cupboards for condoms. He found a half-full box of Benetton Colours and a six-pack of UltraStrong, so I knew we'd be OK for quite a while.

I laid him in the bath and hung over the side, my hands foaming with soap and my tongue almost welded to his. I slipped and slid my fingers along his cock. Tight grip, then soft. Quick then slow. I moved my mouth down his body to his balls and showed him the crushing ecstasy of being brought to climax by a combination of my hot tongue and long fingers.

On the landing I bent forward over the wide oak banister and concentrated on the drop to the hallway far below as he entered me quickly from behind, pushing himself up inside me while rimming the puckered flower of my bottom with a moistened forefinger.

It felt dangerous and scary, leaning right out with only his hands to save me from certain death, and I had trouble relaxing until he chased away morbid thoughts of death by sliding his finger into my bottom, just at the moment when he came. I was hot and cold and shivering as I clenched on to him and achieved my own climax at last.

We spent the whole of Saturday night eating and fucking. I cooked a huge feast of chilli and rice, revelling in breaking the meat-free rule. We found a case of red wine in the pantry and downed two bottles in quick succession so that our drunkenness overcame any lack of energy we had acquired from eating.

We made love twice after dark that night. Once standing up against the french windows in the sitting room, my buttocks spread flat on the pane, Seph's hands pressed to the glass either side of me and his thighs bulging beneath mine. And once in the hall, with me braced over the telephone table and Seph tucked tight in behind me, his mouth glued to my neck and his cock pumping: thundering into me until I cried out, my voice hoarse with a mixture of exhaustion and pleasure.

I had planned another day of frenzied lovemaking on Sunday, ignoring the chafing soreness of my over-used sex, but in the morning things changed abruptly. We had eaten nearly all the food in the fridge, so Seph went out on an old push-bike and came back laden with provisions and wearing his old combat trousers.

He placed a basket of dirty, still-warm eggs on the counter and reached for me. I caught a whiff of aftershave and saw that he wore a clean T-shirt and had shaved away the soft blond stubble that had grown so long over the past day and night.

'Where have you been?' I asked, dodging his kiss and spreading my hands against his chest.

'To get food.'

'No, before that.'

'Nowhere.'

'Liar. You've been home, haven't you?' I stepped back and narrowed my eyes accusingly. I felt jealous and cross. Put out that he hadn't told me where he had intended going. Possessive of his company. Worried that he had been with Sasha. Curious about where he lived. Why hadn't he told me? I stuck my bottom lip out and shoved the basket of eggs to one side.

'Listen to me,' I snapped. 'You go to get food, and you come straight back. If I want you to go sniffing round your sister then I'll tell you.' I grabbed the neck of his fleecy shirt and jerked him towards me. 'You may be pretty, but you're not indispensable. I could have Ross sack you if I wanted. Be sure you ask next time, or else.'

I was satisfied with the look of uncertainty that washed across his features. He was pale under the ruddy country glow of health, and it made me feel big and mean. I knew exactly how Ross must have felt making me bend to his will for the first time, back in his office. That seemed such a long time ago. Light years in fact. I had learnt to submit, and yet I had also learnt to dominate even more effectively than I had before. I banged Seph on the shoulder with the flat of my hand and he dropped to his knees, pressing his mouth to my blue-painted toenails.

I watched him, studying the way that his long back curved down to his neat little bottom. His hands gripped my feet tightly and his thin silver bangle made a mark on my skin where he was pressing so hard. He looked good on his knees, I thought. I must get him down there more often.

A flash of colour at the window beside me caught my eye and I glanced up to see Sasha marching quickly away. Her head was bowed and I felt a curious sense of triumph.

'Oh, look,' I said, conversationally. 'There's your sister. I don't think she liked what she saw. It looks as if she's running away.'

Seph rose up, resting one hand on the edge of the table. He smiled, then glanced at me from under his lashes.

'She's not running away,' he said. 'She's just going home. She's been there all the time. She watches us.'

'Watches us?' I felt cold fingers close around my heart. 'What do you mean?'

'She loves to watch. Ross told her to watch. He will want to know everything when he comes back, so she records it all and he'll get to watch it later.'

'Oh, God.' I stared at her retreating back. She was small now, a tiny figure travelling quickly down the driveway. 'You mean he'll know about us?'

'Yes,' he said, his hands on my waist. 'I thought you knew. I thought you liked that. You must have realised.'

'No,' I whispered. 'I thought it was our secret. Just you and me.'

'Nothing is a secret in this house, that's why he brought you here.'

'Were you really a virgin?' I asked, cupping his face in my hands and willing him to say yes.

He stood tall and gazed down at me, laughter lighting his beautiful blue eyes, then he leant down and kissed me softly on the cheek.

'With girls,' he murmured. 'But I'm just as much Ross's slave as you are.'

Chapter Ten

'You must think I'm stupid,' murmured Ross. His finger hit the pause button and I was left to watch the flickering image of myself with my mouth full of Seph's cock.

I sighed and bit my bottom lip hard. The evidence was absolutely clear – there was no point offering any denials. I couldn't help thinking that Sasha had a very good eye behind the camera. Her angles were great, and shooting the scene through the window added a certain grainy, surreal quality to the footage.

What a bitch. I could hardly bring myself to think of the satisfaction that she must have felt, carrying out Ross's instructions to the letter while I systematically educated and abused her brother. I looked away from the television set, finding that I didn't really like myself very much, certainly not enough to gaze at my own lust-depraved face for very long.

'Did you?' Ross turned to face me, his voice deceptively mild. 'Did you think I was stupid?'

I saw how stressed he was by the tell-tale way he patted his shirt – feeling for his cigarettes. Then he frowned as he remembered he'd given up, and I knew that the memory would probably make him angrier and more unpredictable.

'No.' I interlaced my fingers and pressed my hands together until I saw my knuckles turn white. 'Of course not. I just thought you wouldn't find out.'

He gave a laugh that sounded halfway between mirth and fury, then strode over to the television, yanked all the leads out of it, picked it up and hurled it through the closed french windows as if he were a seventies rock star. I gaped at the jagged hole in the glass. So he was cross, then. It made me feel all weak inside and I sought to catch his eye with my own, but he wasn't playing.

'There,' he said, grinding the remote control underfoot. 'That'll give your beloved boyfriend something to do when he next shows his face around here. He'd better start reading through a glazing manual.'

He strode over to me and grabbed me by the hair, pulling me until I stood upright. My eyes smarted and I reached up to hold my head before he tore anything out by the roots, but he knocked my arm down.

'You'll have to be punished,' he barked. 'You've been just about the worst slave I have ever seen. I gave you some leeway before I left, but you have done nothing but abuse it. You've taken liberties.' He shook me a little by the hair and I winced, but kept my hands at my sides, determined not to let him see how much it hurt. 'Your performance has been so bad that I feel like breaking every bone in your body and tearing up your contract right now. You're stupid. Stupid, d'you hear?'

I nodded, real tears joining the smarts of pain at the corners of my eyes. If Ross was trying to grind me down he was doing well; he sounded so much like my stepmother, Moira, that it sent an icy trickle all the way down my spine. She had revelled in calling me stupid. The boys – my brothers – were always perfect angels, even when they had been bad. But me? Well, if my dad was in earshot then she tempered her wrath and told me that I was just a little bit naughty. But if he wasn't around she really let rip. I was stupid, good-for-nothing, an idiot, and everything else she could think of.

At the tender age of ten you tend to believe whatever grown-ups say, and I had never really outgrown the notion that what Moira said was true. Ross calling me stupid ripped the remains of my self-respect to shreds.

'Please, Ross . . .' I began. His hand tightened on my hair, if that were possible.

'Shut up,' he said. 'I don't want to hear it. There is nothing you can say that will mitigate the evidence on that video.'

'But, I –'

'Silence!' He shook me again, and I couldn't help myself: my hands came up and cupped his, desperately trying to ease the weight of my own body that dangled on my poor hair. 'You will no longer speak unless spoken to. What is it?' I glanced up, thinking that he spoke to me, but then saw that Louisa was standing just inside the door. Her eyes were wide and her lips seemed very dark in the pallor of her face.

'I – I thought I heard something break,' she said. It was the first time that I had heard a note of hesitancy in her voice since the night when Ross had fucked her under the photographer's lamps, when I had been trussed to the ceiling by my wrists. I slid my eyes sideways and studied her with interest.

'It's nothing. Go to bed.' Ross eased up on my hair, but not so that you'd notice.

'The window –' she began. He dropped me and strode to the door. Louisa shrank backwards and looked almost frightened for a moment and I felt a wave of something akin to tenderness as I watched

181

her from the other side of the room. Ross rested one hand on the door and touched her cheek with his other.

'Go to bed,' he whispered. 'It's late.'

'What's going on?' She was persistent, I'll give her that.

'I just –' He took a deep breath. 'I just threw the television out of the window.' Bless him, he sounded quite sheepish. Louisa let him kiss her, but it was me that she looked at, not him. Her eyes were full of concern and one hand came up to hook a length of her soft hair away from her mouth. She didn't seem in any hurry to leave.

'Samantha,' she said, her voice loud in the otherwise silent room. 'Are you all right?'

I considered my options.

One. Cry wolf and escape into her arms.

Two. Cry wolf and find out that her sympathy was a trick, that she and Ross had planned it to subjugate me even further.

Three. Take what I had coming from Ross, and damn well enjoy it.

Blood is thicker than water, they say. I still trusted Ross a whole lot more than I trusted her.

'I'm fine. We're just having a bit of a chat.' The smile on my face must have looked like a rictus, but she was obviously easily convinced. She gave me one last, lingering look, then quickly kissed my cousin's cheek and softly closed the door behind her. I was alone in the lion's den and it scared the shit out of me. But it felt good.

'Where were we?' I said, feeling comfortable again now that it was just us.

'I told you not to speak,' he said. 'You will not speak unless I address you directly. The only word you may utter is the safe word, and then we're all out of here.'

I sighed and flicked my eyes to the ceiling. I could barely remember what the safe word was, so I was hardly about to use it. Anyway, I couldn't imagine Ross would have the wherewithal to punish me enough to make me want to even come close to saying it.

I was wrong. Over the next twenty-four hours I came very close indeed.

To get to the cellar we had to go outside. Into the garden. Around the back of the house. Down some wide steps which led to some shabby patio doors and the cellar beyond.

Although it was dark in the garden, I could see the broken outline of the trashed television set, and feel the brittle crunch of broken glass underfoot. Ross had bound my hands in front of me, and he steered me by the firm pressure of his hand in the small of my back. I shivered with fear and anticipation, but the sensation that his touch gave me was one of warmth and mastery, not cruelty. I knew Ross would never hurt or humiliate me.

How wrong a girl can be.

You don't really know someone until you've seen them *in extremis*. Well, Ross was *in extremis*, for sure. I knew that it was jealousy. And in a funny way that was what made the initial stages of his punishment bearable: the thought that I was worth it. The knowledge that he couldn't bear to share me with anyone made what he did to me a ritual of affirmation. The ultimate token of love and possession.

It was one hell of a token.

First of all he stripped the clothes from my body. He moved without speaking at all; there were no words of comfort or reassurance, just quick harsh hands that twisted and turned me, pulling and tearing until I was naked. The air was cold and damp in the cellar: bare stone walls, no windows and a rudimentary floor. He pushed me into a corner and, before I could see what he was doing, he turned a power-hose on me.

Damn, it was cold. Freezing water hit me and I ducked, twisting out of the way, but the arctic barrage found me wherever I tried to go. I gasped and bit my tongue, remembering just in time that I was no longer allowed to speak. It was torture. And with that thought came the realisation of what the game was.

Through the needling water, I saw Ross in his long black leather coat and polished boots: the Prussian Officer of my Saturday night fantasies. It was as if he had walked straight down off the cinema screen and into the cellar. He didn't look like Ross any more. The icy water streamed down my face and blurred my vision, but I could see that the look on his face was strange and hard. Every ounce of humanity and softness that I had come to know and love seemed to have been eradicated. I felt a twist of fear deep inside me, and it almost chased away the desire I had for him.

The water stopped and I stood against the far wall, soaking and shivering, my hair plastered to my neck, every strand lank and streaming. He tossed the hose aside and strode towards me, grabbed my wrist and yanked me around so that my icy, wet back was curved into his hard stomach.

'Now, Fräulein,' he hissed. 'I will teach you never to disobey me. You thought you could betray me and get away with it? You were wrong. I shall punish you according to your crime.'

It made me want to giggle, until he bent me over and, without ceremony or foreplay, plunged his fingers deep into my unready sex.

'So, you find this amusing. Don't. Never laugh. Never smile. Never do anything but show your remorse.' His fingers widened and stretched me, pushing my soft flesh sideways and outward so that I was totally open. It was almost painful, but not quite. Then a stinging flail caught my buttocks and I squealed and winced. It felt like some old-fashioned cat-o'-nine-tails, but it couldn't be. I twisted slightly in his arms, and he jerked me tight into him so that I wouldn't see. But I had already caught the strange, metallic gleam of the chain-mail glove that covered his hand.

'Close your eyes, Fräulein,' he grated, his mouth close to my ear. We were so close that I could feel the heat of his body through his clothes, and smell the musky, male scent of his sweat. The feral perfume of clean perspiration has a particular odour, and I knew Ross's so well that I could almost read his emotions from it. I knew that he was as turned on as I was. And almost as scared.

I closed my eyes but that was apparently not good enough. He pulled a black velvet hood from his pocket and looped it over my head. The world abruptly turned matt black. And deadly silent. Sounds from outside were muffled and I felt a frisson of fear that was stronger than that I had experienced before. It was just a little too close to the hoods people wear for an execution, and I suddenly wondered how far I really trusted this unfamiliar, angry, jealous Ross.

He smacked me again. It stung like a hundred bees had just landed on my bottom. I had a curious vision of the markings that must be appearing on my buttocks. Tightly linked chain-shaped circlets. A wide hand. Tiny red bite-marks made by the interlocking rings. Pale, milky skin spoiled by a red rash of writhing kinks and lines that expanded in a heated flush across my bottom. A shapely girl with her head shrouded in black velvet – anonymous and naked. Juicy and willing. Fair game.

Despite the pain that licked across my back and thighs, the thought of what Ross could see made a curl of creamy heat surge against the Prussian Officer's thrusting fingers, and I tightened on to him. Fear lent my arousal a dangerous piquancy that I had rarely felt before.

The long and painful spanking made me shiver inside. I felt an electric thrill shoot from my stomach up to my breasts and down again; I was really turned on now. I could feel the familiar swell of arousal deep inside me and I knew that it was making my heart race and my skin goosebump. The slow thrusting slick of the Officer's fingers in my sex was like heaven: he seemed to time the rhythm of his fingers exactly to the smack of his other hand. It hurt me. It hurt a lot. But since the whipping I had taken in the little attic room, the boundaries of pain and pleasure had become blurred and I could hardly tell what was hurting and what felt good.

Just as I was relaxing into it, he withdrew his fingers and slowly slid his hand up to cup my breast. Anticipating a gentle caress of my already hard nipple, I was shocked by the sudden ferocity with which he seized and twisted it. I cried out, but his hand silenced me with a hard slap and I leant against him, waiting for his next move, wanting him to press his fingers back inside me.

I was also thinking very hard about the safe word.

He bent me further over. I was doubled to the floor, my bound hands resting on the dirty floor and my feet spread wide. I was exposed and vulnerable, and quite cold by then. I shivered against him, feeling the hard jut of his cock through the leather coat as he leant against the sore skin of my bottom for a moment.

He steadied me with his hands tight on my hips, and I thought – hoped – that he would fuck me in that leisurely way of his. I could feel the dizzying effect of breathing my own carbon dioxide inside the hood and I knew that I was moving slightly out of touch with reality. I nudged back against him in a suggestive way, but all I got for my trouble was a hard slap with the metal glove, and then cold air on my bare, burning skin as he moved away.

The Officer's boots rang against the floor as he strode across the cellar, leaving me impersonating an A-board. He returned, and slipped his fingers over my raw and exposed bottom. Despite the burning of my skin, it felt sweet and warm and I thrilled at his touch, waiting for him to do what he planned.

I didn't have to wait long. He gripped me hard, steadying me with one hand, and I felt his other hand introduce something to my bottom. It was long, very thin and slick with lubricant. I shuddered against him, pleasure and arousal surging through me at his intimate touch. I heard a moist, sucking noise and realised that something warm was surging deep into my bottom. I tensed every muscle, pulling my legs inward, and felt his knees knock mine apart again to counteract my tightly closed body.

I yelped as I realised what he was doing. He was giving me an enema. Ross was giving me an enema, for God's sake. The safety word came straight to my lips and I inhaled to shout it out. This was one game I was not going to play. This was going way too far, even for me.

He jerked me upright, tight against his chest, and gripped my mouth with his bare hand, holding my lips closed, forcing a little of the hood between my teeth.

'Ssh,' he whispered, his breath hot and sweetly minty through the velvet. 'Ssh. I know you want to say the word, but don't – yet. Just wait. See if you can do this.' He adjusted his grip on me with the other, chain-mail-clad hand. 'I want to cleanse you. Purify you. Punish you. But it will never be more than you can bear. Don't say that word unless you're totally sure.'

I thought very hard. Cleansing and purifying didn't really sound my thing. A little flagellation would always go down well, now that I'd learnt about the pain-pleasure principle: the raised heartbeat and the constriction of breathing that makes fear go hand in hand with arousal. But enemas? No thanks. I was going to say the safe word.

The cold chain-mail slid up my bare front, slipping over my belly and lightly dabbing my nipples. He held me tight against him, whispering against the hood and caressing my breast with metallic fingers that seemed to kiss my sensitive skin.

'I'm going to take my hand away now, Puss. If you do say it, just remember that there is no going back. We all leave. We all go back to the real world. Me to the boats, you to your desk and Louisa to the hospital. End of story.' There was a long pause. 'Here, steady now. I'm taking my hand away.'

The chain-mail made a slow, slipping, sliding journey to my sex and I felt the light metallic caress of his thumb against the gold ring in my labia as I leant against him. A tiny trickle of lube slid down the inside of my thigh and I tensed, then relaxed. I didn't say a word.

'Fräulein,' he murmured in my ear. 'You have made a good choice.'

I groaned as I felt him remove the enema, then clenched as tight as I could to keep the warmth inside. It was the strangest feeling. I'd heard of people going for this sort of thing in a big way. Apparently Harley Street is full of colonic irrigation practitioners. It was not my bag at all: the sensation of fullness, heat and desperate clenching that I had now confirmed that.

But there was a tiny, curious part of me that wanted to find out what it was all about, why the aficionados liked it so much. I held on tight with all the muscles in my lower body, and waited while he loosened the hood and slipped it off over my head.

'Now, Fräulein,' whispered the Officer, twisting me around to face him, 'kiss me.'

I stared up into the face of a stranger. Dark eyes shone with a nameless passion and his lips were narrowed and pale. I wondered where he had come from, this Ross who I had never seen before, then ceased to think as he gripped the back of my head and jerked me up on to tiptoes.

'Kiss me. It's a command, not a request.'

I placed my mouth against his, wondering whether I could bite him when his guard was down. But the sudden sensation of losing control of the warmth inside my bottom made me gasp and clench myself. I kissed him as passionately as I dared.

The intensity of sensation, and the utter steeliness of the muscles in my buttocks, served to propel me forwards and I could feel the leather of his coat against my bare breasts and bound hands. He gripped my elbows and held me steady, then opened his mouth to me.

It was a blissful kiss: both soft and hard, demanding yet yielding. I really felt as if I was kissing a stranger, and it excited me so much that I nearly forgot to keep a hold on things down below.

'Mein Herr,' I murmured against his lips. 'I need the bathroom.'

'Never speak,' he hissed. 'I forgive you this once, but don't forget again. There is a bathroom through the wooden door. You may go when I decree that you may. That time has not yet come.'

The sudden archaic turn of phrase that he had adopted made him seem all the more strange. Foreign even. He seemed to be slipping easily into his role. I breathed heavily, composing myself, and appealed to the real Ross.

'But I need to go. I don't think I can hold on much longer.'

'Silence.' The muscles in his jaw tightened and he thrust me away from him. I was backed up against the damp, bare stone wall and my feet kicked roughly apart. I could feel a slick of the lube slither down the back of my thigh and I held on for dear life, afraid of what might follow.

'Right now your muscles are probably so tight that you think you can't do anything.' Ross leant his body against mine and I felt the breath leave my body in one quick exhalation. He was tall and heavy, and the tightly held clench of my bottom was draining all my strength; I didn't have any energy left for breathing hard or fighting him off. 'So tight. I love how tight you are. If I slip my hand round here I can feel the little dimples in your buttocks where you're holding on so hard.'

My horror must have shown in my eyes and I heard a tiny squeak escape from between my lips. This was torture. This was agony. Utterly humiliated, and dreading the moment when I knew that I'd have to let go, I closed my eyes and hung my head, miserably aware of the cold tendrils of wet hair that stuck to my cheeks and shoulders.

'That's good. That's nice.' He stroked the soft skin of my bottom and I opened my eyes to stare at him. His eyes were like dark pools, part-amused, part-aroused, and he gazed straight back at me, not even blinking.

'Please,' I whispered.

'No.'

'Yes. I need to go now.'

'No.' He was resolute. Steely. I sighed and swallowed hard, fighting back tears which made my throat swell and my neck throb.

'Please, mein Herr.'

That seemed to be the right thing to say, because he smiled slightly: a chilling little curl at the corner of his mouth that had nothing to do with amusement and everything to do with victory.

'Then I'll assist you. Come through here.'

My horror at the thought of his assistance must have shown in my eyes, but he didn't flinch. He propelled me backwards through the wooden door to a cold sterile bathroom. I felt my heart sinking almost to my toes. How was I going to survive this? This was just how I imagined a hospital to be, not the downstairs cloakroom of a country house.

My gaoler twisted the leather that bound my hands and loosened it so that I could move them. The return of blood to my fingers was both a welcome and a painful rush of prickles and heat. He stood back, cast his eyes from my head down to my toes, then clicked his heels together in a way that would have made any dictator jealous.

'Go ahead.'

I pleaded with him with my eyes. I wanted him to go.

Nothing changed. He stood and watched.

Miserably I sat on the cracked wooden seat and felt the tears stinging my eyelids. Three weeks of slavery had exceeded my worst nightmares, I thought, as I did the thing that nature had intended and reached for the roll of paper.

This was bad. This was abysmal. I'd never be able to look him in the face again. My health-conscious friends would never, ever get me to a colonic irrigationist, not if they strapped me to the back of a tractor and dragged me there. I couldn't imagine why it was so popular. I felt drained. An empty hollow shell. I had been sucked dry of all feeling, all passion, all life. Nothing remained except a desiccated husk.

The Officer turned on the taps of the bath, and I

saw the gush of water and the haze of steam. Thank goodness, hot water. I let him hand me in, then slipped down under the surface with as much pleasure as was left in my body. I couldn't look at him, couldn't meet his gaze, although I could feel that he wanted me to. That one act of intimacy had robbed me of the last of my energy and spirit.

I could have stayed in there all night, but it was not part of the game plan. After twenty minutes or so, the Officer pulled the plug and took me out, bundling me into his arms and carrying me back to the outer room. In our absence, someone had erected a huge black board in the centre of the room. It was in the shape of an inverted Y, and had straps at the top and bottom. In the centre there was a strange dark protuberance. A moulded cock. A full nine inches and wide with it.

It looked like some kind of devilish surf-board, and I found out later that that was exactly what it was. A smooth bespoke item fashioned by one of Ross's kinky surfing friends around the headland from the lifeboat station: the man had apparently found a huge market for shiny, curvaceous fibreglass among the local fetishists. It must have cost Ross an arm and a leg, but he got the use out of it that night.

The Officer stood me beside it and ran his hands over the board appreciatively. It was as smooth as glass, and gleamed ominously in the dim light of the single electric bulb that dangled from the ceiling. I could not begin to imagine its purpose, but it soon became clear.

'Come here. Stand by me.' The Officer gestured to a spot just in front of the Y-board and I complied. I had no fight left in me, I was empty and soulless. Let him do what he wants, I thought.

He slowly unbound my hands and stood me in front of the board, with my back to it. It swept the curve of my buttocks and the swell of my calves, cool and sleek where it touched. He lifted my arms and buckled me into the hand harnesses, then lifted me slightly until I felt the bump of the protruding part against my thigh. He smiled: a closed, neutral curving of the lips that didn't reach his eyes.

'You will stay on this board, with this deep inside you, until I think that you are sorry. The more you move, the deeper it will penetrate you. If you wish to struggle, that is your choice. You may find it painful or pleasurable, depending on your movements.'

He lifted me and slotted me on to it. Thick and hard, the colour of polished ebony, it slid into my sex and filled me totally. I was stretched. Opened. Plugged with a thick black cock and there was nothing I could do about it, even if I'd had the energy to fight. I struggled weakly as he strapped my ankles wide to the legs of the board, and my sex swelled around the object, grasping it and pulling it deeper as I moved. I stayed still, waiting and watching hopelessly as I saw the Officer move away.

He had his back turned towards me so that I could not see what he was doing. There was a wooden cupboard high on the stone wall and he reached into it, then turned quickly back and strode over to me. In his hand there was the cold flash of silver and I held my breath, filled with anticipation and uneasiness.

He fixed glinting silver caps to my jutting nipples: they were identical to the ones that I had seen on Sasha and Seph on my first night at the house. Rounded cylinders with scalloped edges that bit into the skin, gripping and pulling and making me feel a flash of life despite the enervated heaviness that pervaded my limbs.

The thought that the cold metal may have been warmed by the twins' lovely flesh made me quiver and squirm, each tiny movement making the protruding black cock sink deeper and press harder into me.

It was blissful, and my pulse thrummed hard through my veins as I tipped my head back against the polished board and watched the Officer from below lowered lashes.

'I'll leave you now,' he stated. 'Think of your crime. Think about how bad you are and try to decide how you will become a better person. Repent.'

Simple words, but I couldn't absorb what he meant. I was tired, I was hungry, and I was cold. My body ached, and the cool, damp darkness that settled around me once he had gone filled me with depression and the feeling of intense isolation. I wondered how long I would be left like that, suspended on the board with a huge replica cock stretching me, and with my limbs firmly manacled.

What was the point of this? I wondered.

The blackness in the room grew more intense as the night progressed, and I grew colder and more alone. My understanding seemed to struggle with what was happening to me. Hunger gnawed at my insides and the cold settled around my limbs like an icy cloak. Then, at dawn, when the darkness became less dense and cool blue daylight crept across the rough floor and chased the shadows away, everything seemed to become clearer in my head.

In *Venus in Furs*, I thought, struggling to remember, Severin is desolate when Wanda leaves him tied to a pillar. She lets her new lover, Alexis the Greek, whip him mercilessly until he bleeds, then the mistress and the Greek depart, for ever. Perhaps Ross was trying to re-create that desolation for me, maybe he and Louisa had departed. I prayed that it wouldn't be for ever. I was cold. My hunger made me light-headed, and I was getting desperate to pee.

The long day passed. The house above me remained silent and the temperature in the cellar icy. My skin became numb, and the only warmth I could feel was the heated clasp of my sex around the moulded black cock. The pressure in my bladder was immense and almost painful. Eventually, having shouted for help until I was hoarse, I let it go.

Heat. Hot fluid. It was bliss for a long moment, but it soon cooled and I felt like sobbing as I hung there. I was purged and emptied, as he had wanted me to be. He had given me an enema. And now I had wet myself. My humiliation was complete.

By nightfall, I thought I was beginning to go mad. Every sound was magnified in the growing gloom. My body was numb but my brain was feverishly overactive. There was a tapping sound. Knocking. Like a stick being rapped against the side of an empty oil drum.

I craned my neck and looked up. It seemed to be the hot water pipes that I could hear. Three of them ran through the ceiling, long and lagged with cotton, as wide as my arm. With the tick-ticking came a slow sense of warmth as the temperature in the room gradually rose.

Within an hour I was comfortably warm. In two I was sweating.

The heat was almost as intense as that in the house, but the damp air made it humid and strange, like a New York bath house. Gleaming beads of perspiration pearled along the length of my cramped limbs, and my skin became rosy, puffy and petal-soft with heat. I could feel my hair cleaving to my neck and I longed to slip my fingers behind my head to stop the tendrils from sticking against my skin, but my hands were firmly bound and even if they had not been, they were so cramped that I doubted whether I could have moved them voluntarily.

My suffering receded with the cold, and by the time my Officer returned I had even forgotten how hungry I was.

195

He pulled up a chair, the squeal of the wood against the floor making my hair stand on end. I watched as he sat astride it, resting his forearms on the curving back. He raised an eyebrow and settled to watch me, one boot resting on the strap that secured my left ankle.

'You look good. Very good. I wonder what Seph would say if he could see you now?'

The unpleasant thought that he might bring Seph down here was almost more than I could bear. I struggled against the bonds, heedless of the deep penetration of the fibreglass cock, and opened my mouth to speak, but he shook his head slowly.

'Not a word, Fräulein. I have ways of making you not talk.' There was a glint of amusement in his eyes. I closed my mouth and kept still. I had been strapped to the board and left for twenty-four hours after being painfully spanked and horribly humiliated. The last thing I wanted was to discover what methods he had for keeping me silent; my imagination simply didn't want to go there.

We both kept very still, eyeing each other warily. The air had become searingly hot, the atmosphere thick with our combined breaths and the warmth from pipes which ran the length of the ceiling. I wondered how long we were going to stay like that, but didn't dare speak as I knew that the sound of my voice – weak and thin – would give Ross another of his victories. I realised that holding out was a waste of time, because he'd already won in so many ways. But it made me feel better to do the thing that he least expected.

Ross glanced down at the puddle at my feet, then leant forward and slid his forefinger up the tender skin of my inner thigh.

'Couldn't hold on, eh, Puss?' He gazed deep into my eyes and I wondered whether I hated him. He smiled briefly and slipped his thumb across my clit. 'Time for a wash, I think.'

I cringed as I saw him unwind the hose; I didn't want another splash-down with icy water. But this time it was different. Steaming, gorgeously hot water washed me clean, reviving my senses and making me feel less empty, more of a person. Ross held a bar of scented soap in one hand and smoothed it across my body with leisurely strokes, slowly working up a lather and massaging it into my creases and folds. His warm fingers lingered under the curve of my breast and in the smooth dip of my navel. His mouth sought mine and he kissed me gently, his tongue searching for mine, and I felt grateful for his every tenderness.

He dried me carefully, his hands gentle and swathed in a fluffy white towel, then he settled back into his chair. I waited. He waited. He glanced at his watch. Then a door opened.

Chapter Eleven

'Good, you've come. I was beginning to think you'd forgotten.' Ross tipped the chair a little and swung on its two back legs, tipping his head to greet whoever had entered the cellar. A cool draught licked my ankles, then I heard the door close, and I flicked my eyes sideways to see who it was.

'I was held up. I came as soon as I could.' I couldn't see the person, but I recognised the voice. It was full of excitement and sexual promise. Closing my eyes, I let my head droop, feeling a strange nausea wash over me as the reality of who was speaking sank in.

'Come here.' I had heard Ross talk like that before, his voice hoarse with suppressed excitement. He used to use that voice on me when we hadn't seen each other for ages. It meant that he was about to tear my clothes off and fuck me senseless wherever I happened to be standing. Usually it gave me a thrill that made my spine quiver, but tonight the only sensation I had was one of dread, because it wasn't me he was speaking to.

'Come here and let me touch you,' he murmured.

The object of his desire, innocently unaware of my

presence, strolled forward into view and I watched him stop suddenly and take stock of the black board with my naked body strapped to it. It was Seph. His eyes widened and he glanced from me to Ross and then back again, his face blank with incomprehension.

'What's going on?' he asked, jamming his hands deep into his pockets.

'She's going to watch us. What do you think?' Ross stood up and pushed the chair away with his foot, then went to stand very close to Seph. I squeezed my eyes shut when he dipped his head to kiss Seph: it was just not something that I wanted to see – my two favourite boys kissing each other. Now, if I was the filling in a sandwich where they made the bread, that would be another matter. But to see them getting it on without me was just too much. I couldn't bear to watch.

'This isn't right.' It was Seph. His voice had dropped almost an octave and I could tell by his tone he was feeling very uncomfortable. I strained my ears to listen to what Ross said in reply. I couldn't make out the words, but the way he said them made me feel strange: his voice was low, caressing, intimate; but the intimacy wasn't for me.

I could tell that he was soothing Seph, telling him that it was all right, probably reassuring him that I was strapped to the cock-board because I wanted to be. Which was true in a way, I suppose. They stopped talking after a while, their already hushed voices dropping lower and lower until the only sound I could hear was my own blood swishing through my veins.

I knew that they were kissing when I heard the sound of lips and tongues and a sudden, quick inhalation. I was desperate to take a peep, but kept my eyes resolutely squeezed shut. Swirls of red and purple danced under my eyelids, like the back projection at an early seventies gig, but that little illusion was soon superseded by the sound of someone obviously sucking cock.

Whose cock? Whose mouth? I tried to push the questions away but they grew more insistent by the minute. I was not going to look. I was just not going to. I didn't need to see real men snogging only three feet away from me.

In spite of myself, I could feel the swell of arousal coursing through my sex, tightening my flesh around the protrusion that filled me and making its shaft sticky with my secretions. I shifted, forgetting that every move I made had me impaled even further. It hurt, but it felt good too. Especially when I heard the rustle of clothing being removed and the whispers and sighs of two people engaged in some very heavy making out.

'You need some lube. It hurts.' God, it was Seph. Seph was letting Ross fuck him. No, Ross was letting Seph fuck him. Which way? Who? Oh, I needed to see.

'Oh, that feels good. You feel so tight, you must be nervous because of the audience. Move closer to her. Do it like that. Yeah, squeeze me.'

That was it. I had to look. I opened my eyes wide, blinked twice to accustom myself to the light, then feasted my eyes. I was an innocent where these things are concerned, but by the time I had focused on the men, I was pretty well hooked on the voyeur thing.

Seph had moved as he had been commanded and was now standing very close, face to face with me. His arms were spread wide and his hands gripped the edges of the black board while his silver bangle tapped the board repeatedly as it swung in time with the movements of his body. If I had wanted to, I could have thrust my head forward and kissed his mouth, but I could tell by the look in his eyes that he wouldn't want me to.

His face was taut, concentrating hard, and his stare had a faraway look that told me that although he was looking at me, he didn't actually see me. His wiry shoulders were sheened with a glossing of moisture – baby oil or sweat, I couldn't tell which – and his biceps were pumped and curved. He was naked, and the sight of his pale, lean body made my belly fill with flickering, fluttering butterfly wings.

Behind him, Ross was still fully clothed: ever in control, the perfect master. He had pushed the sleeves of his leather greatcoat up to the elbow and I could see the bulge and twist of his muscular forearms and the glitter of his Breitling watch as he clasped Seph's wrists and steadied himself.

He had unbuttoned the minimum on his flies, just enough to free his sex, but his cock was buried deep between the cheeks of Seph's arse. I couldn't see, but I could tell by the sweet smell of cock and lube that they were enjoying a tight little fuck that owed nothing to tenderness and everything to control and dependence.

'Can you see him, Puss?' Ross's face was against the side of Seph's head, their cheeks pressing against each other so that the golden stubble of one peppered the black of the other. 'Can you see how much he likes it? You love it, don't you, Seph? You love it when I fuck you good and hard. That's why you nearly came when she pushed that dildo into you on the kitchen table. You were imagining it was me, weren't you, Seph?'

He had been. He didn't have to say anything because I could tell it was the truth from the look of desperation in his blue eyes. I watched as Ross moved faster behind him, his knuckles whitening as they tightened on to Seph's wrists, his thumb nudging the silver bangle aside, and his lips getting thinner as he thrust harder. Seph stared past me, apology and yearning written across his face, while Ross stared straight at me, his eyes burning into mine and a harsh look of unpleasant victory on his handsome features.

He was a complicated man, but I knew that what he was doing to Seph was somehow something that he was actually doing to me, and Seph knew it, too. Poor Seph, who liked fucking girls but loved to be fucked by men. And the man behind him was only fucking him physically because in his head he was giving me some kind of mind-fuck. Me. His cousin. The girl he was close to – closer than all the friendship in the world. Blood close. Family.

I felt Seph come against my belly, his hot spurts surging up around my navel and then trickling through my pubic hair. I desperately wanted to reach up and cradle his head against mine, but the fastenings on my wrists were as immovable as steel handcuffs so all I could do was lean forward in my bonds and press my mouth to his. His lips were dry, his breath slightly sour, and he didn't even attempt to kiss me back.

I let my head rest back against the board and watched as Ross finished himself off and gave one final hard thrust, jerking Seph's body hard on to mine and crushing us both with his weight. He freed one of Seph's hands and reached up to grasp my chin and pull my mouth on to his, bruising and crushing my lips and making me cry out with lust and hopelessness.

It was horrible but good, to feel those two male bodies hard on mine and sense the sticky slip of cooling semen across the skin of my belly. I wished that I could come, too, but I knew that I would not be allowed.

I made my body relax against the board as much as I could and closed my eyes. Feigning sleep was the only way I could deal with this.

* * *

202

Feigning soon turned to reality. It must have been past 3 a.m. by the time I heard the men leave and I had had a long night and day. The previous morning – when Seph had arrived back with the basket of free-range eggs and given me his Judas kiss in the kitchen – seemed like a lifetime ago. As I slept, I dreamt.

I dreamt of suffering and pain. And sexual longing that left me hollow and needy. Strange hunchback dwarves stood between my legs and held my labia wide while their diminutive friends lapped and sucked at my sex. My juices creamed and flowed over their mouths and noses as they took turns, little sighs escaping from their mouths as they brought me closer and closer to orgasm.

'Oh please. Please now. Hurry, please.'

It was my own voice. Begging them to hurry, to bring me off quickly before I died of longing and frustration. Abruptly, I remembered that I was not allowed to speak. And so I bit my lips until they bled; crimson streaks made thin with saliva trailed across my chest, cupping and pooling in my belly-button.

The dwarves stepped back, their strange little faces lit red from below by the glow of a torch. Laughing, they ran away, their retreating feet echoing and harsh in the empty cellar, the laughter reverberating from the bare walls and repeating in my head. I would go mad if I didn't wake up.

I opened my eyes. Louisa stood before me, her face close to mine and her perfume strong in my nose. Her loose hair soothed my shoulders where it fell and she smelt of the outdoors, of lilies and fresh spring breezes. I had been in the dark cellar for so long that I had almost forgotten that there was such a thing as the outside: clean air, freedom.

'I thought you'd never wake up,' Louisa murmured. Her hands felt light on my waist and her nose almost touched mine. 'I imagined he must have drugged you or something. How do you feel?'

'I –' I broke off, remembering that speaking was probably still forbidden. She smiled and stroked my face.

'Poor Puss-cat. You got a little more than you bargained for here, didn't you?' She ran the tip of her forefinger down my nose. 'Did you think you knew Ross? Did you? Nobody really knows anybody. We all just rub along together. Take what life throws at us. For better or worse.'

I gazed at her, noticing the lush thickness of her dark lashes and the way that some of them clumped together and glistened, as if she had been crying. I saw the full pout of her red mouth and the gleam of her white teeth behind.

'You're so alive,' I murmured, conscious that semen was still crisp on my stomach. 'So vibrant, while I feel dead and soiled, and used.'

'I know.' Her smile was lovely. She was everything that I was not – with my dark hair, black brows, moody temper and volatile ways. I sighed wistfully, hoping that she'd either get to the point of her visit or go away and stop torturing me.

'Ross doesn't belong to you,' she murmured. 'He doesn't belong to me, either. None of us own anybody, although you seemed to think that you did. He doesn't want you to change, Puss. You are wonderful the way you are, headstrong and wilful and full of passion. So vibrant.' She smiled. 'Just learn to submit sometimes. Let go of this ownership that you think you have, and we can all live together and enjoy each other. Forget rivalry. I am not your rival. I am not your enemy. You are. And only you can change that.'

Philosophy at six in the morning was hard but I listened. The slow stroke of her fingers on my face and waist soothed me and made being dumbstruck very easy. I closed my eyes and listened to the slow soothing tones of her voice as she slid down my body, talking and stroking, until she was crouched in the same position as the dream-dwarves. Her breath was warm on my belly, and the feel of the black replica cock deep inside me made me sigh and let all the tension out of my body.

'Let me see how you are healing,' she said. 'That gold ring is a little wider than the size I would normally put in for a first-timer. It must hurt.'

I shook my head and kept my eyes tightly closed as she stroked the tender skin of my inner thigh and subjected my labia to an intimate inspection.

'You're swollen,' she murmured, her breath warm on my sex. 'But not from the piercing. You're aroused, aren't you? Did you like it last night? Did it thrill you? I've never seen men together. It must be something pretty special to get you so steamed up. You must tell me about it sometime.'

Her light fingers pushed back the hood of my clitoris. The hot dab of her tongue was unexpected. Thrilling. She moved slightly, positioning herself on her knees just in front of the board and partly under me, so that I could feel the brush of her shoulders on the inner surface of my legs, and sense the closeness of her soft hair just from the little electric tingles I had along the muscles of my thighs.

Her touch was professional at first. She inspected the gold ring closely, her fingers pushing lightly, first on one side, and then the other. I could feel myself swelling out to meet her, my flesh pouting like a mouth around the shaft of the black cock.

'Mmm, you smell of sex and boys.' Her finger traced the silvery, dried line of semen that snaked from my navel into my bush. I heard her little murmur of satisfaction, and then she leant forward.

The tiny pointed tip of her tongue swept up the

205

stem of my clit, sending rockets of crackling sensation up my spine. The effect of her touch was as if she had smothered my whole body in kisses: my nipples swelled out, expanding into the silver cups until the hard metal hurt and pinched the tender flesh of my areola; my belly tingled, butterflies of arousal fluttering through my stomach from ribs to hips; my fingers curled and cramped in the leather bonds that secured me to the board; my sex and anus drew tighter, sending a shudder of lust across my skin and up into my hairline.

I was at her mercy. She could do anything to me.

Her lips looped over the gold ring. I felt her tongue slip under it and down through my plush sex to where the shaft of the black cock entered me. The smooth fibreglass surface was already slick and creamy from my state of high arousal, but then I felt her lick it and wet it even more. Her tongue slid up and into me, alongside the dildo, and pressed upwards so that I was stretched by the combination of her muscular tongue and the sleek sheen of the cock.

I trembled and moved against the board, my bonds seeming to clasp me tighter as I forced the cock deeper, dragging Louisa's tongue in with it until I thought I could take no more. I was full to bursting, and the sensation that I was going to explode became stronger and stronger.

With her nose kissed up to my clit, her lips fastened to the base of the cock, she sucked at it. And me. Her hand slid up to caress the sensitive undercurve of my breast.

I found myself in a paradise that I had never visited before.

I exhaled slowly and carefully, trying not to come on to her beautiful face but feeling the control slipping away from me.

Her movements became rhythmic and insistent, her

hand on my breast slowly squeezing and her mouth a deliciously sweet combination of hard, thrusting tongue and slow, slippery suction. I felt my eyelids tremble and the long muscles of my body curl upwards of their own accord, my limbs only held outward and rigid by the bonds at my hands and feet. A slow throb started in my temples and beat a primitive tattoo across my brain until I felt a wave of shuddering ecstasy surge up and break over me, exploding in a feast of sensation and climax.

I cried out, a hard, guttural sound that was foreign to me, and bit my lips hard against the forbidden noise. I made my lips bleed – just like the dream – and a salty metallic warmth spread through my mouth as I felt the rhythmic grasping of my sex and the muscular shiver of my body. The release felt so good – I let myself drown in the bitter-sweet heat of my orgasm.

As I recovered, I let my eyelids flutter open so that I could see Louisa. She was sitting back on her heels and smiling, her face flushed and her lips glossy with my juices. I felt a trickle of creaminess slick down the inside of my thigh and I knew that it was the heat of my own dew mixed with her saliva. It made me feel warm and sunny inside: there was a post-climax glow that made my mouth curve in a smile that matched hers. I closed my eyes again, my body totally relaxed.

A sudden draught cooled the skin of my ankles, and then was gone as a door was closed. Slowly, I became aware that someone else had entered the cellar. I opened my eyes. Ross had come to sit, cowboy-style, in the chair a short distance from us, an inscrutable look on his dark face.

He was wearing the leather coat from the night before, but had changed into clean black jeans and a fresh white T-shirt. His coat was open and the edges flowed over his widespread thighs to rest on the dirty floor. I followed the line of the black stitched edging until the hem met the matt of his boots, then my eyes slid to the rod-like bulge that followed the line of his fly. He was as hard as a rock. I could tell by the way he fixed his gaze somewhere in the region of my breast that he wanted one of us very badly. Trouble was, which one?

'Very touching,' he said. 'Just girls together, how sweet. Thanks, Lou, that was a nice show.' I glanced down and saw her mouth twist into an ironic little pout as if she were thinking: you wish, Ross. I knew then that although he might have told her to come in here and pleasure me, she had done it for herself, and for me.

I knew that she was genuinely attracted to me. She had sucked me to orgasm because she wanted to, not just because Ross had instructed her to. It was a strange feeling, and one that I wasn't sure that I liked: I had entered into the contract to get Ross, not to turn lesbian.

I looked long and hard at her. She smiled, shrugged and sat further back on her heels. She was wearing a pair of navy combats that had been worn pale in all the right places and a tight little white T-shirt that buttoned all the way up the front, but she had left it undone at the top to show the swell of her cleavage. She looked relaxed and happy – casual enough to go to the supermarket but gorgeous enough to catch anyone's eye.

I suddenly realised that if we'd met in other circumstances we would probably have been friends: drinking on a Friday when she wasn't on call at the hospital; shopping in the West End; chatting over coffee; laughing about our thirty-something singleness; going to parties to find the ideal man and staggering home tipsy and empty-handed.

Louisa smiled at me and broke the spell. She stood up and wandered away from both Ross and me, to stand near the doors that led up to the garden. I could see the silver glint of a simple bangle on her wrist – similar to the one Seph wore – and she played with it as she half-turned back to speak.

'I have to get ready,' she said. 'I'll see you later.'

I expected Ross to go with her but he stayed exactly where he was, his knuckles white as he gripped the back of the chair and swept a look of lingering relish over my nakedness.

'Give me an hour,' he said. Then he stood up and came towards me. I held his stare, then lowered my eyes: submission was suddenly a very attractive prospect.

Ross made full use of the requested hour, and eked out more time besides. I was released from the board, and ordered to stand very still with my hands buckled behind my back while he painted my face. He spent a long time washing and perfuming me, paying particular attention to the creases and folds of my sex, and the puckered rose of my bottom.

His talent as a make-up artist had never been brought to my attention before, but when he held up a mirror for me to inspect the results of his painstaking brushing and blending, I was amazed and pleased. A pale oval face gazed back at me. My already almond-shaped eyes had been lengthened with a thick line of glistening black eyeliner so that I looked oriental. The mascara made my lashes luscious and thick – huge fringes above and below my eyes that looked so luxuriant that if I didn't know better, I'd think they were false. My eyelids and cheeks had been darkened with a bruised chocolate shade, and my lips stained the darkest vampire red that I had ever seen.

I looked exotic and unusual. Not at all like myself – more like a geisha girl on acid.

Ross stood very still while I examined my reflection,

a smile of pride mixed with sexual hunger on his handsome face.

'Sometimes I think you're the most beautiful girl I know,' he murmured. He rested his fingers lightly on my shoulders and pressed his cheek lightly to mine so that I could see both of our faces in the mirror. I smiled uncertainly, then felt a wave of relief as he smiled back. He cupped my chin in his hand and turned my face first to one side, then the other. 'You always were the most exciting-looking girl in the school, even before you grew breasts.'

I raised an eyebrow and felt my smile widen to become a grin. His words had reminded me just how much shared history we had, how far back we went. We had memories of each other from the time before sex became an issue and I could feel the bonds of kinship and intimate knowledge pulling us closer.

I met his gaze, and felt my pulse skip a beat. The obsession I had for him did not seem to have dimmed one bit, in spite of the horrible and humiliating things he had subjected me to. He had screwed his way through the household before my very eyes, but I still wanted him to be mine. Why was that? I wondered. Did I love him? Was this what love felt like? Would we end up together, for ever?

I didn't know, and I didn't really care. The present was the only thing that mattered, and in the present Ross was lowering the mirror and cupping my breast with his hand, applying the tip of the lip-brush to my taut and expectant nipple. He painted them a deep red to match my mouth, then dropped to his knees and applied the lipstick to my sex until I looked like a hungry, gorgeous Venus flytrap – pouting, open and ready to grasp all those who fluttered by.

Then he slipped the velvet hood back over my head.

* * *

I blinked my eyes as the hood was removed, and found myself at a party. I was in a baking hot room where a long, polished oval table formed the centre-piece. Elaborate floral displays, mostly lilies and long green leaves, stood in tall-stemmed vases around the edges of the room. Tall red candles lit every surface and the saffron-coloured walls of the dining room gleamed like a tropical sunset.

I remembered that in *Venus in Furs*, Wanda had a pre-theatre dinner for a small group of men and women. But their party was nothing like this. Nine people lounged on the chairs around the table, all wearing outlandish fancy dress and looking comfort-able despite the heat. There was an African dandy; a Pierrot doll; a Georgian lady in wig and mask; a monk in a Jesuit gown; a fetishist in rubber lederhosen and zipped full-face mask; a soldier in Napoleonic battle dress; a Knight Crusader with chain-mail headgear and a red cross on his chest; a lifeboatman whose face seemed vaguely familiar – my eyes whipped back to his face. It was Mike, the mechanic with whom I had my baptism of fire at the very start of my slavery.

I squinted and looked closer at the faces of the other guests to see if there was anyone else I knew. Sasha was there as the Georgian lady, but no Seph that I could see. At the far end of the table sat a woman who looked like Snow White's wicked stepmother – all clinging indigo silk and face-hugging wimple – but whose inscrutable grey eyes and pale skin identified her as Louisa.

I stared at her and she regarded me calmly, no emotion or hint of complicity anywhere in her demeanour. Then suddenly, as I began to look away, I saw her eyelid drop in a slow wink and she curved one corner of her full mouth in the suggestion of a smile.

That tiny movement on her otherwise still face made

me feel warm and safe. Whatever was about to happen, I knew that she was there for me. Watching. Waiting. Monitoring Ross's excesses. I swallowed and kept my face plain and expressionless: she knew I had seen and understood.

I stood in the doorway on my high-heeled shoes and bathed in the admiration of nine pairs of eyes. I knew I looked good, and the image of myself that was reflected on their hungry faces was enough to turn a lesser mortal's head.

Ross was behind me, his leather coat creaking slightly in the warmth, the heat of his hand at my waist the only part of him that I could feel. But I didn't really need to feel anything more. The past hour had welded us firmly together so that I could once more read his mind, anticipate his moves. It was just like the old days.

He gently urged me forward with his fingertips until I stood near the table, my hips level with the gleaming surface. The guests waited, watching. There was a hesitant expectancy in the warm air. A stillness. I waited for further instruction, then I saw that there was no food laid on the table. I realised that I was to climb up on to the empty surface. I was the feast.

I shivered, fearful yet full of anticipation, then stepped lightly on to a stool that Ross had placed in front of me. From there it was just one short step up on to the warm wood. The surface was slightly slippery, as if it had been greased, and I slid easily to the centre.

'Lie down,' said Ross, pushing the stool away with one booted foot. 'Make yourself comfortable and we will begin.'

I was wearing a thong made of gossamer-thin rubber, so my buttocks slid easily into position across the oiled surface. The only other garments were the cat collar, two metal slave bangles, the nipple grips, and a new, jewelled butt-plug.

Ross had inserted this just before we had left the cellar, making me present myself on all fours for him to widen me with his fingers and press it in. He had shown it to me first, and I had been fascinated with the pretty jewel. It was about an inch in diameter, and had a gold rim that fitted to the wearer's anus, holding it wide. The part that was worn inside was smooth and tapered, while outside tiny emeralds and rubies winked and glittered. It looked precious and beautiful. Ross had told me that I was to show it to whoever asked to see my jewels, presenting myself on all fours for intimate inspection.

I lay on my back, my skin glowing in the heat, my knees bent and head resting sideways so that I could look into the lifeboatman's face. His weathered skin crinkled around his eyes in the suggestion of a smile, but his mouth remained straight and firm, surrounded by dark blond stubble that looked to be at least three days' growth. His eyes were a curious mixture of brown and green, and his teeth gleamed white and straight below the suggestion of a moustache.

I met his gaze and held it, then looked away as I heard Ross draw a chair to the table and sit at my feet, his eyes locking with Louisa's above the length of my body. I could feel the warmth of his hands on my ankles as he gripped them and spread my legs wide.

'Who wishes to see her jewel?' he enquired.

No one moved, then I saw the Knight Crusader stand up, his chain-mail rippling slightly.

'You first, then.' Ross smiled and generously extended his arm. The Knight Crusader moved so that his hips butted up against the table and I swivelled round, feeling slightly like a dish on a rotating table in a Chinese restaurant. I lifted my knees to my chest to show the knight the jewel.

'On your knees, I think.'

I glanced at Ross, interested to see him from the sideways position that I lay in. His eyes were dark and hooded, his brows drawn slightly together. I obeyed him, kneeling in front of the Crusader with my bottom in the air and my face tilted to the person opposite. It was the Georgian Lady, and I could see Sasha's eyes glittering between the slits of her black velvet mask. She looked lascivious and dangerous, ready to pounce.

I jumped slightly as I felt the Crusader's metal-clad hands on my hips. He slipped them round until he had gripped me fast, then I felt the warmth of his breath on the naked cheeks of my bottom. He took the slender thong in his teeth and moved it aside, before sliding his forefinger over the jewelled butt-plug.

It felt strange, but pleasant: metallic fingers striking hard gems and hot lips brushing the crease that separated my cheeks. I shivered as an electric spark shivered through my body and made a curling creaminess form in my sex. I could feel the calm steadiness of my pulse beginning to flip faster, and I stared resolutely into Sasha's eyes, determined not to blink.

Beside her, the Jesuit slid his hand under his dark robes and I could see that he was caressing the steely shaft of his slender cock. The rounded head pressed against the rough fabric and his hand moved slowly, then gradually faster as he saw that I had seen. I cast him a hot look from under my lashes, then glanced back at Sasha.

She moved forward in her chair, her tight, boned corset forcing her upright and making her small breasts look like rounded fruit just ready to spill from the frothy lace of her bodice. She leant forward and placed her hand under my chin, making my neck curve unnaturally, then she lowered her mouth to mine.

Her lipstick smeared across my mouth in a taste of Givenchy and peaches as she moved in for the kill, thrusting her tongue so far down my throat that I almost gagged. I caught her with my teeth and sucked hard, revelling in the taste of her, and in the feel of the Knight Crusader who still caressed my bottom.

I could hear tiny sighs and breathy whispers from the other guests. Opening my eyes, I slanted my gaze sideways to see that the Jesuit had pulled up his robes and was openly wanking his long red cock. I felt a surge of libidinous heat catch in my chest as I stared at the small, tight balls that kissed up under his sex as if they were nesting birds.

Sasha released me, and I felt myself rotated smoothly on the table until Ross was at my bottom and the Jesuit's lap under my nose. His sweet smell pervaded my senses until I felt almost faint, then, as Ross slipped his tongue over my creamed and hot groove, I felt Sasha's hand cup the base of my skull and urge me forward towards the Jesuit, one of his hands caressing his primed cock.

He thrust at my face, and Sasha held me fast. I closed my mouth around him and felt the burn of his ready flesh on my lips and tongue. I latched on to him, sucking and drawing my way down to the base of his cock where his sparse hair crinkled against my nose with its peppery scent. The other guests moved in, breathing hard, touching where they could reach.

I felt Ross's tongue hard in the cleft of my bottom, then his fingers possessed my sex with a slick plunge. I could hear how wet I was as he slipped in – hot and swollen, very juiced up, as well as sticky with the lipstick he had painted there. He kept my rear jealously to himself, so that the others had to cluster around my shoulders, their hands grasping my breasts and fingers trailing down the length of my spine.

I felt at once used and delicious, subservient yet in

control. They all wanted a piece of me, but I wanted all of them, so we were quits. And Ross had the best bit. It was just how I wanted it.

The Jesuit jerked out of my mouth. I thought he was going to come, but glancing from under heavy eyelids, I saw that the Fetishist in rubber had turned to reveal a neat cutaway in the seat of his lederhosen. He bent over the wicked stepmother's lap, gripping her knees to steady himself as the Jesuit slipped into him with a thrusting, screwing motion. I held my breath, conscious of the rub of Ross's fingers in my sex, as I watched one man screw the other.

The muscular pumping of the Jesuit's strong thighs and the grunts of the Fetishist combined to make a visual and aural feast. When Sasha and the African Dandy gripped my breasts and kneaded them in unison I thought I would come just from watching the spectacle.

The Jesuit tensed, and I fixed my eyes on the tight little balls that jerked up with his final thrust. I could see the underside of his shaft, dark with lust and creamed with my lipstick, and the Fetishist's arse. I wanted to see him come. I wanted him to pull out and pump his white-hot, sticky come over my face. But I was suddenly swung around so that I could see nothing but the lifeboatman's face.

'No, let me,' I gasped, craning my neck round. The lifeboatman gripped my chin and jerked my head back so that I was facing him. He pushed me upright until he could stand close and press my aching breasts together, frotting himself hard between them. His thick come sprayed hot and salty across my chin and neck. At the same time, I heard the Fetishist groan and protest as the Jesuit pulled out and turned to me, removed the butt-plug and – straight away – thrust hard into me, hilting himself and coming instantly. The muscular throb of his climax made me gasp and

216

cry out. My sphincter was tight and painful, gripping him as I closed my eyes against the lifeboatman's intense stare.

From then on it was open season.

Part Three

Completion

Chapter Twelve

I sucked and licked cocks until I could no longer differentiate whose I had in my mouth. My body slid around the table, partly on my own impulse, partly on the propulsion of many hands.

I was sodomised by the African Dandy and I thought for a moment that I would split around him. He was short and squat, but very thick. His curved penis plunged into me after he had lubricated it with a handful of juice from between Sasha's wide-open legs, where he had nestled a moment before.

The Napoleonic soldier, complete with bristling-moustached upper lip, held my legs wide and thrust his tongue against the gold ring in my labia. Then I felt his forefinger delve deep into my sex, then two fingers, then three. He slid them back and forth in a leisurely fashion, his eyes fixed on my face to watch my reaction as he almost buried his hand in me. Then, as I glanced down and saw the curve of his forearm moving rhythmically between my legs, I knew from the beautifully painful sensation of fullness that he was fisting me.

I cried out and leant back against the person behind

me. Rough hands cupped my breasts and mouths sought my nipples, sucking and pulling until I could only just see straight. I watched the soldier, and he watched me, and I could feel the trembling beginning of some deep spasm, an orgasm from so far inside my body that I could hardly breathe properly.

The stretchy rubber of my thong gripped the soldier's wrist, pulling him in like some sexual catapult. I could see where my thick cream had crusted the gusset, and so could he, for he met my eyes, then bent his head and inhaled deeply.

I let my head fall back against someone's warm shoulder and revelled in the bristling of the soldier's moustache against my quim as he licked all traces of me from the thong, then pressed hard against my clit until I felt the vibrating waves of the building climax tighten and thrum across my lower body, clenching my womb and oscillating through my pelvis with a white-hot, agonising heat.

I cried out and felt my body go taut for one long, spell-binding minute, then I slumped against the supporting bodies. The soldier carefully slipped his hand out of me, folding his fingers and gently disengaging from the deepest parts of my sex. He dropped a tender kiss on my lipsticked quim, then turned to let Sasha take his aching cock in her ready mouth.

Hands turned me over and I found myself facing the Pierrot. He was strange, with a pierced cock, which he called his Prince Albert. He made me slip my tongue under and around it, then he looped his fingers into my hair and held me close while I slid my mouth all the way on to him. I could feel the stud at the back of my throat, and I listened as he whispered what it would do to me if he was allowed to fuck me, how it would press and throb inside, stimulating me until he knew I would come on to him, gripping and shuddering and crying out.

222

The words he chose were filthy, language from a place my grandmother would probably have called 'the gutter'. But it turned me on so much that when I felt the lifeboatman behind me, caressing the groove that ran between my painted labia, I came anyway. Hard and jerking, my eyes closed and my lips curved around my teeth so that I didn't damage the Prince Albert. I felt hands all over my body, stroking and pulling, fingers at my nipples and thumbs against my clit, and I fell forward on to the table, exhausted and shaking.

But they hadn't finished with me. The girls were waiting.

Ross sat back in his chair, the front of his breeches tented by his unspilt erection. His face was inscrutable but suffused with pleasure, tiny blush spots high on his cheek bones, as if he had a fever. He watched as the men turned me over on the table and big masculine hands nestled my head against Louisa's silk-clad breasts. Then Ross's face darkened and his eyes slid sideways to watch Sasha.

She had taken off her skirt and stood just to the left of my feet in her tightly laced bodice and a velvet mask. She wore white cotton bloomers which she shucked down over her hips, and I saw that she cupped her groin in one hand.

As she advanced, I saw thin black straps that curved over her narrow hips and thighs, then in her hand I saw the thick length of a strap-on penis. It looked almost real with its beautifully carved head and veiny length, and I felt my insides contract at the realisation of what she was going to do. The men could use their fingers and tongues on me or use my bottom, but the girls were going to be allowed to actually fuck me as if they were men.

My legs were stretched wide and I felt my bare feet being hooked on to the muscular shoulders of the lifeboatman and the Pierrot. Sasha stood still between my thighs, her dick resting against the soft skin of my inner thigh, while her hands slipped over my stomach and lingered in my belly button.

She massaged me, her fingers rotating across my flesh in circles that came ever nearer to the base of my breasts. When she reached my nipples, her fingers latched on to the silver nipple grips and squeezed until I bit my lips to stop myself crying out. Her eyes were hard and glittering, and I knew she wanted to hurt me: but I wasn't about to give her the pleasure of hearing me whimper.

She hooked her long fingernails under the grips and, without opening them, tore them away so that my nipples lengthened and became scarlet in protest. It hurt like hell, but only for a moment, then the softness of two mouths closed over the burning little nubs, and strangers' tongues caressed the sore flesh.

It felt good and I glanced down to see that the Dandy and the Knight Crusader were lapping and suckling at me like two babies. The slashed mouth in the chain-metal headdress settled around my warm breast and I wondered who was inside the helmet. His mouth felt delicious against my nipple and I thrust myself up to meet him. His hand curved up to cup the underside of my breast, and I saw a familiar silver bangle in the gap between sleeve and glove. Seph. I smiled at him and his blue eyes met mine, shadowed by the chain-mail mask.

Louisa leant forward, her hands brushing Sasha's as she stretched the rubber of my thong away from my sticky skin. Her wimple-clad head bent to my legs and I felt the soft caress of a lock of escaped hair as she pressed her mouth to my thigh, then bit through the narrow ribbons of rubber that secure the thong. It fell away, and although it had been such a small piece of fabric, I felt its absence keenly. I was undressed now. Vulnerable. Open to anyone.

I looked for Ross. He was still at the head of the table, a goblet of dark wine in one hand. He propped one foot up on a chair and raised one eyebrow when he met my eyes. As Sasha moved forward between my thighs and held her dick carefully to my pouting, creamed sex, I held his gaze.

Sasha moved into me with one thrust, her hips taut and her rounded buttocks tightened against the force of her plunges as she moved faster and worked herself into a rhythm. Ross and I stared at each other, neither one of us flinching. It was like a staring match: but one where it didn't really matter who won.

The Napoleonic soldier moved up behind Sasha, his breeches open around his sex. He bent to press his tongue to her tight little bottom, and I felt her clench against me momentarily, then ease back slightly to grant him access. He opened her slowly, with care, lubricating her hole with his saliva before gentling his way in. She was still, her eyelids fluttered for a moment and cast long shadows on her pale cheeks, then she remembered what she was supposed to be doing, and she moved hard against me, thrusting and rutting with an intent look on her face.

I held my breath, drowning in the heat of the mouths at my breasts and the hardness of her cock inside me. I was full but wide open, my legs held sideways to the utmost and my flesh stretched by a girl's dick. It was blissful. Ross was still holding my gaze and I stared into those drowning pools of darkness for a moment. Then I closed my eyes to increase my pleasure.

Sasha moved faster, giving me a hard, rhythmic fuck despite the fact that she really shouldn't have been physically able to do that to me. It was strange, having a girl between my legs like that. I opened my eyes again to watch her.

Fingers joined Sasha's at my sex. I saw Louisa's hand cover hers and both pressed against my clit until the swirling sensation that threatened to sweep me over the edge became a throb. My heart pounded wildly in my chest and I felt an electric charge start in my toes and curl up my legs to my womb.

The thumping of Sasha's hips against me, and the combined rubbing of the girls' hands and fingers, made my breathing come raggedly undone until I was panting in time to the fucking. Harder. Harder. All the way in. Deep so that the rounded head of her cock nosed against the entrance to my womb. Her golden curly bush brushed and tangled with mine. Her hard little clit poked under the cock and took a battering just as mine did.

I widened my eyes to see them all better: the predatory faces, the sucking mouths, the wanking hands. Glazed blue eyes met mine but I knew Sasha was not really seeing me. She was in some sex-obsessed world of her own where the ultimate power had been granted to her and she was in control. I was her slave. The slave to be fucked and pinched and made to cry out.

And cry out I did. Harsh and guttural, I grunted and then screamed as the orgasm scorched through me, exploding in my belly and making my sex spasm. My muscles oscillated and gripped at the hard cock that plundered my depths.

I reached sideways and wound my arms around the men's heads that concentrated on my breasts, crushing them into me so that I could feel their suffocating breaths against my rounded curves and hear their moans of pleasure as they came on the table-top: milky hot spunk that slipped and jetted across the greased surface until I could feel it soaking into my ribs at the back, searing my skin.

Sasha fell forward on to me, her breathing harsh and unsteady, her hands clutching at my waist as she came against the old soldier's fingers and her little bottom tightened on to his pumping cock. It was a red-hot, bitter-sweet, treacle-sticky orgy and I loved it. I felt a thrilling echo charge through me and I came again, clutching and curving myself on to the girl-cock, my teeth clamping on to my bottom lip and my legs suddenly wrenched free from the men's shoulders to entwine Sasha.

I was no longer merely Ross's slave, I was their slave. All of them. Subjugating myself to them. Opening myself to pleasure. In fact, if I really thought about it, they were my slaves. I was the centre of the orgy. I was the one getting sexual ecstasy from all comers. I was the taker, drowning in sensation at their hands. When I fell into a deep sleep that night, under the softness of the duvet in Ross's big bed, my last thought was how sad I would be when the month was up. Only six more days of lust and gratification.

But it was shorter than that. Because when I woke up, there was the warm stickiness of blood between my legs, and I swore softly as I ransacked the bathroom for the little blue box I had seen there the previous week.

Louisa came to say goodbye on Thursday. I was curled up in the corner of the sofa, a hot-water bottle in my lap. I had been enjoying the spring sunshine that sparkled through the window panes on to my face, and flipping the pages of *Venus in Furs*.

I had read that day's *Independent* from the front page to the business section, and, running out of things to do because Ross had relieved me from slavedom for a few days – in recognition of what he referred to as my 'womanly condition' – I had retrieved my dog-eared paperback from the attic bedroom.

Re-reading it had been a strange experience. Everything was subtly shaded with my own memories of the past three-and-a-half weeks, and with the knowledge that slavery to a person, or group of people, was also a liberation of the senses. I hadn't felt so good about myself and my body since I was twelve, before the arrival of breasts and hips.

'Sam?' Louisa spoke softly, and I looked up at her, placing my book face down on the arm of the sofa.

She was dressed in a pale grey sweater that hugged her every curve, and a long silky skirt, above which I could just see a centimetre of bare waist. Her hair was piled up in a soft chignon with long wisps that framed her face. She wore her simple silver bangle, matched with tiny silver studs in her ears and no make-up; just a slick of vaseline glistened on her lips and eyelids. She was the picture of understated beauty and elegance.

I felt clumsy and scruffy in comparison, wearing the obligatory borrowed jeans and an oversized sweater that had definitely seen better days. So I hugged the hot-water bottle tighter to my tummy and waited to see what she would say.

She dropped her gaze and studied the cover of my book, seeming at a loss for words. The meek Louisa was back. I wondered which was the real her. Somehow, I imagined that the strident dominatrix in the fur coat and Manolo Blahniks would be the better approach for the cut-throat world of modern surgery. An image of her in a navy suit and minimalist jewellery, with a plethora of medical students trailing in her wake, flickered to the forefront of my mind and I smiled.

She caught the smile and it seemed to help her find her tongue.

'I'm going in a few minutes. I just thought I'd say goodbye.'

I nodded but didn't speak. She tried again.

'Ross said you're leaving on Saturday.' I nodded again. 'Is he driving you back?' She really seemed unsure of herself. The fact that she was leaving and I was staying had put her in a weak position, I realised. But somehow I didn't feel inclined to capitalise on it – I liked her too much. I took a deep breath and found my tongue.

'I don't think so. He said something about the train.'

'That'll be nice.' She grinned suddenly. 'Make sure he pays for you to go First Class.'

'I will.' I turned the hot-water bottle over and curled my feet tighter up under my bottom. She watched me, and then perched next to me on the sofa.

'Are you taking any painkillers? You seem to be in a bad way.'

'Actually I'm not, this time.' My voice dropped to a whisper. 'But he doesn't need to know that.'

Our eyes met and we smiled like conspirators. Louisa leant forward and kissed my cheek, her warm perfume lingering in my nose and the wisps of her hair caressing my neck and chin.

'Take care,' she whispered. 'Maybe we'll see each other again.'

'I'd like that.' I suddenly didn't want her to go without giving some sort of invitation. 'Maybe next time you come up to the city we could meet for a cappuccino somewhere nice.' I told her the name of the firm I worked for and she nodded.

'I'll give you a call, then. Maybe.' She smiled as she turned away, one finger toying with the silver bangle on her wrist.

It was nice leaving it open-ended like that. I knew

that she and Ross weren't finished, and I knew that I wasn't looking for an affair with her. But it would be exciting to have that thrill every time the telephone rang on my desk. I would pick it up wondering if a soft velvet voice would say, 'It's Doctor Richmond.'

It was just the sort of titillation I needed to get through the nine-to-five.

That evening, Ross cooked while I sat on the edge of the kitchen worktop, swinging my legs and sipping chilled Chardonnay. It was just like old times, except that there seemed to be a new shyness and restraint. Somehow the past four weeks had imbued our relationship with a mutual respect that it had never featured before. Every so often our eyes would meet, almost accidentally, then we would both quickly look away, just as if it was our first date.

I watched the way his hands moved across the wooden surface of the chopping board as he skilfully carved up onions and garlic cloves. He had never cooked for me before. We usually ate out when I had spent weekends with him. His home town boasted a wealth of seafood restaurants, and we never felt like staying in with beans on toast when there was Rick Stein in all his glory available in the next street.

'I'm doing spag bol,' said Ross, reaching for a bunch of bay leaves that hung from one of the overhead poles. 'I think you need the red meat. You don't want to get anaemic.'

'Honestly, anyone would think I was pregnant. It's just a period.'

'It's not just a period. It's your period. I've never been with you when you've been having one before – I want to look after you.'

This was true. We never had been together like this before. The searing sexuality of our relationship had always made me cry off visits to Ross if a trip to the chemist was in order. The intimacy that was now rearing its unfamiliar head made me feel strange.

It was like opening a fortune cookie and finding the slip of paper inside said 'Greet old age together'. I wasn't sure that I liked it. It hadn't really been the idea. All I had had my eye on at the beginning of the four weeks was getting Ross away from Louisa. Wholesome togetherness and two beaming, pink-faced children were definitely not in my life plan.

'I thought there was no meat in the house,' I said drily.

'Lou went shopping before she left. There's a great little butcher's shop in the village.'

'Louisa bought it? But I thought she was a vegetarian.'

'She is.'

The thought of Louisa going into a butcher's and buying meat that she hated just for me was so amazing that I nearly choked on my wine. I knew I could never be that selfless. She was actually a *nice* person. A real live nice person. I couldn't remember ever having met one of those before. I sloshed some more Chardonnay into the glasses and took a healthy swig.

I really must try to be nicer, I thought. Like Louisa. No wonder Ross had hooked up with her.

We ate the meal in undemanding silence, then Ross opened another bottle of wine and we curled up on the sofa in front of a blazing fire with our glasses and a bowl of juicy black olives.

'What do you want to do?' he asked. 'Is there anything on television?'

'On a Thursday?' I thought back to civilised life. Wednesday was the good TV night with reruns of *ER* – lots of drooling over George Clooney and arguing with myself over who I fancied more, Dr Ross or Dr Carter – so Thursdays were always a real let-down. 'Nothing. Anyway, I think you're forgetting that we don't have that choice.' I stared pointedly at the space near the fireplace where the television had once stood.

'Oh, yeah,' he said, grinning shamefacedly. 'I ought to replace that before we leave. Do you fancy a trip into town tomorrow?'

'Maybe.' I shrugged. 'Although I don't really have any suitable clothes to wear outside this house.'

'I'll buy you some. Come on, we've never done anything like shopping together before. It'll be fun to spend a day in town. You can choose whatever you like. I'll pay.'

It would have been rude to refuse.

'Try it on again. Go on. Put it on for me.' Ross leant against the sitting-room door-frame and folded his arms. I was momentarily distracted by the way his biceps bulged under his long-sleeved T-shirt, but then the pull of the Jigsaw skirt and top he'd bought me won over the attractions of his physique.

I peered inside the bag and smiled. It was beautiful. Pink – not my colour usually, but pink was apparently the season's black and I couldn't argue with the fashion pages of *Cosmo* and *Marie Claire*.

'OK. I'll just go upstairs.'

'No. Here.'

I glanced at the netless windows.

'Well –'

'Go on. Who's going to see? We're in the middle of nowhere, that's why I chose this place.'

'Someone might be around,' I said.

'There's no one around. Anyway, if there was, we'd see them.'

'I didn't see Sasha and her video camera.' I turned and glared at the broken television that still littered the path outside. That shut him up for a moment, then he strode over and parked his broad-shouldered form in front of the window. The glass still had stickers on, and smears of putty and fingerprints from the local glazier who had replaced it.

'There. Privacy. Go on. Get changed,' he said. I looked at him, wondering why I suddenly felt so shy. It could have been to do with the period thing, I suppose. Or it could have been to do with the weird, shy intimacy I'd felt in the kitchen the previous night.

Reluctantly, I unbuttoned the old shirt that he'd lent me to wear into town. Then, seeing the exasperated look on his face, I decided to make it fun with a little striptease. The room was comfortably warm, everything I had on was easy to remove, lots of buttons and long sleeves for whisking around. It would be fun to tease him.

I began to dance. My fingers strummed over the buttons on the shirt and I undid them slowly, swaying my hips and arching my back so that my breasts jutted forward.

'That looks good.' Ross smiled. He moved to the CD player, not taking his eyes off me for a second. 'Let's put some music on. What do you want to dance to?'

'Something hard and rocky. With a good beat.' I dropped the shirt off my shoulders and held it tight around my arms and breasts, sashaying over to stand near him and peer over his shoulder. 'You'd better stop watching me and pay attention, you're putting it in upside down.'

'Damn.' He flipped the CD over and I smiled as I saw the name of the album etched into the silver: *Exile on Main Street* had been a passion of ours one summer when we had rediscovered the Rolling Stones. The intro of *Tumbling Dice* always reminds me of the smell of a burning joint and the feel of Ross's fingers against the back of my neck. We'd smoked and played poker and turned the cassette player up too loud, out in my old wooden Wendy house. Each raucous waver of Mick Jagger's voice had taken us closer and closer to that moment when we took off our clothes in front of each other for the first time as adults.

We had stretched out – on a makeshift bed fashioned from the cushioned seating of the tiny sofa – and I had found out for the first time why every girl in my class at school had looked at Ross in that special way that screamed lust and longing: word had got around by the time we were fourteen that Ross had a way with his fingers, and the girls were virtually queuing up to sample a taste of his dexterity.

That hot summer afternoon, two days after my eighteenth birthday, I got more than a taste and it left me dazed and desperate for a repeat performance. The sound of the Stones along with the vivid memory of my defloration made a pucker of goosebumps flicker up my spine and I could feel my nipples constricting to strain through the cotton shirt.

I decided to get on with the job in hand and make the memory of his touch a reality. I moved away and slowly warmed to the task, my eyes fixed on Ross as he strolled back to stand in front of the window.

The shirt dropped around my feet in a pale, striped drift and my fingers stroked their way down to my belly button, where I lingered a moment before popping the button on the borrowed Levi's. Several sizes too big and cut for a man, the denim hung around my hips in a sexily fashionable manner, making me look like a cross between someone in an All Saints video and a harem girl. All I needed was a pierced belly button and some fab abs, and I could wiggle and groove my way along with the best of them.

Ross's eyes were fixed on my fingertips, his dark gaze watchful and half-amused. I could see his tension by the way he leant back against the window and shucked his hips to one side as if he could only weight-bear on one leg. He always dressed to the left, and I could see that he was trying to relieve the sudden tightness of his Dockers by leaning sideways like that. The khaki fabric was pulled tight over his groin, the pockets giving that little flare inward that showed he was packed so tight that he didn't even have room for a clean hanky in there.

I was pleased with the success of my admittedly timid strip. I danced across the carpet for a while and then decided to heat it up a bit. Slipping my hands up over my breasts and round the back of my neck I thought of Demi Moore in *Striptease*. It wasn't my choice of Friday night viewing, but I'd been dragged along to see it by an old part-time boyfriend who had a thing about Demi. And now I was glad because it meant that I sort of knew the moves.

I piled all my hair up on top of my head and looked out at Ross from under seductively lowered eyelids, all sultry pout and come-hither eyes. He didn't come hither at all; he just stood very still, his cock straining the seam of his trousers and his face getting a little pink. In the background Mick sang his rocks off and I was tempted to hum along.

'You look gorgeous,' Ross whispered.

I simply smiled. And slipped the wide lace straps of my brand new Triumph Flaunt bra – cranberry red and very sexy – down my arms so that the cups cleaved to my breasts and my flesh threatened to spill right out. It was tantalising, I knew, and, as if to confirm it, Ross tucked his fingers into the tight pockets of his Dockers and clasped his bottom lip with his teeth. His eyes fixed on to my skin and never left me.

I did a little wiggle, clad only in the jeans and bra, then twirled around to shake my buns at him. I didn't actually hear him move, but he strode across the floor in record time and was tucked up behind me before I knew it, thighs bulging into mine and strong arms wrapped around my bare waist.

His mouth sank to my neck. I leant my head to one

side to feel his kiss as he sucked his lips on to my skin, exhaling hard through his nose. His arms felt good around me, so comfortable, and the pulsing beat of his rigid cock against my left buttock was just swoon-worthy.

We swayed like that for a while, then his fingers slipped down over my belly and into the jeans. Five weeks' growing time on my previously shaven bush had made it thick and curly, a luxuriant glossy pelt that parted for his probing fingers. He gave the little gold ring a sensual stroke that made my eyelids flutter closed and my heart speed up to double-time.

But when he reached further and felt the thin white string he froze. Then his hand jumped away as if I had a nest of angry hornets down there.

'Sorry, I forgot,' he breathed against my neck.

'So?'

'Well. So.'

'We can still do it.'

'We can?' He was not at all sure. How strange that he was adventurous in so many things, but that having sex during my period remained a taboo. Nicole had told me she'd done it once with an impatient date that just wouldn't wait. And she'd liked it, too. Sensitive and hot, she'd said. And totally relaxed because there was little fear of the dreaded nine-month penalty. I'd made up my mind to try it, just the once. And so I reached up to pull his hand back down to the fly of my jeans.

'Keep going,' I murmured. 'If you can give me an enema then you can fuck me with a little mess, right?'

And so we did. Several times. Over the sofa with him behind. Against the wall with my legs up around his hips. Up in the bedroom across his big bed, in the reliable old missionary position with a towel under my hips to stop any tell-tale crimson blushes on the pristine white sheets the next morning.

Nicole was right; it was good. The hard shagging with props and toys, the use of other people and the dressing in rubber and slave-chains was gone. All we did now was a sensuous, warm low-gear screw that made me curl up with happiness inside. I preened myself underneath him like a cat, stretching my limbs along his, enjoying the rough feel of his hairy legs against my smooth calves, and the sleek movements of his muscular shoulders under my fingertips.

It was cosy and nice, sweet, slow fucking that made all the hard horniness of our past feel a million miles away. When it was over, I lay tucked into his side with my nose in his armpit hair. Ross had found Louisa's discarded, crumpled pack of Camel Lights, and he extracted a slightly bent cigarette and propped it into the corner of his mouth. He lit it and took a deep drag, slowly letting the smoke trickle out of his nostrils.

I watched him smoke his first cigarette since New Year's Eve, enjoying the smell of burning tobacco and the gentle odour of his armpit. As I watched, I noticed that there was a subtle difference about Ross that I hadn't noticed before: his hair had gone grey at the temples. Just a little. A few salt and pepper streaks that only added to his attractiveness. They definitely hadn't been there at the beginning of the month. It made me wonder what silent toll all this slave and master thing had had on him.

'Will you be glad to go home?' I asked.

'In some ways.' He raised his head and crushed the half-smoked cigarette into the ashtray, then wriggled down to lie next to me, nose to nose. 'What about you?'

'Oh yes. My own bath. My own toilet. My own bed.' The latter was something that had been preying on my mind for the past few days: stretching out in my own bed, with cool fresh sheets and a good book.

Alone. No one else around. Doing what I wanted to do, when I wanted to do it.

'Yeah, that's something I miss too. Sleeping sideways across the bed if I want to, getting up at five and going for a run, keeping the light on till three in the morning when I feel like listening to music. Not having to consider another living soul.'

I lay there staring into the deep caramel brown of his eyes and realised that I had read all the signals wrong the previous evening. Ross and I weren't looking at a 'together for ever' thing. There would never be two shiny kids and an estate car. Thank goodness. No, the recent intimacy and consideration for each other meant that we were each saying goodbye in our own way. We liked each other – loved each other even – but we enjoyed being on our own too much, were too independent, to ever submit to any conventional relationship.

The new softer Ross and the new contented me were the products of a month of submission and slavery that had shown us both where our paths lay. We were separate beings for the first time in more than a decade. This really was goodbye. And it didn't feel bad at all.

And I never did get to model the new Jigsaw skirt and top for Ross; it stayed in its bag until I left the house for the last time on Saturday.

'Are you going?'

I was standing in the doorway at the front of the house, waiting for Ross to bring the car round. Seph stood uncertainly on the path, his eyes searching mine hesitantly while the fingers of one hand slowly twisted the silver bangle on his slender wrist.

'Yes.' I frowned, feeling immensely tender towards him. He looked very vulnerable, standing there in the dusk in his combats and T-shirt, shivering slightly.

I reached out and looped my finger around his bangle, more to stop him fiddling with it than anything else. 'Will you miss me?'

'You know I will. Thing is –' he glanced down at the cracked pavings beneath his booted feet '– will you miss me?'

'Yes. Yes, I will. You know I will.'

There was a long silence. Then, from the back of the house, I heard the purr of Ross's car as the engine started. Everything felt suddenly very hurried, secretive, too much left unsaid.

'Come and see me,' I said. And I whispered my phone number into his ear.

Chapter Thirteen

*R*oss slowly untied the thick, soft rope from my wrists and ankles. We had driven for what seemed like miles in his car, but we could have been going round in circles for all I knew, because he had also tied a black scarf around my eyes. It served the dual purpose of blindfolding me and muffling my ears. Now he untied the scarf as well.

'This is it,' he said, his lips pressing to mine for an all too brief kiss. 'This is goodbye, Puss. Or au revoir, depending on which way you want it. I'll let you decide that one.'

I searched his face, but didn't find any answers there, just eyes that burnt like black fire in the darkness, and a solemn expression that could have meant regret or relief.

'Bye, then.' I felt funny inside, sort of sick, but there was nothing I could do except go along with him. I frowned. 'How will I get home? What shall I do?'

'You'll find out, someone will be waiting here for you. Now, go in and do your penance, Puss. Repent of your sins. When you come out of the church, you'll know that the contract is finished.' He smiled. 'You're lucky – Severin never had it this easy at the end.'

Ross stroked the side of my face, his thumb playing softly along my jaw. I swallowed and thought of all the things I ought to say to him, but no words came.

I watched him as he turned and walked away, his footfalls crunching bleakly on the gravel. He stopped when he reached the road and I thought for one heart-stopping moment that he was going to turn round and come back to me. But he simply paused, his shoulders stiff and broad, then reached into his pocket and pulled out his car keys.

I closed my eyes for a minute so that I didn't have to see him leave, and stood motionless until I heard his car purr away into the night. Then I turned slowly, pushed open the lych-gate and walked into God's Acre.

At the far end of the path was a little church, the white gravestones which surrounded it gleaming like an old man's teeth in the cold moonlight. I glanced around and realised that I was totally alone in the dark. An icy tremor of fear washed over me and I resisted the strange urge to make some sign – cross myself perhaps – although I had never done such a thing in my life before.

The darkness was soft and velvety around me, but cool on my skin. There was a slight rustling in the undergrowth to my left as if something, or someone, moved there. I strained my eyes, but could see nothing except inky blackness highlighted by the uneven white of the gravestones. I could feel superstitious terror beginning to close its cold fingers around my heathen heart, and I coughed loudly to break the deathly silence. Nothing happened, the fear remained. I wondered what to do next.

Ross had said to go and do penance, so I was obviously supposed to enter the church. I took a few tentative steps forward, my legs trembling a little and my stomach clenched tight with fright.

Inside the building it was warm and musty, the smell of dusty, well-thumbed prayer books making my nostrils flare in protest. Incense from evening mass still lay heavily on the air, and I could see dust motes floating in candlelit dimness.

I walked slowly along the aisle, listening to the dry echo of my footsteps and wondering if I was alone or whether someone watched me from the shadows. Churches after dark have their own peculiar creepiness for unbelievers, and I could feel a tiny tight nugget of panic in my guts that I fought to control. I reached the low, partly carpeted steps that led up to the altar and then stood still, gazing at the huge arching, stained-glass window ahead of me. The smell, the soft darkness and the weight of hundreds of years of tradition and ritual made me feel very odd, so I thought I would sit down quietly and await my fate.

To one side of the nave was a tiny Lady chapel, half-hidden by a fretted woodwork rood screen and long red and gold tapestries. Stepping inside, I perched on the nearest pew and gazed at the gleaming golden cross that stood on the small altar at the front of the wooden pews.

I sat still, deep in thought, for a long time. My thoughts jumped from memories of the past four weeks, to long-forgotten snippets of childhood with my brothers and Ross. The silence in the church was overwhelming – almost threatening – but gradually I relaxed and breathed deeply, sliding comfortably back into the pew and letting my hands rest on my knees. A feeling of peace stole over me, like a balm after the month of storm and riotous emotion. I hoped whoever was coming hurried up, or I'd be getting religion next.

There was a slight rustling sound to my right. My heart skipped a beat and I jumped at the harsh sound of my own sharp intake of breath. I glanced up to see that a priest had entered the little chapel. Tall and willowy, he moved with the infinite grace and elegance of a gazelle, his long hands and fingers folded over each other in front of the smooth ebony cloth of his vestments.

As I watched him approach, he walked past lighted candelabra and the soft glow lit his face and head, shining on his unruly black hair and lighting it with silver streaks. The white in his hair, and the widow's peak over his forehead, made him seem very old, but as he drew close, I could see that his face was unlined and that his keen grey eyes shone with the energy of youth. He stopped abruptly on seeing me.

'I'm sorry, my child. I didn't know that anyone was in here. I have no wish to disturb you.'

'I was just waiting for someone. Perhaps I should go.' I stood up, wondering whether he was the person I was waiting for, and how I would know it if he was. The silver cross that hung on a fine chain around his neck made me feel small and guilty, as if I had no right to be in a church at all. I moved to walk past him but he held out one hand and laid it gently on my arm.

'It's very late. Who are you waiting for?'

'I don't know.' I felt embarrassed at trespassing in the church. The priest couldn't be the person I was expecting; Ross would have said. Or maybe he wouldn't have – maybe this wasn't a real priest. I cast my mind back, trying to remember the exact words Ross had used.

Repent of your sins, he had said. The contract is finished when you come out of that church. I looked up at the priest, seeing interest and expectation in his deep-set eyes. Well, there was only one way to find out whether he was here for me, and that was to talk to him.

'Father, I –' I took a deep breath. 'Father, will you hear my confession? I don't usually go to church, so I don't know the form. But I think I am here to repent of my sins. Can you help me?'

'I am at your disposal.' His voice was beautiful. Low, velvety tones seemed to reach out and wind round me like a cashmere scarf. He moved a little closer and I felt his hand at my elbow; gentle fingers touched my arm, smoothing and stroking until they stopped just above the wrist.

I felt a helpless languor steal through my limbs, a heaviness that made me want to sit down again and stay, just to listen to his voice. I stepped back, feeling the hard edge of the nearby pew behind my knees.

He knelt before me, his eyes fixed on mine and his face very close. I could smell the dusty scent of his official robes and the floral perfume of the violet pastille he seemed to have just finished sucking. If I had wanted to I could have leant forward and kissed him.

I shook my head to clear it. Get a grip, Bentley, I thought. This man is a priest and you're in the house of God. What on earth would everyone think? There's no proof that Ross dressed him up and sent him here for you.

Was he a real priest? I had to know. The only way was to hit on him during confession and see what he did. If he turned and fled, then I'd know for sure that he was the local clergyman. If he responded, then it would mean that he was just one of Ross's friends in fancy dress. Probably one of the lifeboatmen – up for anything, as usual.

I looked him straight in the eye, my breathing deliberately shallow as I slowly wet my top lip with the tip of my tongue. As I had thought he might, the priest swallowed visibly and placed his hand on my leg, just above my knee.

'Do you wish to confess your sins, child?'

'Oh, yes. Bless me, Father, for I have sinned.' The words came from nowhere, and I realised that movies and literature had a lot to answer for. 'It is four full weeks since my last confession, and in that time I have been a bonded slave of lust and depravity.'

His eyelids flickered very slightly, but that was the only expression of his surprise. He leant forward a little and I could see the masculine body hair that protruded from his stark white collar. I imagined what he would look like without his robes: his body pale with a distribution of hair that covered his chest and belly to lead the eye ever downward . . .

I shivered and tried to pull myself away but he pressed his hand firmly on my thigh, the fingers long and pale against the dark blue of my skirt. I sat very still, my mind protesting but my body strangely silent as I studied the elegance of the carefully tended oval nails and the slender grace of the wrist that showed beneath the black cuff.

'Will you continue?' asked the priest. I nodded.

'Yes, Father. I came here to a house with my cousin. I intended to be his slave, to bind him further to me by the use of feminine wiles. However, he set me a series of tasks and tests which included sexual acts with his housekeeper, her brother, another woman and finally a party of ten.'

'And did you perform these tasks and tests?' His eyes were fixed on mine, unblinking, and the only sign of emotion was the tightening of his hand on my leg. His fingers were like slim bands of steel clamped to my thigh and I moved a little to escape, but found that his hand slid further up, bunching my skirt a little.

I made up my mind then: he wasn't really a priest. But I'd play along and see what the last instalment of the contract brought me.

'I did, Father. With extreme pleasure.' I stared at him, daring him to punish me or give me thirty Hail Marys or whatever it is sinners have to do. He did nothing, merely smiled and nodded slowly.

'I think you have been sent to me by the Good Lord,' he said. 'As punishment for my own sins.'

'You must have been very bad, then, Father,' I said with a wry smile.

'Indeed,' he replied. 'I am a very bad man, but a very good priest. Kneel and pray with me.'

I knelt between the pews on the hard stone floor. His hands grasped mine and pushed them together in an attitude of prayer, then he intoned several canticles: long, complicated verses which included old-fashioned references to the Flesh and the Devil. I sneaked a look at him half-way through and was struck by how genuine he looked, and by how real and unhesitating the prayers were. Ross was really very good at choosing the right people to play these roles, I thought.

When we had done the Amen bit, he remained kneeling on the stone floor but motioned for me to sit back up on the pew before him. His face was impassive but his eyes gleamed with a strange zeal and I felt a wash of something akin to superstitious fear as he placed his fingertips on my knees. Then I remembered that he was only acting, and I experienced a rush of erotic sensation that brushed all the hair on the nape of my neck upwards, and made me shiver.

'Are you cold, child?'

'No, Father. I'm just wondering what we are to do now.'

'What would you like to do?'

'I think you know what we are both here for.'

'Indeed, I am beginning to know. You are very wicked. But then so am I. Thus we shall be partners in repentance, shall we not?'

He had such a strange and archaic turn of phrase. It was really quite charming. To be called wicked by a man dressed as a priest was a new turn-on, and I could sense the pink, silky skirt Ross had bought me sticking to the underside of my sex.

I leant forward a little to press myself on to the hard wooden seat, and experienced that familiar electrical tingling in my body. The sight of the heavy gold cross gleaming on the altar over the priest's right shoulder made me feel mad, bad and very guilty. That's the only excuse I have for letting him do what he did to me in that church. And for what I did to him. Willingly.

I breathed out slowly, feeling the air sigh between my parted lips. I suddenly found that I couldn't speak: it seemed as if the only sound I was capable of making was that tiny, breathy sigh. He asked me a question and I nodded very slowly, my eyes fixed on his.

His thumb slid under the hem of my skirt, then the whole hand continued its upward slide along my thigh, drawing back the soft fabric with infinite care. My peripheral vision caught the sight of his other hand coming to join the first so that they lay like two long lilies on a pink cloth, then I dropped my head and watched properly as he bared my legs.

Almost without thinking, I let myself slide forward on the pew, my bottom slipping easily on the heavily varnished wood. I watched with fascination as he folded the skirt back on itself and I could see his sudden start at the sight of my bare flesh and the short glossy curls that nestled between my pale thighs.

'Fur coat and no knickers,' he breathed. 'Men should be wary of women like you.'

'Fur coat? I wish. It's pretty cold in here.' I felt a nervous giggle bubble up from somewhere deep inside and struggled to quell it. I jumped slightly as his hand brushed lightly across my pubic hair.

'Fur coat,' he repeated. 'I have a thing about fur. And yours, my dear, is simply the most beautiful fur coat I have seen for many weeks.'

I watched, mesmerised, as his fingers burrowed into my soft hair, caressing and luxuriating. I felt my pulse skip a beat and a thrill travel across my nerve-endings that made me shudder. It felt so good, so forbidden, so delicious, to sit in a quiet, incense-laden church and let this devilish priest impersonator run his long, soft hands over my lower body. I tilted my hips up towards him to give him better access. Unhesitating, he placed his thumbs at either side of my plump sex and opened me, very gently, until I was exposed to his gaze.

'Jewellery. How divine,' he breathed, gazing at my gold piercing. 'But there is something I must do first. Allow me.'

His hand disappeared into the pocket of his long black robes, then withdrew. I saw a metallic gleam, and stared – fascinated – as he slipped his fingers into the circular grips of a tiny pair of silver scissors. I stiffened as he leant towards me, then slowly relaxed as he soothed me with his free hand, stroking me as if I were some half-tame animal that needed to be gentled into submission.

I felt his breath on my thigh as he bent to his work, snipping the edges of my mound so that my bush was made into a shape that pleased him. Watching, feeling relaxed and warmed by his touch, I saw him carefully remove the hairs from around my sex.

He trimmed and snipped, sending small clouds of chestnut fluff down to the dusty floor with tiny exhalations and delicate brushings of his little finger. He shaped me carefully, leaving the top and middle in place but scything hair from the sides until my pubic triangle had gained the geometric shape of a cross –

tall and dark with perfect arms and the main body formed by the darker flesh of my vulva.

He brushed the remaining hair from my thighs, sweeping it into the palm of his left hand and surreptitiously slipping a souvenir lock of dark curls into his pocket along with the scissors. Then, as I silently watched, he knelt between my spread thighs and murmured a prayer.

Crossing himself, he stood and stepped back to murmur a benediction over me, his eyes moving over my body, caressing me as surely as his hands had done, and I felt a hot gush of cream ooze from my pouting sex and trickle – so very slowly – down over my perineal skin to my bottom.

The priest smiled, then knelt again and inspected me from very close range, his nose almost touching my skin and his warm breath washing over the most intimate parts of my body. He leant forward and touched the tip of his tongue to my golden ring, then slowly circled my clit until I could feel heat swelling in my sex. He nestled in closer, and his tongue began to bathe me. I closed my eyes, sinking low in the pew so that my neck was hooked on to the hard ridge at the top of the back-rest and my hair spread out, its colour almost indiscernible from that of the polished chestnut wood.

He was very skilled, his touch light then firm as he worked across my swelling skin. He began by sliding his tongue into the groove between my lips, working his way deeper and drinking me in until I could feel his face buried into the cross of hair that he had pruned. His long nose pressed wonderfully against my clit and I could feel him burrowing – snuffling as if he sought the most expensive truffles – until he had found my most sensitive spot.

His tongue looped up to replace his nose and I felt the thrill of the quick, muscular caresses as he brought

249

me to a fever pitch of desire and longing. I could sense the lengthening of my clitoris as it swelled and enlarged under his expert mouth, then he sank his lips on to me and sucked as if I had become a hard and very delicious sweet. I knew that I would come if he carried on; I could feel the first spicy waves of climax hovering at the edges of my senses.

He slipped one long forefinger into my moist sex and I felt his thumb apply a very slight pressure to my flowering bottom. It was irresistibly sublime. The light quick waves shuddered over me and I gasped under the intensity of sensation as his tongue worked me quickly while his finger frigged my juicy sheath and his thumb circled around my anus.

My orgasm was powerful, hitting me hard and repeatedly as I jerked against his mouth and fingers, my hands grasping wide and stiffening against the slide of varnished wood. It was sacred bliss.

I stayed still for a long moment, my eyes closed, my limbs gloriously heavy and full. I could feel the priest's hands still between my legs, I could sense the tiny, gentle movements he made with his slender fingers. I opened my eyes and gazed at his strange, silver-streaked hair.

I could see his excitement in the slight tremble of his hands and his quick little intake of breath. He glanced up at me, then suddenly reached up with one hand to grasp my chin. He drew my face to his and crushed my mouth with a devouring, violet-scented kiss, then took both of my hands in his and led them to the front of his surplice.

His cock had tented the front of the dark fabric, pushing it out and against my knee. I closed my fist around him and felt my own arousal shoot like sticky treacle through my stomach. He was short, but thick and very, very hard. I could see where his control had eluded him and left a small, darker stain of dampness on the front of his robe. The knowledge that he was so turned on increased my own ardour.

'Let me,' I murmured against his mouth. 'Let me lift this off.'

He leant away from me and I caught at the dull black fabric, pulling it up and away until I could get my fingers on to the zip of his fly. He wore dark trousers, and underneath that a pair of crisp shorts that mirrored the brilliant white of his clerical collar. I thrust my hands into the starched warmth, almost unable to contain myself.

His cock was hot and steely hard. I slid my fingers up and down until I saw another drop of salty moisture bead the end of his shaft. Leaning forward, I pressed the tip of my tongue to it, sliding into the little slit and drawing out his juice. I heard him inhale sharply above me, and felt his balls tighten beneath my hands as I smoothed my fingertips across the dark-haired, pepper-fragrant skin of his groin.

I licked him rapidly, polishing the hard red glans, then I leant back in the pew, lifting my feet and tucking my toes into his waistband so that I could use my feet to push his trousers down, just as I had once seen Louisa do. His thighs were pale, covered with vibrant black hair, and muscular, with a barely restrained power that I anticipated him using when he would thrust into me.

I slipped my hand into the pocket of my skirt and silently handed him the condom that Ross had given me earlier. He raised one eyebrow, looked at the little packet and then raised his eyes to gaze heavenward. I thought he said a prayer, for his lips moved, but I couldn't hear what he said. I hoped that God did.

When he had finished, I placed my feet, the soles flat, against his chest and gazed at him from under heavy, blue-bruised eyelids.

'Quickly,' I whispered. 'Do it now.'

He obliged. Leaning forward, he gripped my waist in those long, elegant hands and held me still while he searched for my sex with the straining tip of his cock. He paused for a moment, his helmet searingly hot against the pout of my labia, then with one hard, powerful clench he entered me, hilting himself on the first thrust.

I gasped. I was so full – he was incredibly wide but it felt heavenly to be stretched like that. I spread my fingers on his shoulders, grasping handfuls of black cloth and moving my hips wantonly against him as he withdrew for a second, mind-spinning entry.

'Oh God!' I was aware of the irony of my cry as it echoed against the stained-glass windows, but the knowledge of my surroundings, and the supposed priestly status of the man who thrust powerfully and repeatedly between my stretched thighs, heightened my sensations and I felt a slick of pure ecstasy cream his cock.

It was fantastic, a spiritual experience that was everything I needed and more, a wickedness that filled the void left by Ross Peterson, and pushed all my experiences of the past month down into the black depths of my soul.

I cried out again and felt his hand, dry and floral-scented, come across my mouth. It was like being gagged. No speech, no noise could escape me and the only way I could get enough oxygen was to flare my nostrils and concentrate hard on my breathing. His eyes were a pale limpid grey, fixed on mine, and I could see every one of his long thick eyelashes.

Suddenly his pupils contracted to pinpoint dots of ebony and I gasped as he withdrew abruptly, pulled off his condom, and came in hot, pumping spurts, anointing my warm belly and crumpled skirt. The surprise, and the evidence of his extreme desire for me, made a sweet reverberation start somewhere deep in my stomach and I could feel the muscular clamping and grasping of my suddenly empty sex as I climaxed unexpectedly against the hard pressure of his thumb against my clit.

It didn't stop there. He was hungry for me, his mouth pressing urgent, burning kisses across my forehead and down the side of my face. His lips felt searingly hot against my neck and I arched my chin upwards, opening myself to him. He grasped me suddenly, pulled me up from the pew and turned me quickly around so that I half-staggered, half-fell towards the altar.

I braced myself with my hands, my eyes fixed on the dark colours of the stained-glass arches before me, while he tucked himself into me from behind, his thighs pressing mine and his hands moving beneath me to open my sex in readiness for his desperate cock. He took me quickly, savagely, and I gasped and grunted as his hips thrust hard against my bottom while his hands reached round my body to grasp my breasts, kneading them through the thin fabric of my top and almost hurting as he pinched the sensitive flesh of my nipples.

At last he achieved his climax, his breathing ragged and hoarse against my hair. I moved on him then, anxious to achieve my own sweet release, but it was a long time coming. He held me tightly, pressing my stomach against the crimson velvet of the altar cloth, and pushing his fingers hard against my clitoris until I came. A gasping, clenching, quick little release that made me droop my head with relief.

Afterwards, I carefully wiped myself with his silk handkerchief and smoothed my skirt down over my trembling thighs.

'Thank you, Father. I feel that I have truly repented of my sins. I feel cleansed,' I said. He nodded, then stood to tuck himself neatly into his robes.

'Perhaps if you return to this part of the country, my child,' he said, 'you will call in again. I will always be here.'

'Oh, yes.' I grinned. 'I'm sure. I expect I'll see you at the harbour sometime, on one of the boats.'

'Boats?' He looked genuinely puzzled. 'No, I think you must be mistaken. I have no plans for a coastal ministry. Unless, of course, His Holiness sees fit to send me elsewhere in the future.'

I had a sudden horrible feeling that he really was a priest. I stared at him, trying to imagine him in the blues and yellows of Ross's uniform. It was incongruous but not impossible. Then something else struck me and I grabbed one of his hands, holding it up to the candlelight and stroking it with my thumb.

His palm was as soft as a baby's. No mooring ropes, no briny sea and no oily rags had ever roughened it. It was an indoor hand. A bookish hand. There was a smoothness to his forefinger, as if he regularly licked it and used it for turning the pages of his bibles.

'You really are a priest,' I breathed. 'Oh, my God.'

'Sssh,' he said. 'Do not take the Lord's name in vain here, child. You are too free with your profanities.'

Thoroughly chastened, and not a little confused, I was aware of his grey eyes boring into my back as I walked quickly away, around the rood screen and into the main church. My footsteps echoed loudly on the stone flags as I walked, and I willed myself not to look back. The big timber door closed behind me with a heavy finality.

In the stone porch, under the wooden table laden with old pieces of oasis for church flowers, stood my own battered suitcase that Ross had thrown over the hedge on the A303 a whole month ago; I couldn't imagine how he'd got it back. Resting on the top was a dark green plastic bag with the name of a bookshop printed in black. I picked it up and peered inside:

254

there was a brand new copy of *Venus in Furs*, and a first-class train ticket to London.

The book had some pages folded down at the corners, and I flicked through them out of interest. They were all references that Ross had obviously drawn on over the past month, and the very last was the page that detailed Wanda going off with the Greek Prince, and Severin being left desolate and alone.

It was obviously a message, I thought. But interestingly, I didn't think it applied to me. I might be alone, but I wasn't desolate. I was strong and full of hope. The future looked bright. The future was mine.

I almost jumped out of my skin when a car horn sounded and I looked down the gleaming moonlight-white path to see a taxi just beyond the dry-stone wall.

'Hurry up, love. Last train's in ten minutes,' yelled the driver. I gave him a wave and hauled the case out from under the table. I was going home.

Epilogue

'Who is it?' I croaked sleepily. The telephone by the side of my bed had been ringing for what seemed like hours before I could rouse myself enough to answer it. The LED on my clock-radio said one minute after midnight, and I rubbed one eye while wondering who on earth was phoning me so late.

'It's me.'

The voice was familiar but I was just not awake enough.

'Who's me?'

'Me. Ross.' I could hear the exasperation in his voice and it made me smile. I leant up on one elbow and hugged the phone to my ear in the dark.

'Oh. Hi. What time d'you call this? It's past midnight, Ross.'

'I know that. I just felt like calling, that's all. Are you OK? I haven't heard from you for a while.'

'I'm fine. Are you?'

'Yes. Busy, but I like it like that.'

'Mmm, me too. Are you going to Moira and Dad's for Easter Sunday?' It was still a week away but I was dreading it already. Easter Sunday was a big thing in our family – roast goose and all the trimmings with stacks of stodgy pud for afters. Ross's presence was usually the only thing that made it any fun.

'I'll be there.' His voice was warm and soft, like melted chocolate dripping down the phone lines and into my ear. I drew my knees up to my chest and revelled in the balmy feeling his voice gave me.

'Are you bringing anyone?' I asked.

'Probably not. I wanted to see you. Are you coming on your own?'

There was a movement in the bed beside me and a warm arm was sleepily draped over my thigh. I caressed the soft inside of the wrist idly with my forefinger, then ran the pad of my thumb over the silver bangle that encircled it. I smiled into the phone as I replied to Ross's question.

'I haven't decided yet.'

'Sam, I love you.'

I felt my pulse skip a beat and I held my breath as I realised that I had never heard him say that before. It gave me a strange feeling of yearning and regret deep inside me and I couldn't reply straight away. I had thought myself over him, and completely besotted by the person who breathed softly under the duvet next to me. Did I love Ross? I chose my next words very carefully, unwilling to commit. Just yet.

'I know you do.'

BLACK LACE NEW BOOKS

Published in October

THE TIES THAT BIND
Tesni Morgan
£5.99

Kim Buckley is a beautiful but shy young woman who is married to a wealthy business consultant. When a charismatic young stranger dressed as the devil turns up at their Halloween party, Kim's life is set to change for ever. Claiming to be her lost half-brother, he's got his eye on her money and a gameplan for revenge. Things are further complicated by their mutual sexual attraction and a sizzling combination of secret and guilty passions threatens to overwhelm them.

ISBN 0 352 33438 X

IN THE DARK
Zoe le Verdier
£5.99

This second collection of Zoe's erotic short stories explores the most explicit female desires. There's something here for every reader who likes their erotica hot and a little bit rare. From anonymous sex to exhibitionism, phone sex and rubber fetishism, all these stories have great characterisation and a sting in the tail.

ISBN 0 352 33439 8

Published in November

VELVET GLOVE
Emma Holly
£5.99

Audrey is an SM Goldilocks in search of the perfect master. Her first choice is far too cruel. Her second too tender. When she meets Patrick – a charismatic bar owner – he seems just right. But can she trust the man behind the charm, or will he drag her deeper into submission than she's prepared to go?

ISBN 0 352 33448 7

BOUND BY CONTRACT
Helena Ravenscroft
£5.99

Samantha Bentley and her cousin Ross have been an illicit item for years. When Ross becomes involved with the submissive Dr Louisa, Sam senses that Ross's true passions aren't compatible with her own domineering ways. Then she reads the classic novel *Venus in Furs*, which inspires her to experiment with being his slave for a month. When Dr Louisa shows up at Ross's country hideaway, there are surprising shifts in their ritual games of power and punishment.

ISBN 0 352 33447 9

To be published in December

STRIPPED TO THE BONE
Jasmine Stone
£5.99

Annie is a fun-loving free-thinking American woman who sets herself the mission of changing everything in her life. The only snag is she doesn't know when to stop changing things. Every man she meets is determined to find out what makes her tick, but her wild personality means no one can get a hold on her. Her sexual magnetism is electrifying, and her capacity for unusual and experimental sex-play has her loves in a spin of erotic confusion.

ISBN 0 352 33463 0

THE BEST OF BLACK LACE
Ed. Kerri Sharp
£5.99

This diverse collection of sizzling erotica is an 'editor's choice' of extracts from Black Lace books with a contemporary theme. The accent is on female characters who know what they want in bed – and in the workplace – and who have a sense of adventure above and beyond the heroines of romantic fiction. These girls kick ass!

ISBN 0 352 33452 5

If you would like a complete list of plot summaries of Black Lace titles, or would like to receive information on other publications available, please send a stamped addressed envelope to:

Black Lace, Thames Wharf Studios,
Rainville Road, London W6 9HA

BLACK LACE BOOKLIST

All books are priced £4.99 unless another price is given.

Black Lace books with a contemporary setting

PALAZZO	Jan Smith ISBN 0 352 33156 9	☐
THE GALLERY	Fredrica Alleyn ISBN 0 352 33148 8	☐
AVENGING ANGELS	Roxanne Carr ISBN 0 352 33147 X	☐
COUNTRY MATTERS	Tesni Morgan ISBN 0 352 33174 7	☐
GINGER ROOT	Robyn Russell ISBN 0 352 33152 6	☐
DANGEROUS CONSEQUENCES	Pamela Rochford ISBN 0 352 33185 2	☐
THE NAME OF AN ANGEL £6.99	Laura Thornton ISBN 0 352 33205 0	☐
BONDED	Fleur Reynolds ISBN 0 352 33192 5	☐
CONTEST OF WILLS £5.99	Louisa Francis ISBN 0 352 33223 9	☐
THE SUCCUBUS £5.99	Zoe le Verdier ISBN 0 352 33230 1	☐
FEMININE WILES £7.99	Karina Moore ISBN 0 352 33235 2	☐
AN ACT OF LOVE £5.99	Ella Broussard ISBN 0 352 33240 9	☐
DRAMATIC AFFAIRS £5.99	Fredrica Alleyn ISBN 0 352 33289 1	☐
DARK OBSESSION £7.99	Fredrica Alleyn ISBN 0 352 33281 6	☐
COOKING UP A STORM £7.99	Emma Holly ISBN 0 352 33258 1	☐
SEARCHING FOR VENUS £5.99	Ella Broussard ISBN 0 352 33284 0	☐
A SECRET PLACE £5.99	Ella Broussard ISBN 0 352 33307 3	☐

------ ✂ ------------------

Please send me the books I have ticked above.

Name   ....

Address   ....

           ....

           ....

         .... Post Code ....

Send to: **Cash Sales, Black Lace Books, Thames Wharf Studios, Rainville Road, London W6 9HA.**

US customers: for prices and details of how to order books for delivery by mail, call 1-800-805-1083.

Please enclose a cheque or postal order, made payable to **Virgin Publishing Ltd**, to the value of the books you have ordered plus postage and packing costs as follows:

UK and BFPO – £1.00 for the first book, 50p for each subsequent book.

Overseas (including Republic of Ireland) – £2.00 for the first book, £1.00 for each subsequent book.

If you would prefer to pay by VISA, ACCESS/MASTER-CARD, DINERS CLUB, AMEX or SWITCH, please write your card number and expiry date here:

....

Please allow up to 28 days for delivery.

Signature ....

------ ✂ ------------------